NIK

THE STRANGELOVE GAMBIT

The red-haired woman offered her right hand to him. "I'm Tempest."

Dante kissed the hand, adding his wickedest of grins. "Enchanted," he whispered before moving on to the other twin. "And you must be Storm. How delightful to make your acquaintance." She did not offer Dante a hand, folding her arms instead. "I'm told you two do everything together."

"Almost," Tempest replied. "We find two heads are better than one."

"Still, three needn't always be a crowd," Dante countered. "Perhaps we could get together and talk about it sometime."

"I doubt that will be possible before the end of term," Storm said brusquely before walking away. "Come along, sister." Dante watched them walk away, admiring the rippling muscles in their thighs and buttocks.

You're out of your depth, the Crest warned. *Those two would eat you for breakfast and leave nothing behind.*

"But what a way to go," Dante murmured. "What a way to go."

NIKOLAI DANTE

THE STRANGELOVE GAMBIT

David Bishop

BLACK FLAME

For Robbie, who let me have fun with his character.

A Black Flame Publication
www.blackflame.com

First published in 2005 by BL Publishing, Games Workshop Ltd.,
Willow Road, Nottingham NG7 2WS, UK.

Distributed in the US by Simon & Schuster, 1230 Avenue of the
Americas, New York, NY 10020, USA.

10 9 8 7 6 5 4 3 2 1

Cover illustration by Simon Fraser.

ISBN 1 84416 139 0

A CIP record for this book is available from the British Library.

Printed in the UK by Bookmarque, Surrey, UK.

PROLOGUE

"The wicked flatter to the face, then stab in the back"
– Russian proverb

The scent, smoke and sweat of a casino are nauseating at three in the morning. But the Casino Royale was a different place at three in the afternoon. Its windows and doors were thrown open, allowing fresh air and natural light into the crimson chamber normally designated Members Only. Ashtrays were emptied and polished, carpets cleaned and deodorised, lingering fingerprint smears of desperation removed from the brass fixtures and fittings. The casino interior was being scoured clean with a surgeon's precision.

James Di Grizov watched the preparations and smiled. All his life he had been a grifter in the Vorovskoi Mir, the Thieves' World. Di Grizov had developed and nurtured a reputation as a master escapologist, able to get himself out of almost any situation. But the big score, that single, career-making heist, had eluded him – until now. In a few hours this casino would be choked with the Empire's rich and famous, all gathered for the most talked about event of 2660: an auction. A single item was going under the hammer, but it had generated more interest than any lot in living memory – and Di Grizov planned to steal it.

Satisfied with the results of his final reconnoitre, the silver-haired thief returned to his suite in the adjoining hotel complex. The Casino Royale had trebled its room rates for the week of the auction. The sale was being handled by Sotheby's of Britannia, preventing the casino from claiming any percentage of the final price. But the indirect benefits were plentiful and the casino's management was determined to gouge all they could from them. Di Grizov had spent every kopeck he possessed to cover the deposit on his suite. Fortunately he would be absconding long before the final bill was due for payment. Di Grizov was known in the Vorovskoi Mir as a grifter who had never paid a bill in his life.

A retinal scanner outside the hotel room confirmed his identity and the door slid open with the silky ease of an Imperial courtesan's lingerie coming undone. Inside, the suite was wall-to-wall luxury, its gold and black decor reminiscent of a painted whore. Di Grizov ignored the glitzy interior and strode out on to the balcony. Sprawled below was Monaco, a tiny principality whose sole purpose for hundreds of years had been the pursuit of hedonism. Fewer than fifty thousand people lived in this Mediterranean enclave, but its borders contained many of the Empire's wealthiest individuals. Only the richest and the most beautiful dared venture out on the streets, strolling along the boulevards and nodding to those they deemed worthy of recognition.

The bay was awash with pleasure cruisers, each costing more than the gross national product of minor provinces like Domacha or Rudinshtein. The azure sea stretched out lazily to the horizon, merging seamlessly with the cloudless sky. All was bathed in brilliant sunshine, the resort bronzed and magnificent. If I believed in God, Di Grizov thought, He would come here to relax.

Only one thing spoiled the ambience, a recurrent snoring with all the timbre and tenderness of a chainsaw. Di Grizov sighed and turned to where his teenage assistant was slumbering on a sun lounger. They had first met six months earlier, when Di Grizov caught the upstart trying to pick his pocket at Tsyganov Black Market in St Petersburg. The veteran had almost turned the callow cutpurse in but something had stopped him. Perhaps I recognised a little of myself in him, the grifter thought. But was I ever this stupid?

His protégé had dozed off while reading a book, *Masterpieces from the House of Fabergé*. The hefty tome now rested on the youth's chest, masking a section of skin from the sun. The rest of the recumbent body was now a livid red, except for a triangular area covered by a pair of minuscule black trunks. The most vivid area of crimson was the youth's face. Surrounded by unruly black hair, the features were plain and unremarkable. Age and experience would give his face character but for now it was like an empty page, waiting for a life story.

Di Grizov slapped a hand down hard on his assistant's sunburnt thigh, shocking the sleeper into a sudden consciousness.

"Bojemoi!" Nikolai Dante shouted in pain and surprise, jolting upright.

"Never fall asleep on a job," Di Grizov said sternly. "And certainly never fall asleep in the sun, lest you suffer the consequences."

Dante looked down at his angry pink skin. The neglected book slid out of position, revealing a pale white rectangle where it had been resting. "Fuoco," the teenager muttered. "I always knew I was hot stuff, but this–"

"Is not what I meant by 'Get to know our target'," Di Grizov interjected. "You were supposed to be learning more about the reason we're here, not working on your tan!"

Dante shrugged sheepishly. "Sorry. I couldn't resist."

"That's your problem in a nutshell, boy. You can't resist anything." Di Grizov tried to sound angry but Dante's cherry-red face was too comical. "Take a cold shower and then I'll grill you on what you've learned."

The youth pointed at his sunburn. "Don't you think I've been grilled enough for one day?"

"The auction begins in five hours. We have to be ready. Now go!"

• • •

Kurt Brockman raised an eyebrow. "Good afternoon. Tonight on the Bolshoi Arts Channel, we bring you live and exclusive coverage of the bidding for one of the legendary Imperial Easter Eggs, created nearly seven hundred and fifty years ago by fabled jeweller Carl Fabergé. So make sure you tune in to catch all the auction action, live and exclusive, here on the Bolshoi Arts Channel. Don't miss it!" Brockman maintained his pose for five seconds before the red light above the camera filming him blinked off. His sculpted chin, piercing gaze and broad chest all suggested authority, intelligence and an athletic physique worthy of any Adonis. Once the brief transmission was over, Brockman abandoned his masculine on-screen persona and became a simpering bundle of nerves, shoulders slumping forwards, hands flopping about limply in the air. "Yuri, darling. How was it that time? Yuri?"

"Lovely, sweetie. Lovely," a camp voice replied via Brockman's earpiece. "Now we need you to interview the Fabergé expert, Kenworth Snowman. Lots of open-ended questions this time, love – let him do the talking for once, alright?"

"Are you saying I talk too much during interviews, Yuri?"

"Darling, the only time you don't talk too much is when you've got your mouth full," the director snapped back archly. "And try not to stand in front of the bloody egg this time, alright love? We need to see what the expert is talking about, not you trying to hold in your gut."

Brockman muttered an obscenity under his breath.

"What was that, darling?" the director asked.

"Nothing you need to worry about, love," Brockman cooed back. He beckoned to a short, bespectacled man sitting patiently nearby. The bookish expert scuttled over to join Brockman, self consciously brushing specks of dandruff from the shoulders of his tweed jacket. "Now, Mr Snowman–"

"Professor Snowman, actually."

"My apologies, Professor Snowman," Brockman continued, smiling thinly. "Perhaps you could tell our viewers about the fascinating history of this rare and unique objet d'art?" The presenter gestured expansively to the item displayed behind him on a pedestal of black onyx, guarded by a fearsome laser defence grid and a quartet of muscular casino security men.

At the centre of these defences was a steel egg, slightly larger in size than an ostrich egg, with two fine rings of inlaid gold encircling the polished silver surface. Set around the widest part of the circumference were four golden crests, while a small gold replica of an Imperial crown was fixed to its top. The egg sat in the centre of a square formed by four bullet-shaped cylinders, each made of polished silver and ringed with gold. These protruded from a sculpted square of green marble, itself edged with gold. The object was both beautiful and sinister, a work of art made in praise of military might.

"Well, the Steel Military Egg is certainly rare but we cannot say for certain it is unique," Professor Snowman began. Short, wild-eyed and frantic of hair, the expert from Britannia had been flown over especially for the auction coverage. It was a rare opportunity for the crusty academic, his enthusiasm evident in the hushed reverence of his words. "The House of Fabergé jewellers are believed to have constructed more than fifty Imperial eggs between 1885 and the first Russian revolution in 1917. Each was commissioned and given away as an Easter present by the Romanov Tsar of the time to his family and friends. In those days Easter was among the most important dates of celebration for those of the Russian Orthodox religion. Inside each egg was an exquisite surprise, handcrafted wonders that were often automated. Examples of these hidden delights were tiny birds that sang or miniature walking elephants.

"Nearly three-quarters of a millennium have elapsed and it was believed all the fabled Fabergé eggs had been lost or destroyed – until this one came up for auction. It's possible others have also survived and still remain in private hands. So to call the Steel Military Egg unique may be misleading your viewers. Obviously, all the Imperial Easter Eggs were unique in and of themselves, but there may still be other eggs out there. It's a not unimportant distinction, I feel."

"Fascinating, I'm sure." Brockman rolled his eyes before nodding to the camera. The red light on top of it blinked on and the recording began. "Professor Snowman, you've been telling me about the significance of the item up for auction today. Perhaps you could share that knowledge with our viewers?"

The flustered expert peered at the camera in dismay. "I thought I just had. You mean to say that thing wasn't switched on before?"

"Cut!" Brockman shouted, stamping a foot petulantly.

"Did I do something wrong?" Snowman asked ingenuously.

"No, no, professor, nothing at all," the reporter replied, his voice dripping with sarcasm and disdain.

"So that was your fault?"

Brockman resisted the urge to scream. "Yes, professor, that was my fault. Shall we start again?"

Dante stifled a yawn while watching the interview on Channel 88. The expert was droning on and on about the changing styles of late nineteenth century jewellery design, not a subject for which the apprentice thief had much enthusiasm. His interest was stirred when Brockman began asking about a legendary curse that was said to afflict anyone who touched a particular Fabergé egg.

"Superstitious nonsense," Snowman snapped grumpily. "Just because every member of the Tsar's family who touched the egg was dead within a year doesn't mean this item is cursed. As a scientist I cannot endorse such a fanciful and, frankly, implausible notion!"

"But isn't it true that you yourself have refused to lay a hand upon the Steel Military Egg?" Brockman persisted.

"That is simply to preserve the lustre and appearance of the object."

"You might say that, professor, but I'm sure the viewers can reach their own conclusions," the presenter replied smoothly, winking slyly to the camera.

Dante shouted across the suite to his mentor. "You never told me about this egg being cursed, Jim!"

Di Grizov was busy in the luxurious bathroom disguising his appearance with the addition of a false goatee beard and moustache. "It's all in the book, if you'd bothered to read it."

By now the coverage on Channel 88 had switched to outside the casino, showing the arrival of various celebrities and representatives from noble houses. Dante's interest was soon aroused by something on screen. "Fuoco! You could have somebody's eyes out with those," he enthused.

A transformed Di Grizov emerged to find his apprentice staring lustily at a considerable décolletage filling the viewscreen. "Do you ever think of anything besides sex?"

Dante grinned wolfishly. "When you're packing as much manhood as me, you can't help but appreciate those just as well-endowed in other areas."

"The endowment in question belongs to whom?"

"Er, can't say I caught her name..."

Di Grizov sighed wearily. "That's Princess Marie-Anne from the House of Windsor in Britannia. Ambitious, ruthless and utterly amoral. Her father is supposed to be going insane, leaving Marie-Anne free to spend his wealth as she sees fit. We can expect her to be in at the kill when the auction gets going."

"Sounds like my kind of woman," Dante announced. "Think she'll fancy a diamond in the rough?"

"Nikolai, you may be rough, but the princess would be polishing a long time before she transformed you into a diamond of any sort."

"Long as she doesn't give me friction burns, she can rub me up the wrong way anytime."

"Try having a thought that originates above your waist for once in your life, please?" Di Grizov pleaded in exasperation.

Dante held up both hands in mock surrender. "Sorry. I just enjoy making you despair."

"Nevertheless, we are here on a job, so let's concentrate on that. Who's arriving now?" The grifter pointed at the viewscreen where a handsome man with light brown hair was alighting from a hovercar. A double-headed eagle crest was sewn into the fabric on the upper arm of his pristine white jacket.

"That's the symbol of the Romanovs," Dante said. "They're the oldest of the noble houses, the family line dating back to before the creation of the Fabergé eggs. Judging by the beauty of his companion that must be Andreas, the playboy of the Romanovs. He never sleeps with the same woman two nights in a row, according to legend."

"Very good," Di Grizov said. "I'm glad to see you've done some research!"

"He's my role model," Dante admitted sheepishly.

"I should have guessed. No doubt Andreas will be bidding on behalf of his father, Dmitri. Doubtful the Romanovs will stay the course. Most of their resources are tied up in a cold war of attrition with the Tsar. Andreas is here to be seen and to see what everyone else does."

Next on to the red-carpeted steps outside the casino was Mikhail Deriabin, media baron and House of Bolshoi patriarch. His curly brown hair swept back from a pinched face, a monocle held in front of his right eye. He was clad in a finely tailored dinner jacket of black and blue, his head tossed back at a haughty angle. At his side stood a poised, elegant woman in a simple silk gown of red and orange. Brockman appeared from inside the casino and began interviewing his boss, simpering with obsequiousness.

"Arse-licker," Dante sneered. "Who's the woman with Deriabin?"

"The Firebird," Di Grizov replied, his face alive with admiration as he watched her on screen. "She is Ballerina Queen of the Danse Macabre, the greatest dancer of our age.

I saw her perform once when I was playing a long con. Such elegance, such finesse."

The last to arrive for the auction was a cruel-faced man with closely cropped black hair. He was alone and refused to be interviewed by Brockman, waving the presenter away with a curt gesture.

"Doctor Fabergé – I wonder what he's doing here?" Di Grizov stroked his chin thoughtfully, watching the final guest disappear inside.

"Fabergé? Like the egg guy?" Dante asked.

"Carl Fabergé was the jeweller who designed the Imperial Easter Eggs. He died hundreds of years ago. The man who just arrived is a scientist called Dr Karl Fabergé. He and Raoul Sequanna co-founded GenetiCo, a genetics research company much favoured by the Tsar. But why come to an event like this? He can't imagine being able to successfully bid for the egg…"

Dante shrugged. "Guess we'll find out tonight. The auction starts soon."

"Hello and welcome back to our live and exclusive coverage of the Auction of the Century! I'm Kurt Brockman, your host for this evening's event here on the House of Bolshoi Arts Channel." The presenter paused and looked over his shoulder at the assembled throng of the rich and famous. "Well, it seems anybody who's anybody is here in this room tonight, waiting for their chance to bid on the fabled Steel Military Egg. The only noble dynasty not represented is that of our beloved Tsar, the House of Makarov. Could the Tsar be the mystery seller of this much-vaunted item? Sotheby's have refused to be drawn on the seller's identity, but speculation remains–" Brockman stopped to hold a finger up to one ear, his face a mask of concentration. "I'm hearing the auction is about to begin, so I'll let the action speak for itself from now on…"

In the auction room a hush descended upon those assembled. All one hundred seats were occupied by some of the best-fed posteriors in the Empire. Ladies fanned themselves with sale programmes as heat from the television lights began to overwhelm the casino's air conditioning system. Those who had arrived too late to claim a seat stood around the walls, Di Grizov and Dante scattered among them, the two men careful to avoid each other.

After an awkward pause a chubby auctioneer appeared from between two curtains of crimson velvet and approached the podium. At his signal the curtains parted to reveal the egg on its pedestal, surrounded by security guards. The audience found their voices again, a babble of excitement passing round the chamber. The auctioneer dabbed a white cotton handkerchief against his sweaty brow and gripped the podium. He clasped a small wooden gavel and rapped it three times against a wooden disc. "Thank you, my lords, ladies and gentlemen. It is now time for the main event of the evening: Lot forty-two, the Steel Military Egg, designed in 1916 by Carl Fabergé." The auctioneer paused, then leaned on the podium. "Ten million roubles I am bid."

A whisper of awe rippled through the room. This opening sum was more than had been bid on the previous forty-one lots, auctioned a day earlier, including some of the most precious artefacts of the millennium. History was being made and everybody knew it.

"Twelve million. Fourteen. Sixteen. Eighteen. Twenty. Twenty million roubles I am bid. And five? Twenty-five million. Thirty. Thirty-five. Forty. Forty-five. Fifty. Fifty million roubles I am bid." The auctioneer paused to let the audience applaud and mopped his brow once more. So far the bids had been almost non-stop, but the world record price was fast approaching and most would blanch at exceeding that psychological barrier. "Do I hear fifty-five million?"

Dante wiped his palms on the legs of his trousers. Fifty million roubles! The sum was astronomical, almost beyond imagining. In his young life Dante had rarely possessed more than a few hundred roubles at once, but as soon as the auction was completed he would be helping Jim steal lot forty-two. Just watching the sale was causing an unpleasant quiver in Dante's lower intestine. How would he cope with being part of the greatest heist in history? If they pulled it off, his reputation as a leading light in the Vorovskoi Mir would be assured. If they failed and were caught, well, he'd be lucky to survive the night. "Live fast, die young, leave a handsome corpse," Dante told himself.

He concentrated on trying to detect who was still in the bidding. Most of the signals to the auctioneer were almost imperceptible, unless the bidder wanted others to know their identity. Andreas Romanov had made no secret of his interest, expansively gesturing with a waft of his catalogue. When the top bid passed forty million he had waved the auctioneer away and smiled broadly to those among him. Honour had been satisfied, it seemed.

Fifty million proved to be the pain barrier for Princess Marie-Anne. She closed her catalogue and rested it on her lap, the merest shake of her head indicating her with-drawal. But who had bid the top price? Dante peered at those present but remained none the wiser. The auctioneer was still calling for fresh bids, hoping to push the price on to the world record and beyond.

"Fifty-five? Do I hear fifty-five? Last chance for this rare and very special lot, going once at fifty million roubles. Going twice. Go–"

"Sixty million!"

All heads turned to see who had called out. In most auc-tions it was considered bad form to look over your shoulder in search of rival bidders. Calling out your bid was also sneered upon but the figure standing against the back wall did not seem concerned by that.

The auctioneer arched an eyebrow at the newcomer. "We have a fresh bidder – sixty million roubles."

Dante smiled at the audience, all of whom had twisted round to stare at him. He couldn't explain what had hap-pened, even to himself. One moment he was scanning the crowd, the next he was yelping out a bid despite not having two roubles to rub together. Keep a low profile, Jim had reminded him a thousand times; a good grifter never draws attention to himself. Dante did not dare look in his mentor's direction, lest he be struck dead by the venomous glare no doubt being directed at him. Instead he nodded to the auctioneer.

"Sixty million it is," the rotund man with the gravel confirmed. "Do I hear sixty-five? Sixty-five it is."

"Seventy," Dante squeaked, his voice an octave above its normal pitch.

"And seventy, I am bid. Now seventy-five." The auctioneer looked at Dante once more. "The bid is seventy-five million roubles, against you sir."

Dante smiled, shrugged and waved him away. Only when the audience had resumed ignoring him did the youth let out a sigh of relief.

The auctioneer was close to concluding the sale. The world record price of eighty-seven million roubles had been too much to hope for, but lot 42 had gone close. "The bid is seventy-five million roubles. Final chance, selling now at seventy-five million roubles?"

In the audience Deriabin had suddenly begun to smile broadly, unable to quell his pride any longer. Plainly he was the top bidder. His hands clutched the sale catalogue tightly, waiting for the gavel to be struck for the last time.

"Selling now at seventy-five million roubles... Eighty million!"

There was a collective gasp of astonishment. Who was this new bidder? Why had they entered the fray so late on? And who could afford to spend such a sum on anything, even an item this exquisite?

Deriabin's face was a snarl of anger, his knuckles white on the hand clutching the catalogue. The media mogul made no attempt to hide his next bid, visibly twitching his catalogue.

"And eighty-five. Any advance on eighty-five? I'll accept eighty-seven and a half," the auctioneer offered. "No? Then the final bid is eighty-five million roubles. Eighty-five million…" The gavel twitched. "Eighty-seven and a half million roubles! I am bid eighty-seven and a half million roubles!"

The audience began to applaud spontaneously; each of them knowing this would be a story to tell their grandchildren. Only Deriabin refused to take part, his arms folded severely across his chest. When the congratulations had died down he flicked his catalogue once more.

"Ninety million. Ninety-two and a half. Ninety-five. Ninety-seven and a half. One hundred million roubles!" More applause but it quickly died away as the bidding continued in a frenzy. "And five. Ten. Fifteen. Twenty. Twenty-five. Thirty. Thirty-five. Forty! I am bid one hundred and forty million roubles!"

At last Dante had detected who was the other bidder. In a corner of the room Doctor Fabergé was signalling his bids with the faintest of nods. Now Deriabin had the upper hand again. Surely this ludicrous sum could grow no higher? A collective madness seemed to have gripped everyone in the room, Dante included. Where would this insanity end?

"A hundred and forty-five million roubles," the auctioneer said after another tiny nod from Fabergé. In the middle of the room Deriabin sat fuming, all eyes staring at him. The egg had only been expected to fetch fifty million roubles, talk of breaking the world record thought to be merely media hype. Now the bids were close to doubling the old mark. After a long, agonising silence Deriabin stood and stalked from the chamber, flinging his crumpled catalogue to the floor.

"I am bid a hundred and forty-five million roubles. Do I hear any advance on that figure?" The auctioneer paused, then slammed his gavel downward, signalling the end of the sale. "Sold!"

Di Grizov found his apprentice in the melee that followed and dragged him to one side. "What the hell were you thinking? Why did you start bidding?"

Dante just shrugged. "Sorry. The excitement got to me!"

"Diavolo, do you ever listen? I should have followed my instincts and reported you to the authorities when we first met. You're a menace, Nikolai Dante, and you're in danger of dragging me down with you. It'll be a miracle if you live to see twenty!"

"Calm down, Jim. Nobody will remember me, not after what just happened – the auction smashing the world record, Deriabin storming out."

Di Grizov had to concede the truth of this. "Nevertheless, pull a stunt like that again and you're finished. I'll person-ally hand you over to the Raven Corps!"

"Yeah, yeah," Dante replied, having heard it all before. "Shouldn't we be getting close to Fabergé? He's the winning bidder."

The senior grifter jerked a thumb over his shoulder. Fabergé was surrounded by a scrum of cameras and reporters, all demanding to know why he had bid so much for the egg and where the money had come from. "Trust me, the good doctor isn't going anywhere for a while. Let's get back to the suite and prepare for tonight. I may have thought of how we can turn your little display of stupidity to our advantage."

"I don't like to talk about money, it's unseemly." Fabergé was surrounded by reporters, all jostling for a chance to question the winning bidder, hoping to catch his eye. The doctor had escaped the auction room but was now holding an impromptu press conference in the corridor outside. Fabergé kept smiling, even if the expression sat oddly on his severe features. "If you must know, yesterday I sold my half-share of GenetiCo to my co-founder, Raoul Sequanna. The dividend from that transaction enabled me to bid with confidence."

"If I may be so bold, why?" The interrogator was Kurt Brockman, determined to keep his face close to the centre of this story. "What possible reason could you have for spending a small fortune on a piece of jewellery?"

"The Fabergé Eggs have great personal significance for me," the scientist replied. "I was raised in an orphanage by nuns and one of the sisters named me after Carl Fabergé, the acclaimed jeweller who fashioned the eggs. Alas, the nun spelled my first name wrongly on the paperwork!"

His joke was a familiar one to the reporters, since he used it in every interview, but they dutifully laughed along with him. For once the weak jest had acquired an extra significance, just as Fabergé was now a man of greater importance than usual thanks to his bidding coup.

"The concept of the eggs with their hidden surprises has inspired a daring and innovative new direction for research I shall be conducting over the coming months and years. It is work of the utmost importance, with the full support of our glorious leader, Tsar Vladimir. This new project means I am no longer able to involve myself in the day-to-day running of GenetiCo – hence the sale. But the company is in safe hands with Raoul and shall go from strength to strength under his leadership. In the meantime it is enough for me to say I shall treasure this day for many years to come and look forward to having the Steel Military Egg as my most prized possession. That is all."

Fabergé forced his way through the melee, waving away any further questions as he struggled towards the lifts. A man distinguished by the characteristic crimson blazer of a Sotheby's official shoved his way through the journalists and took the doctor by an elbow. "Sir, if you'll follow me. I shall escort you safely back to your suite. The egg will be delivered to you there later."

"Thank you," Fabergé said once the two men were safely inside a lift, sliding doors shutting out the media. "The gutter press are tiresome, but one must give them a quote or else they make your life a misery!"

"Indeed. Forty-fourth floor, is it sir?"

"Forty-fifth, actually," Fabergé replied. "Some usurper persuaded the casino management to surrender my usual suite! Probably the red-faced upstart who tried to get himself noticed by bidding against Deriabin earlier. I soon showed that gross pretender!"

The lift sighed to a halt on the forty-fifth floor, its doors parting to reveal a tasteful penthouse suite. A dozen Sotheby's employees were waiting, their faces suffused with obsequious civility.

"Welcome to your suite, Doctor Fabergé!"

"Congratulations on your purchase!"

"A wonderful piece of bidding, if I may say so. Audacious yet assured!"

"You lived up to your famous name in every way today, sir!"

"Silence!" Fabergé bellowed. "I've heard enough questions and false compliments to last me a lifetime. All I want is some peace and quiet. Get out of my suite – NOW!"

The auction house staff scuttled towards the lift, eager to satisfy their most important client. Fabergé stopped them with another barked command. "Wait! Where's the man who rescued me from that unseemly mob downstairs? He can stay. The rest of you – get out!"

Di Grizov emerged from the cluster of cowering staff, one hand stroking his false moustache and beard. "Glad to be of service, sir."

Dante took a deep breath and placed a call to the Casino Royale's concierge. "Yes, I'd like to be put through to Doctor Fabergé. No, I'm not surprised to hear he's not taking any calls, but he'll want to take mine. Why? Tell him I have evidence the Steel Military Egg for which he just paid a world record sum is a fake. If he wants to know more, I will be happy to visit his suite in twenty minutes' time. My name? Dante, Nikolai Dante. He'll know me when he sees me."

Since the age of five Karl Fabergé had known of his own genius. Across the Empire all five year-old children were required to undergo intelligence, aptitude and personality testing. From this the authorities could identify potential soldiers, scientists, athletes, artists, thinkers and trouble-makers. Those that could be of use were channelled into the best schools and academies, set on a path to best fulfil their latent talents. Those that posed a danger were watched, detained, and in some cases, exterminated with extreme prejudice. There was no mercy for those who could have been a threat to the Tsar and the glorious Empire.

This reign of terror had been the making of Fabergé. A sickly baby, he had been abandoned on the steps of a convent orphanage. One of the nuns doted on this weakling runt, keeping it alive and secretly suckling the infant on her breasts. She was the sister who misnamed the child, calling him her little jewel. Fabergé could still remember her scent, warm and flowery. By the age of four he had rejected the nun's beliefs as superstitious nonsense, substituting science as his catechism. On his fifth birthday Karl was tested by the local education official and declared a genius, with superior intellect and a brilliant scientific mind. The boy was removed from the orphanage and began his studies at the science academy in St Petersburg.

There he emerged as the leading mind of his generation, revolutionising techniques in several fields and challenging accepted scientific thinking. As Fabergé's fame grew, so did his egotism and self-regard. But being the most acclaimed scientist of the twenty-seventh century was not enough for him. Fabergé wanted to be famous across the Empire. Out-bidding the media baron Deriabin for the Steel Military Egg was a bold first step towards that goal. Deriabin's competitors would replay the auction footage over and over again to humiliate their rival, putting the name of Dr Karl Fabergé on everyone's lips. But to now be told the egg might be a fake – it did not bear thinking about.

The man from Sotheby's assured Fabergé these allegations must be spurious. "My firm is utterly scrupulous in checking and rechecking the provenance of every lot it sells, especially one so prestigious as this. What was the name of this individual who claimed to have evidence to the contrary?"

Fabergé was pacing back and forth in front of the penthouse suite's lift doors. "Dante, Nikolai Dante."

Di Grizov shook his head. "Never heard of him. He isn't a known authority on the Fabergé eggs. That can only mean he is either a liar trying to dupe you, or a thief with some knowledge of an elaborate confidence trick involving the egg. In either case, you should trust little of what he has to say."

The scientist nodded hurriedly. "Very well." He strode to the centre of the suite, where the Steel Military Egg glistened behind an elaborate security screen of deadly lasers. That such an exquisite item should be sullied by claims of falsehood and fakery, it made Fabergé's blood boil. Whoever was responsible for this would suffer the consequences.

Di Grizov noted the lift approaching from below. "He's nearly here."

Fabergé whirled round, his features spiked with suppressed rage. "Good."

Dante stepped from the elegant lift straight into a clenched fist. The blow smashed into his nose, cracking the bone and unleashing a gout of blood from both nostrils. The dazed youth staggered backwards, only the closing doors preventing him tumbling into the lift. He cupped a hand up to his chin, trying to stop the blood from staining his tunic. "Why'd you do that?" he demanded.

Di Grizov stood to one side, nursing bruised knuckles. "I recognise this dolt, Doctor Fabergé. He was the upstart who bid for the egg."

"Yeah, so?" Dante demanded, the words thickened by his throbbing nose. "That's no reason to punch me in the face!"

"Should I hit him again?"

Fabergé held up a hand. "That won't be necessary – yet." The doctor approached the new arrival. "Young man, you claim to have information about a potential fraud involving my egg. Speak up or I shall have this gentleman from Sotheby's strike you again. Well?"

"Just give me a chance to explain!" Dante cried out.

"You have one minute." Fabergé retreated to an antique chair and sat bolt upright in it, his fingers forming a steeple in front of his face.

Dante moved away from the lift doors, still trying to stem the blood flowing freely down his face. "There's a conman here at the Casino Royale who plans to steal the egg and replace it with a copy, a forgery. For all I know he's already done it." The red-faced youth pointed his free hand at the laser grid surrounding the bejewelled egg. "All the security in the Empire won't be enough to stop this fiend from stealing your precious objet d'art."

Fabergé smiled. "And the name of this terrifying individual?"

"Di Grizov. He's called Jim Di Grizov. A very slippery thief."

The scientist laughed. "Hardly a name to inspire fear."

"He's the best escapologist in the Empire, able to break into or out of any enclosed space known to man. Master of disguise too, you'd never be able to recognise him." Dante pointed at the man in the Sotheby's uniform. "For all you know this thug could be Di Grizov. He's stolen from kings and queens, even–"

"Enough." Fabergé shook his head. "And why are you telling me all this? Why did you bid on the egg if you had such fears?"

"Because I'm working with Di Grizov, I'm his apprentice. He wanted me to drive the price up so the egg would be worth more on the black market once he'd stolen it. But when I heard about the curse... I got cold feet. Figured you'd offer me a handsome reward for tipping you off."

Fabergé consulted a gold pocket watch. "Your time is up. I must thank you for this fanciful little tale but the entertainment is over. Leave now and I won't have you beaten by the casino's security personnel."

"But what about my reward?" Dante protested.

"Here's your reward!" Di Grizov replied, driving a knee up into the youth's groin. Dante collapsed to the carpet, breath whistling out between his gritted teeth. Di Grizov aimed a vicious kick into his protégé's ribs, sending Dante rolling away towards the lift doors. They slid open and Dante crawled inside, glaring up accusingly at his partner.

"Why?"

Di Grizov smiled. "Got to make it look convincing," he whispered.

"The fabulous Fabergé Steel Military Egg has been stolen!" Kurt Brockman beamed into the camera, unable to believe his good luck at having the lead story on Channel 88's news bulletin for the second day running. "Yesterday the legendary jewelled item attracted a world record price at auction when its creator's namesake, Doctor Karl Fabergé, won the egg with a bid of one hundred and forty-five million roubles. Now it seems lot forty-two has been stolen from inside the doctor's penthouse suite here at the Casino Royale in Monaco. An investigation has been launched but there are no clues and even fewer suspects for what is already being described by some as the crime of the century!"

Dante watched the bulletin with dazed resignation. He knew who had stolen the egg but the knowledge would do him no good. After spending the night in a hospital bed suffering from concussion, broken ribs and other injuries, Dante had hurried back to the hotel after hearing about the audacious theft. The suite he had been sharing with Di Grizov was empty but for a message hastily scrawled on headed notepaper of the Casino Royale: "There is no honour amongst thieves – sorry!"

"Honour be damned," Dante snarled as he tore the note apart.

Heavy fists began hammering against the outer door of the suite. "Hotel security! Open this door or we will be forced to break it down!"

No doubt Fabergé told the authorities what Dante had claimed the night before. With Di Grizov gone and the egg missing, that leaves me to take the blame, the youth thought ruefully. Me and my big mouth. The hammering from outside was getting ever more forceful. Dante cast one last, lingering look around the sumptuous chamber. No way of knowing when he would savour such luxury again.

The doors to the suite began to splinter inwards from a concerted attack. Dante retreated to the balcony, leaning over the railing to see what was below. Another balcony was directly beneath, with its sliding doors open to provide a potential escape route. Even more inviting was the beautiful woman bathing topless on a sun lounger, her voluptuous body bronzed and glistening in the warm sunshine. Behind him Dante could hear the doors giving way. No time like the present to make a new friend...

Dante swung himself over the railing and dropped to the balcony below, landing on the balls of his feet. He almost overbalanced and fell backwards, but succeeded in throwing himself forward instead. The youth landed unceremoniously on top of the sunbathing beauty's chest.

"Sorry, m'lady," he said. "Do you need anyone to rub oil into your back?"

The woman would have screamed but for Dante's groin covering her mouth. Instead she flailed at him with her arms. A shout from above indicated the would-be thief's escape route had been detected.

"I'll take that as a no then, shall I?" Dante got to his feet, glancing round to see security men climbing down from the balcony overhead. "You'll have to excuse me, I have a pressing engagement elsewhere!" He paused to kiss the startled woman before running inside. Behind him he could hear the shrieking sunbather shouting at his pursuers.

"Stop that gentleman! He stole a kiss from me!" she cried.

A gentleman thief, Dante thought. That could be my next career...

ONE

"The thief protests his innocence all the way to the gallows"
– Russian proverb

Di Grizov opened his eyes and winced. Overhead lighting stabbed at his vision, harsh and unrelenting. An acrid mixture of antiseptic and fear assaulted the nostrils, forcing its way into his lungs. But worst of all was the face looming over him; the features cast a sickly yellow by the brutal illuminations. Di Grizov thought a woman was watching him, but couldn't be sure.

Her features were broad and ugly – a bulbous nose with fine white hairs sprouting from both inside and out, two small pink eyes set uncomfortably close together above grinning lips of flaccid skin. Dabs of rouge suggested where cheekbones should be, while double and triple chins wobbled for attention and a single eyebrow stretched across the brow. All of this was punctuated with dozens of warts, some home to clumps of dark hair, others flecked with red veins. As she leaned over Di Grizov, the woman's dank breath, heavy with the odours of sweat and decay, bombarded his senses. Quite simply, this was the most grotesque creature in the world.

"Where am I?" Di Grizov was startled by how thin and weak his voice sounded. He had no memory of how he came to be in this place, or why his throat felt so sore. Beneath his neck he felt nothing, just numb weightlessness. The grifter tried to raise his head but could not summon the strength. For now he would have to gather information by questions alone.

"Your new home," the woman replied, her voice made thick and guttural by its Siberian accent. She stood upright, resting two meaty fists on the rolls of fat where her waist should be. "Allow me to introduce myself. I am Madame Wartski."

Wartski by name, warty by nature, Di Grizov thought. Best not to say so out loud, I doubt this whale would find it funny. There was a dry, humourless aspect to her face that did little to inspire frivolity. Wide as she was tall, Wartski was clad in a navy blue matron's uniform, fabric bulging across her drooping breasts and rotund hips. Her flabby hands sported as many warts as her face, each finger encrusted with a selection of fleshy growths.

"Di Grizov. James Di Grizov," the grifter replied. "I'd shake your hand but can't seem to feel my fingers at the moment."

"The anaesthetic is still wearing off," Wartski said.

"Anaesthetic? I don't understand – have I been undergoing surgery? Was I in an accident?"

The masculine matron smiled. "Not exactly. The doctor will explain." She moved to the end of his bed and studied a medical chart. "Good, everything's coming along nicely. I'll tell him you're recovering well."

"Recovering? From what?" Di Grizov tried pushing himself into an upright position, fighting against his body's numb inertia. "Tell me what's going on!"

Wartski tutted imperiously. "Getting agitated will not help. I suggest you remain calm and get some rest. You'll need it for what is ahead."

The grifter felt his sphincter contract involuntarily. There was a threat within the matron's words, an unpleasantly sadistic twinkle in her eyes as she spoke. I'm in trouble here, Di Grizov realised, and I don't even know where I am. He decided to keep bluffing, hoping to find a way out of this place.

"You're probably right," he said in a soothing voice, relaxing back into the pillow. "I'll try and get some more rest. Thank you, Madame Wartski."

She smiled and left the room, an automatic door closing behind her more than ample posterior. Once she had gone, Di Grizov hurriedly examined his surroundings, searching for any clue to his location or method of escape. The chamber was small, with a low ceiling and obtrusive strip lighting. No windows punctuated the walls, denying any hint of the world beyond. The room was sparsely furnished, just a bare table and chair in one corner – no cupboards; nothing that might contain his possessions or a potential weapon. Even the bed was a bare hospital cot, utterly utilitarian and without adornment. Everything was a queasy yellow colour, accentuating his feeling of unease.

Di Grizov tried to haul himself into a sitting position, but his arms were still too weak to support any weight. There was a nagging itch below his right knee but he lacked the energy and strength to reach it. If I could remember how I got here, he thought, maybe I'd have a clue about how to escape. The grifter closed his eyes and focussed on pushing aside the blurring in his mind. Last thing he could recall was a New Year's Eve party. The Year of the Tsar 2671 was coming to an end and Di Grizov had purloined an invitation to the richest event in St Petersburg. The Tsar had created three new noble houses as recognition for their help in defeating the Romanovs during the war, and the recipients were celebrating their enhanced status with a joint party.

Di Grizov had arrived early and begun circulating among the guests, acquiring useful gossip about who was going where for their winter holidays, leaving their homes vulnerable. The grifter saw a familiar face during the gathering but couldn't recall where he had known it before. The man appeared just as startled to see Di Grizov at the celebration. Deciding discretion was always the safest option, the grifter decided to make an early exit; in a life of crime without punishment, he had wronged many people. In his experience revenge was best avoided by not staying around long enough to suffer it.

He had arrived home safely, but after stepping through
the front door everything was lost in a haze. All he could
recall was a male voice, sneering and arch. "I thought it was
you. I would congratulate you on possessing such audacity,
but since it shall be your undoing, there is little to praise..."
After that all was darkness until waking beneath Wartski's
repulsive face.

The grifter snapped open his eyes, terror suddenly evident in them. That voice! He remembered where he
recognised it from now. "Not him. Please don't let it be
him," Di Grizov prayed. "Anyone but him!"

Jena Makarov looked out of her flyer's window as it
skimmed over the Black Sea coastline. Below the water
gleamed and rippled, flecks of white and silver appearing as
gusts of wind created waves or schools of fish broke the
surface. A trawler chugged its way into shore, laden down
with another day's catch. Soon the fishermen would be
unloading their haul, counting their takings and going
home to eat, drink, fight and make love to their partners.
How Jena longed for such a simple life. The grass is always
greener, she knew that. No doubt the fishermen had just as
many cares and worries as she – fruitless catches, dilapi-
dated boats, falling prices. What was the old saying? *Expect
sorrows from the sea and woe from water*. But their lives
could not be any more poisonous than hers, trapped amidst
the intrigues of the imperial court.

She had known neither poverty nor hunger; nor wanted
for any material object. She had been pampered and privi-
leged beyond all others; yet that was no compensation for a
childhood without love or affection. Jena's mother had died
long ago, leaving two daughters in the care of their father.
But when that father was Tsar Vladimir Makarov, the most
feared man in the Empire, happy families were not on the
agenda. Any man who bragged about his ability to create
ingenious tortures such as the corrosive acid enema was not
one to dote on his children. He was a murderous, monstrous

creature with ice for a heart. Instead Jena had kept close to her younger sister, Julianna. They argued as many siblings did, fighting over trivial possessions and experiences to distract themselves from the horrors perpetrated in their father's name. All the while he was training them to take his place, to inherit his reign of terror.

The Tsar's long, bitter struggle with the House of Romanov came to a head in 2669, when decades of sabre rattling became a war encompassing the entire Empire. It was Julianna's murder that provoked the bloody conflict, her life stolen by one of the Romanov siblings. At the time Jena thought this event had hardened her father's heart, forced him to take arms against the pretenders to the imperial throne. But the glee with which he had pursued the war soon persuaded her otherwise. The Tsar had wanted his war and done everything in his power to make it happen. Sometimes she suspected he had deliberately sent Julianna into harm's way, turning her into a suitable target for the Romanovs to assassinate and thus create the justification for war. But Jena did not dare investigate these suspicions. She was the Tsar's sole surviving heir, but even that would not be sufficient protection from his wrath.

No, it was not Vladimir Makarov's heart that had been hardened by the death of Julianna – it was Jena who lost a little of her soul that day. At the time she was in love with a key figure from the Romanov side of the conflict. After years of fighting and flirting, the pair had finally consummated their passion for each other. But by the time they decided to tell the world of their union, the war had already begun. Jena would not let herself think of her lover's name, let alone say it out loud. Just remembering his face, the touch of his hands on her body, the look in his eyes as they... No, she would not torture herself with these memories again. Leave the demon behind, lest the mere thought of him conjured his presence into her life again.

The war had been bloody and brutal. Jena fought like a woman possessed: every victory a memorial to her dead sister, every enemy soldier she slaughtered another stain on her heart. Even during the war she found herself face to face with *him* several times, forced to confront her feelings all over again. But the Romanovs eventually lost, betrayed by one of their own, and the Tsar swept aside their forces. The Romanov name became accursed across the Empire, with Jena's former lover a wanted man with a massive bounty on his head. Any sensible, sane individual would get offworld, find a quiet corner of the Empire and disappear. Jena could not help laughing to herself. *Somehow I doubt he would follow such advice.*

Since the war ended, her father's regime had been crueller and more tyrannical than ever. Purge squads mercilessly took revenge against anyone suspected of betraying the Tsar. Noble houses that had displayed any loyalty or partiality towards the Romanovs were ruthlessly destroyed and new dynasties built on their ashes, fiercely loyal to the Tsar. Amidst it all Jena did her duty, fulfilled her father's wishes. That was all she had left now.

"Approaching our destination," the flyer's pilot announced, snapping Jena back from her reverie. "Beginning final descent to the island."

"Very good," she replied. "Once we're down begin preparations for our departure. I don't want to be here any longer than is absolutely necessary."

"Yes, ma'am."

Doctor Fabergé could not help laughing. To think this was the brigand who had eluded him for a dozen years. The thief lying on the hospital bed was smaller than he remembered, and older – almost wizened. Time had not been kind to Di Grizov. His features were lined and careworn, his hair thinning, his body a shadow of its former strength and agility. Most intriguing were his eyes. Once they had shone with intelligence and bravado. Now they showed terror and foreboding. *Yes, I'm going to enjoy this immensely,* the doctor decided as he chuckled.

"What's so funny?" the patient demanded.

"You are," Fabergé replied, failing to wipe the smile from his face. "In my mind I had built you up into this powerful figure, the only man ever to get the better of me – my nemesis, my hubris, if you will. When I saw you across the room at that tiresome party I struggled to accept that you were the same person. You're just a thief and an old thief at that."

"You don't scare me, Fabergé."

"Your words say one thing but the fear in your eyes says another. Quite right, too. You would do well to be afraid of me. I've spent twelve years planning my revenge. Now the glorious day is finally here, it seems something of an anti-climax. When you stole my Imperial Easter Egg, you stole more than just a priceless piece of jewellery – you stole part of my reputation, my honour. Revenging myself upon you was a matter of principle at first, then a matter of need. Eventually it became an obsession, driving me onward in my work, pushing me to prove I was more than just the victim of this century's most famous theft." The doctor clicked his fingers and Wartski entered the room carrying a silver box. She rested it on the table at the end of Di Grizov's bed.

Fabergé removed the lid with a flourish to reveal the Steel Military Egg, its lustre undimmed. "I must thank you for keeping my egg safe and in such pristine condition for the last twelve years. I feared you might try to break it into pieces for sale or destroy it altogether."

"I'll be happy to see the back of that damned thing," Di Grizov snapped. "It's been the bane of my life since I first set eyes on it."

"Perhaps your assistant was right after all," Fabergé said. "Perhaps the legend of a curse against all who touch the egg is true?"

"We both know you turned that thing into poison," the grifter snarled. "By the time I reached the black market in St Petersburg, word had already been spread that anyone who bought or traded the egg would be hunted down and exterminated, by order of the Tsar himself. How'd you ever swing that, Fabergé?"

"Let's just say our glorious leader and I have a long-standing alliance."

"I couldn't give the egg away, let alone sell it! Nobody would melt it down for me either. I should have just thrown it into the Volga and had done with it."

"Twelve years on the run, a marked man, always looking over your shoulder, never able to relax. That can't have been easy," Wartski interjected.

"Indeed," Fabergé agreed. "But your running days are over now."

Doubts joined fear on Di Grizov's features. "What do you mean?"

"Centuries ago slave labour was used to extract diamonds from mines on the continent of Africa. But the owners had problems with workers trying to escape, taking the precious gems with them to buy a new life. All those who were caught had to be punished and the penalty needed to be so severe it would serve as a warning to others, to dissuade them from fleeing. The process was called hobbling and proved most effective."

"Oh no…"

Fabergé reached down towards the bed covers. "Yes, your running days are definitely over. In fact, to make sure of that," the doctor pulled aside the bedclothes to reveal two bloody and bandaged stumps where Di Grizov's legs had been, "I've amputated both your legs."

Jena heard a scream, stark and terrifying, as she stepped out of the flyer. It felt unnatural to the ears, almost unworldly. During the war Jena had heard many, many men crying out in agony, begging for their lives, but such screams still cut her to the core. What horrors was Doctor Fabergé perpetrating here in her father's name? She turned back to the pilot. "Remember what I said. We don't want to spend a minute longer here than necessary."

"Planning your departure already?"

"But you've only just arrived!"

Jena spun round to find herself facing the chests of two women. She looked up to their faces, more than a head's height above her own. The pair were identical in appearance, but for the colour of their hair – one red, one black. Otherwise they were exactly the same, with high cheekbones, powerful jawlines and wide, intensely blue eyes. "How's the air up there?" Jena joked.

"My name is Tempest," the red-haired woman replied humourlessly. "This is my sister, Storm. We're the Strangelove twins."

"Of course," Jena said. "Sorry, I've never seen you up close before."

The twins exchanged a look before marching away from the landing pad. "Doctor Fabergé is expecting you," Storm announced.

"Follow us, please," Tempest added, not bothering to look back.

Jena jogged after them, struggling to keep pace with the twins' mighty strides. Both women were said to measure exactly two metres in height, but seemed taller in person. The pair became famous at the last Imperial Games, winning all but one of the seven disciplines they entered. Only the marathon title had eluded them, after the Tsar publicly expressed his opinion that it would be nice to see someone else collect the gold medal. Tempest had finished second, with Storm in third. Despite standing on the rostrum's lower steps, both women had towered over the marathon winner.

After the games had finished, controversy had filled the news media. Where had this pair of goddesses appeared from? What was their background? It was then that Doctor Fabergé stepped back into public life. For ten years, after suffering one of the most famous thefts in recent history, the scientist had remained in seclusion on his private island off the Black Sea coastline. Fabergé said the twins were his students but refused to divulge any more about their personal history. The Strangelove women declined a small fortune in offers to become professional sports stars or advertising icons, instead returning to their mentor's home. Their sudden emergence and subsequent disappearance enhanced the enigma surrounding them, with the media nicknaming them the Furies. All the attention further enhanced the myth of Doctor Fabergé, even if it was one of his own making.

Tempest stopped at a high wooden doorway and gestured for Jena to step inside. Above them towered an old castle, reconstructed on this island stone by stone after being transported from its original location in Britannia. Fabergé had purchased the castle with a fraction of his enormous insurance payout for the stolen Steel Military Egg, along with the island. Gargoyles leaned out from the castle's battlements, their faces curled into grotesque shapes and expressions. Everything about the building hinted at menace. "Lovely place you have here," Jena said with a cheerful smile.

"Inside," Tempest growled, the muscles around her jaw rippling.

"Whatever you say."

"Why? Why did you take my legs?" Di Grizov whimpered, his hands pawing uselessly at the stumps.

"Revenge, that was certainly a motivating factor," Fabergé conceded. "I wanted you to suffer as I have suffered – humiliation, despair, anger. I wanted you to be left scarred, to be hurt, to be transformed by our encounter, just as I was transformed by what you did to me."

"I never touched you!"

"But you crippled my reputation! You turned me into a laughing stock, a cocktail party joke across the Empire! I was forced to hide myself away. But I used that exile as a challenge, an opportunity to further my studies, my research. I emerged stronger, better for the experience – perhaps you will too."

Di Grizov stared at the scientist incredulously. "You're insane!"

Fabergé shook his head. "Passionate, yes. Driven, yes. Even a tad obsessed – that might well be true, too. But insane? No, I think that's little strong in the circumstances." He nodded to Wartski, who strode to the bedside and punched the grifter in the face. Di Grizov's head snapped to one side, the sound of a cheekbone breaking like a rifle shot in the small room. "You would do well to remember I am in charge here, not you."

Di Grizov spat a mouthful of blood and phlegm at Fabergé. The scientist sighed and nodded again to Wartski. She punched the patient again, this time cracking his nose with her meaty fist. The hefty woman drew back her arm, ready to strike again, but Fabergé stilled her with a gesture.

"False bravado will only bring you more suffering," the scientist said to his captive. "Wartski here would happily administer such pain. She's a true sadist, gaining a sexual thrill from each bout of agony she inflicts. Unless you're a true masochist, I suggest you keep your opinions and spittle to yourself. Do we have an agreement?"

Di Grizov nodded weakly, crimson coursing from his broken nose and down his chin, pooling in the hollow in the middle of his collarbone.

"That's better," Fabergé smiled. "You should be honoured. I have chosen you as the guinea pig for an exciting series of experiments to be conducted over the coming days. I have developed a hormone that enhances the body's natural healing abilities. I want to use you as the control subject. Every day at this hour you will be given an injection of the hormone and then be made to suffer the most excruciating agony. Wartski will take notes on how you respond to such treatment and determine how much benefit you are gaining from it. And please, be honest in your replies to her enquiries – this *is* for the advancement of science." The doctor gestured to the matron. She removed a pill from a case in her pocket and pushed it roughly between Di Grizov's teeth.

"Swallow," she hissed. "Swallow!" When the grifter did not obey, Wartski reached down beneath his hospital gown and clenched Di Grizov's testicles in her right hand. One squeeze was enough to open his mouth; another squeeze persuaded him to swallow the pill. "That's better," she said approvingly.

Fabergé nodded his agreement. "Now, what should be the nature of today's agony? Considering what you've already suffered, we don't want to go too much further, lest the results be compromised."

A firm knock from outside the room interrupted the discussion.

"Who is it?" Wartski demanded impatiently.

"Tempest and Storm, ma'am. We've brought Doctor Fabergé's guest."

The scientist's face lit up with pleasure. "Ahh, the beautiful Tsarina! Show her in, please, show her in."

Jena was ushered into a small room where Fabergé was waiting for her. He strode forward and bowed deeply, kissing her hand while mouthing some platitudes. Jena was taken aback to realise the doctor's assistant was a woman, and not an obese and obscenely ugly transvestite in a nurse's uniform. They shared an uncomfortable handshake, Jena all too aware of the clump of warts grasping her own slender fingers. Finally Fabergé waved grandly at an unfortunate soul lying on a hospital bed.

"And this is one of my experimental subjects, a thief known as James Di Grizov. He did me a rather infamous disservice some twelve years ago, but is now making recompense by taking part in one of my studies."

Jena frowned. Di Grizov? Where have I heard that name before? Leaving her subconscious to ponder, she took in the horror lying on the bed. His face was a bloody mess: one cheek swelling up and blood still dribbling from a recently broken nose. Jena noticed the bloody stumps where the patient's legs must have been. Some kind of accident? Jena decided not. The glee in her host's voice told her this double amputation had been utterly unnecessary.

I've seen what shelling and bullets and bio-wire can do to the human body, Jena thought, but that was amidst the atrocities of war. To see such injuries in peacetime made her shudder. What other horrors would she have to bear witness to on her father's behalf during this visit?

"Well, that's enough about this patient," Fabergé continued. "Shall we move to the main laboratory? I've got something that the Tsar has expressed great interest in. With his support, my work here could provide the Empire with a weapon far beyond anything wielded in the last war."

Jena nodded. "Yes, that's why I'm here, to assess your progress. But perhaps I could freshen up first? It's been a long journey…"

Her host smiled placidly. "Of course, of course. Wartski will show you to the nearest facilities, then we may began the full inspection."

Di Grizov waited until he was alone before letting himself cry, the tears mingling with the blood and perspiration on his face. If he had the strength and the opportunity, he'd kill himself soon – maybe one day, maybe two. A lifetime among the Vorovskoi Mir had taught the grifter much about the ways of people, their weaknesses and vulnerabilities. Di Grizov knew he would not be able to endure this torture for long. Better to end it now, put himself out of their clutches. If truth were told, he had contemplated suicide more than once in the last dozen years. The curse of the Steel Military Egg had haunted him beyond reckoning, grinding away at his heart and mind. And now this fate…

To the grifter's surprise, the door slid open and the Tsar's daughter stepped back into the room. "What are you doing here?" Di Grizov asked.

"I have to ask you something," she replied, standing beside the entrance. "Have we met before? I know I've heard your name."

"No. I'd remember encountering a woman as beautiful as you."

Jena frowned. "Perhaps someone else mentioned you?"

Di Grizov shook his head. "Unlikely. My name's been mud in the Thieves' World ever since I stole the egg and left my last apprentice to carry the can."

"The egg?"

"The Steel Military Egg – the auction at Casino Royale in Monaco?"

Jena's eyes widened. "That was you?"

"Yes, with a little help. I got away untouched with the egg, leaving my assistant to find his own escape route. I should have been set for life; instead I've ended up like this... And him! Who ever knew he'd become so famous?"

"Lady Jena? Where are you?" Wartski's approaching voice and heavy footfalls signalled imminent danger. "Lady Jena?"

"Your apprentice – what was his name?"

Di Grizov grimaced. "He was cocky and arrogant even then, seemed to think he was too cool to kill. How he's ever survived this long I'll never know. His name was Dante–"

"Nikolai Dante," Jena said, shaking her head. "I should have known."

"You've met him?"

Jena rolled her eyes. The grifter almost smiled. "That's a yes. Well, if you ever see him again, tell Nikolai that I–"

"Lady Jena!" Wartski was standing in the doorway, scowling at the Imperial visitor. "What are you doing in here?"

"My apologies, Madame Wartski. I heard your patient coughing and thought he might need assistance."

The slab-faced matron narrowed her eyes. "I'll be the judge of that."

"Of course," Jena replied swiftly, letting herself be ushered out of the room. She gave Di Grizov one last compassionate smile before the door shut between them.

The grifter lay back on his pillow. So Dante knew the Tsarina? And from that twinkle in her eye, the rogue knew her in quite an intimate manner. *What I wouldn't give to swap places with him now*, Di Grizov thought bleakly.

It was close to dusk before Jena was back on the landing pad, having finished her inspection of the island's facilities. Doctor Fabergé bowed and kissed her hand in an elaborate show of deference, while flanked by the statuesque menace of the Strangelove twins. "I hope you have been impressed by what you've seen here today, Tsarina."

"An exceptional display," Jena replied. "I've never witnessed anything to rival such scientific... daring."

"Then I can hope for a positive response to my request for your father's personal assistance in the next stage of this project?"

"I will deliver a full and frank assessment of everything I have seen here today. I would not dream of second-guessing his reaction, but I am certain you will have it within twenty-four hours of my return to the Imperial Palace."

Fabergé smiled broadly. "Excellent. Then I shall not delay your return to his side a moment longer, ma'am."

Jena began climbing the steps into her flyer before pausing to ask a final question. "Doctor, what will happen to Di Grizov? After you have finished the experiments involving him, what shall be his fate?"

"You need not worry, Lady Jena, he will not trouble polite society again with his criminal ways. All those who survive this phase of the trials are being sent to join work details in an Imperial gulag, probably one in Murmansk. Di Grizov is due to be transferred there tomorrow. Should he make it, I doubt he will last long. I understand from Madame Wartski that such places can be quite bleak, apparently. She was born and raised on a gulag, albeit a Siberian one, so she knows them well."

"I don't doubt it," Jena said with a thin smile. "Well, thank you again for the hospitality. A most illuminating visit. Farewell!" The flyer's passenger door closed behind her and the vehicle rose majestically into the sunset.

Fabergé waved goodbye, still smiling as he spoke to the twins. "Well? What did you make of her?"

"Too curious for her own good," Tempest sneered.

"Too good for her own curiosity," Storm countered.

"But still loyal to her father," the doctor replied. "No matter how much her stomach was turned by what she saw here, the Tsarina can still be trusted to give an accurate report on our progress. Indeed, her disgust may be to our advantage." Once the flyer was clear of the island, Fabergé stopped waving and snapped his fingers at the two women. "Come. We have much to do."

Jena wished she could strip off her clothes and burn them, so nauseating was the effect of being around Doctor Fabergé and his experiments. But purging her loathing would have to wait until after seeing her father. Jena knew she had been sent by the Tsar as a test, both of her nerves and her loyalty. Well, two could play at that game. She would give him a full and frank description of every horror, every atrocity she had witnessed inside that castle. Then she would watch his reaction. Any sane man, any man with a scintilla of morality, ought to reject the Fabergé experiments as an abomination against nature. Knowing the Tsar, he would probably embrace them with both arms.

Jena pushed such thoughts aside; they would do her no good for the moment. Better to focus on something else, anything but what she had seen today. As the flyer began the long journey back to St Petersburg, Jena recalled her conversation with Di Grizov. She remembered now where she had first heard the grifter's name mentioned. After the Romanovs had fallen at the end of the war, a quirk of fate had thrown her and Dante together one last time. But instead of lovers they were bitter enemies, Dante her prisoner.

Nikolai had talked about partnering Di Grizov during his thieving days, being taught everything he knew. No prison in the Empire would be able to hold him – a typical Dante boast. Several times during the war the former lovers had been presented with opportunities to kill each other, yet had been unable or unwilling to do so. Rather than deliver Dante for execution, Jena let him escape, urging him to get to safety offworld. "I never want to see you or hear the name Nikolai Dante again," she had said before turning away.

Where was he now, Jena wondered? Despite herself, she combed daily bulletins from across the Empire, looking for his name. The bounty on Dante's head had reached fifty million roubles, with half as much again if anyone should succeed in delivering him alive to the Tsar. Several times Dante had apparently been captured, only to escape again. His apprenticeship with Di Grizov had not been wasted experience, it seemed.

If he had any common sense, Dante would go beyond the reach of the Empire. The ridiculous rogue possessed many qualities, Jena thought, but common sense was not among the strongest. If I know Nikolai, he's probably in trouble right now – up to his neck.

TWO

"Without a ruse the thief won't steal"
– Russian proverb

Dante liked dressing in black. For a start, it hid a multitude of sins and stains, both of which he had considerable experience with. Secondly, it enabled him to disappear into the shadows. Thirdly – and most importantly – it added a hint of danger to what he considered was his already considerable animal magnetism. Few ladies could resist having a kiss stolen from their lips by Dante when he adopted his guise as the Gentleman Thief!

Dante had first pulled on the black mask while staying at the Hotel Yalta, not long after his acceptance to the House of Romanov in 2666. To celebrate his new status, the black-haired brigand had thrown a month-long debauch at the hotel, one of the Empire's most expensive resorts. It was only after the bill arrived that Dante discovered being a Romanov did not also grant him access to the considerable family purse. Ever inventive, he quickly returned to his thieving ways, reviving the skills honed while growing up amongst the Vorovskoi Mir.

He dressed from head to toe in black, pulled on a matching mask and proclaimed himself to be the Gentleman Thief – robbing the rich and then robbing them again. Soon, under-sexed, over-excited ladies were flocking to the Hotel Yalta in the hope of being ravaged by this virile young cut-purse. But all of that was before the war, before Dante's name became a curse upon the lips of millions. A conventional job was beyond his imagination or skills, and laying low for the next fifty years held little appeal. Live fast, have fun and let tomorrow take care of itself was Dante's motto. But you still needed roubles and kopecks to fund such a lifestyle, and so the thief's mask was coming out of retirement.

Dante studied his reflection in a mirror while knotting the mask into place. His eyes sparkled with wit and intelligence, he liked to think – or at least a hint of mischief. A neatly trimmed black moustache and goatee helped enhance his roguish good looks while a lustrous mane of black hair was swept back from his forehead, reaching down almost to collar length. With the mask, few women could resist my considerable charms, he thought.

You're not going out in that I hope, a pious voice said inside Dante's head.

"Why not? It's always been a hit with the ladies."

It does have the advantage of covering half of your face, yes.

"I haven't got time for this, Crest. I've an appointment to keep."

The prim voice sighed heavily. *More petty thievery? If so, you can do it without my help. I wasn't created to enable ease of entry for minor felons.*

"I resent that remark," Dante protested. "I am not a minor felon!"

Really?

"Don't you know what we're going to rob?"

I dread to think.

"The Imperial Mint," Dante announced triumphantly.

The Imperial Mint?

"Yes."

The most heavily guarded, impenetrable and implacable building in all of St Petersburg?

"That's the one." Dante waited but was rewarded with only a lengthy silence. "Well, aren't you impressed?"

Yes.

"I thought you would be."

This must be the stupidest idea you've ever had, Dante, and that is setting it against an already impressive list of stupid ideas.

Dante finished adjusting his mask. "Whine all you want, Crest, but sometimes I think you actually enjoy my little adventures."

Nothing could be further from the truth! I am a Weapons Crest; one of the most advanced battle computers known to mankind, a repository of vast knowledge and wisdom, charged with the task of training my symbiotic host to become a potential ruler of the Empire! I should have been bonded with a pure-born Romanov – instead I got stuck with you, a lust-driven, sewer-spawned, gutter-rat who acts first and thinks last. You have turned me into an accessory for your petty crime sprees and rejoiced in my discomfort!

"Yeah, yeah, yeah," Dante replied. He looked down at the double-headed eagle tattoo on his left arm, the only physical manifestation of the Crest's presence within his body. "Anytime you want to shut up, just let me know."

I wouldn't give you the satisfaction! Our bonding has given you abilities far beyond most men. You have a vastly enhanced healing ability, so you can survive almost any wound. You can extend cyborganic swords from your fists, giving you a significant advantage in hand-to-hand combat. And with the knowledge in my sentient computer brain, you can access and override any computer in the Empire! But what do you use all these gifts for?

Dante sighed. "You nag worse than my first wife, Crest."

You've only been married once – and she's dead.

"Don't remind me."

You still haven't answered my question, Dante.

"You seem to be doing enough talking for both of us."

Lying, cheating, debauching, crime, infamy and indolence!

"And nobody does it better, Crest."

I despair for you.

"Despair all you want, but lower the volume while you do. It's hard to concentrate with an extra voice offering a running commentary in your brain."

Well, at least you've got one intelligent voice inside here, the Crest snapped. *If it wasn't for me, cuckoos could nest in your skull undisturbed.*

Dante clutched the sides of his head. "Diavolo, just shut up!"

Fine!

"Good!"

I will!

"Suits me!"

After a few moments the Crest spoke again. *But you'll be needing me later to break into the Imperial Mint?*

"Yeah, of course."

In that case I'll start hacking the Imperial Net for security logs, alarm codes and other useful information.

"Thanks."

Let me know when I'm needed.

Dante waited a moment; but the prim, haughty voice had gone silent – for now. "Finally, some peace and quiet," he muttered, before emerging from the bathroom into the suite's living room. An unwelcome fug, redolent of death, spoiled fish and horse liniment, hung in the air. Dante's nose crumpled involuntarily as he sought to avoid breathing too deeply. "Bojemoi, did somebody die and leave us their corpse in the will?"

"Worse – tonight is Spatch's turn to cook," an aristocratic voice replied. Dante peered through the fumes to see the speaker. Lord Peter Flintlock was standing by the balcony doors, breathing the night air of St Petersburg in preference to whatever vileness was being concocted inside the suite. Tall and thin, with a carefully coiffed tangle of blond hair, Flintlock acted like a fop and dressed like a dandy. He still wore the scarlet uniform with gold braid from his days as a conscript in the Romanov army. Disgraced and deported from his native Britannia for some unknown depravity,

Flintlock had joined the fighting forces rather than be executed. Cowardice kept him alive, as did an unlikely alliance with the other occupant of the hotel suite.

"Fuoco, what he is making? Mustard gas?" Dante approached the corner when Spatchcock was stirring something toxic in a pot on a portable stove.

"A little something of me own invention," the grubby chef replied in a gruff and uncultured voice. "Not as lethal as mustard gas but get one drop on your skin and you'll be retching your guts out for hours. I call it purge juice."

"Charming," Dante said.

"Thought it might come in handy for our raid on the mint."

"*Our* raid? I've already explained – you and Flintlock wait outside while I go in alone. One man might get in and out alive, but never three."

"Still, you never know," Spatchcock maintained. "It might go wrong. We might have to launch a rescue mission for you!"

"If something goes wrong, I know exactly where you two will be headed – straight for the hills, looking after your own asses."

The sly-faced poisoner grinned, displaying a mouthful of decay and broken molars. "Heh. You're probably right." Like Flintlock, Spatchcock had chosen conscription ahead of execution during the war. The pair had met when they were selected to serve under Dante in the Rudinshtein Irregulars, a motley collection of thieves, murderers and human effluent. Flintlock and Spatchcock had fitted in perfectly.

But the grubby little man was unlike his aristocratic comrade in almost every other way. A liar, forger, extortionist and purveyor of filth, Spatchcock had murdered a dozen men with potions, pills and poisons before the war. Fond of eating his own lice, he could make a meal out of anything – but few would want to consume it. Any clothes he wore seemed to attract grease and stains, and the only baths he took usually involved falling into rivers, lakes or oceans.

"Heard you arguing with the Crest again. Surprised you two don't get a divorce."

"I've thought about that more than once," Dante admitted, before leaning forwards to whisper in Spatchcock's left ear. "Secretly I think it enjoys all our misadventures but just can't bring itself to admit that." He straightened up again, not wanting to stay too close in case of catching something unpleasant. "How long before this stuff is ready?"

"Any minute. Just got to let it cool down."

"Good. I want to hit the mint just before midnight, as the security guards are changing shift. While they're busy comparing notes–"

"You'll be nicking the bank notes?" Spatchcock interjected.

"Not exactly. I have something far more valuable in mind."

The Imperial Mint stood to the east of St Petersburg, its imposing stone and marble structure surrounded by cybernetically-enhanced attack dogs, a constantly shifting laser defence grid and a cadre of Berez Enforcers. Recruited from the colony world of Berezova, these fearsome aliens were renowned for the thickness and resiliency of their mottled brown skins. Gravity on Berezova was twice the strength of that on Earth, making the Enforcers vastly more powerful than any human. Anyone who took on an Enforcer without the aid of a large tank was considered foolhardy or insane.

"Should be a piece of cake," Dante said, standing in the shadow of a building opposite the mint's main entrance. Behind him Spatchcock and Flintlock looked less certain, the Englishman hopping nervously from foot to foot while his lice-infested associate scratched at a facial scab.

"You want to take some purge juice, just in case?" Spatchcock asked.

"No thanks," Dante replied. "I'd rather rely on my wits."

"There's a doomsday plan if ever I heard one," Flintlock muttered, earning a baleful glare from his former commander. "Sorry, did I say that out loud?"

"Just stay here and keep the getaway vehicle ready. If I do make it out of there in one piece, I'll probably be running for my life." Dante checked his mask was still in place and then began strolling towards the mint, bold as brass. "Crest, how are those security specs coming along?"

All was silent but for Dante's footsteps.

"Crest, can you hear me?" he hissed under his breath. "This is no time to give me the silent treatment." Dante was close to the mint's security perimeter, but knew retracing his steps now would only attract suspicion. Instead he crouched and began retying the laces on one of his black leather boots. "If this is about what I said earlier, I'm sorry, okay? However I've upset you, I'm sorry!"

By now one of the Enforcers had noticed the stranger lingering just beyond the pulsating laser defence grid. It stumped towards him, carefully choosing its steps across the marble flagstones outside the mint. Dante noticed the guard approaching and continued fiddling with his laces, now retying those on his other boot. Beads of sweat were gathering under the black silk of his mask. He swiftly pulled it off and shoved it into a pocket. Hanging around the mint at midnight wouldn't be easily explained, but wearing a black mask over your face at the same time could complicate matters further.

"Please, Crest, tell me what I've done wrong before that guard realises why I'm *really* here!"

Well, you're tying that lace into a double knot, for a start, the Crest finally replied. *You'll have a terrible time undoing that later.*

"Forget the lace! Tell me how to evade the alarms and get inside!"

Not until you apologise.

"I'm sorry, okay? I'm sorry!"

Now say it like you mean it, the Crest replied with a sniff.

"How can I mean it when I don't even know what I'm apologising for?"

Saying I nag, for a start. Telling me to be quiet. That sort of thing is very hurtful. You should think before you speak.

By now the Enforcer was within earshot of Dante. The would-be intruder stood up and smiled, giving the guard a friendly wave. "Nice night for it!"

The Enforcer glared back, its monolithic features impassive.

"Couldn't sleep!" Dante offered by way of explanation for his presence. "Thought I'd take a stroll, stretch the legs, get some air into the lungs."

Still nothing from the Enforcer.

"Well, guess I'll be moving along. Maybe I'll be see you later!"

Maybe I'll see you later? the Crest spluttered inside Dante's mind.

"Bye!" Dante called to the guard, before turning and slowly walking away, whistling tunelessly. After a few seconds he risked a glance back over his shoulder. The Enforcer was returning to its post outside the mint's entrance. "Okay, I think I fooled him," Dante whispered.

Congratulations, the Crest replied. *You've found someone even stupider than you. That's quite an achievement.*

"Very droll. Now how do I get in?"

Turn and start running towards the laser defence grid. The beams are on a complex rotational system but time it just right and you should be able to pick a way between them.

"And if I don't?"

Even your enhanced healing abilities will have trouble reattaching your head or limbs.

"You're filling me with confidence, Crest."

Makes a nice change. Normally you're just full of sh–

"Shut up!" Dante hissed. He spun round and started running towards the laser defence grid. In front of him red beams danced through the air, appearing and disappearing in a dazzling light show that defied interpretation. "Crest, are you sure about this?"

As sure as I can be. There is one factor I can only guess at.
"What's that?"

Your incompetence. Prepare to jump forwards into a somersault.

"Fuoco," Dante whispered.

Now! the Crest commanded. Dante dived into the air hands first, then tucked his legs up underneath himself as he cleared a red beam that suddenly appeared below him. *Now kick out and tumble into a forward roll when you hit the ground!* The black clad figure followed the Crest's instructions, wincing as his body hit the ground. *Stand up – quickly!* Dante was on his feet in a moment. *Run five paces to your left!* The fleet-footed thief set off in one direction. *Your other left!* Dante twisted round, reversing his direction. *Stop! Stay absolutely still!* Laser beams sliced through the air in a dizzying cycle of movement, each accompanied by a low buzz and flash of heat. One zipped between Dante's legs, searing the fabric just below his crotch.

"Ahhh! Hot, hot, hot!" Dante winced.

Now, run three steps forwards and then go into a cartwheel!

Dante began running again. "What's a cartwheel?" he asked.

Just jump!

"I can't look, I can't look," Flintlock whimpered, peering between his fingers as Dante danced around inside the laser field. "Is he still alive?"

"He's still in one piece," Spatchcock chuckled gleefully, "but I'm guessing he won't need his bikini line waxed anytime soon."

"What are you talking about, Spatch?"

"The lasers have – oh, never mind! He's done it, he's through!"

"Bravo!" Flintlock cheered loudly before realising where he was. "Well done," he continued in a much quieter voice. "I always knew he'd pull it off."

"Hmph! That was the easy part," Spatchcock said. "He's still got to penetrate the building, slip past all the security and unlock the vault."

"Oh dear. And that's more difficult?"

"Put it this way, your lordship – no thief has ever made it out of the Imperial Mint alive."

Dante was thankful for the drop in danger levels once inside the mint. He entered via a side window, its lock picked by a combination of the Crest's sentient computer mind and a cyborganic key extruded from one of Dante's fingernails. Inside there were no lasers to dodge, as the mint did not want its staff sliced and diced as they went about their jobs. Instead security rested with a series of alarms and motion sensors, all swiftly neutralised by the Crest. The Gentleman Thief needed less than ten minutes to reach the centre of the building, the mint's world famous Vault of Doom.

"Bit of a melodramatic name, don't you think?"

The Crest ignored Dante's sarcasm. *Nobody has ever deduced the correct combination for this chamber. It is said anyone hoping to crack the safe could spend a millennia of millennia upon the task and still not succeed.*

"Media hype, just a smokescreen to put off the easily discouraged."

I've scanned through the files for every attempt ever made. This task is almost impossible. I don't know why you persist in setting yourself such unobtainable goals; it's irrational and self-destructive.

"I like a challenge," Dante replied. "Besides, I have an advantage that none of my predecessors ever possessed, Crest. You."

Flattery's the food of fools. Jonathan Swift said that, a thousand years ago.

"Spare me the quotations, Crest. Can you open this vault or not?"

It won't be easy.

"I have every confidence in you."

Stop smirking when you say that, it'll be far more convincing. Dante did his best to comply. The Crest sighed in mild exasperation. *Now place your hands against the vault and cede control of your cyborganics to me.*

"How do I do that?"

Empty your mind of all thoughts – hardly the work of a lifetime.

"Just get on with it, Crest, we haven't got all night." Dante flattened his hands against the vault's door and tried to think of nothing. Tendrils of cyborganic circuitry emerged from his fingertips, a mixture of purple and silver, part flesh and part machine. The tendrils crept between the edges of the vault door and its housing, working their way into the locks.

"Getting anywhere yet?"

Have some patience! I'm trying to concentrate.

"Sorry." Dante pursed his lips and whistled a tune, the notes sliding carelessly from one key to another. The Crest sighed loudly inside Dante's head. "Sorry, sorry. Just passing the time."

Let's hope you never have to make a living with your musical talents.

"My mama said I had a beautiful singing voice as a child!"

Parents frequently lie to protect the feelings of their untalented offspring. Now let me concentrate! The Crest continued its investigation of the vault's locking mechanism. *Nearly got it–*

"So you're saying I don't whistle very well?"

Dante! For once in your life stop prattling and let me do what I do best!

A stony silence followed for the next thirty-seven seconds, until the vault's locks undid themselves one after another, each retracting with a heavy *thunk*. When all were disabled, Dante removed his hands, the cyborganic circuitry already being absorbed back into his fingers. The massive door swung open to reveal a circular chamber, all burnished brass and gleaming silver. The thief stepped inside the vault and examined the rows of sealed boxes set into the walls. "I can whistle as well as the next man," Dante muttered under his breath.

I estimate you've less than thirty seconds before the central alarm is triggered and the vault flooded with nerve gas. Even I can't override that.

Dante tapped a box with the numbers 027 etched into its front. "This is the one." He opened the container and removed a slim wooden case from inside. "Funny, I didn't think it would be that easy."

Presumably the owners believed their external security system and the vault door were enough to keep that safe, the Crest ventured.

"I guess so." Dante wedged the wooden case inside the waistband of his trousers and shut the door to box 027.

Suddenly sirens and flashing red lights filled the vault. A noxious yellow gas billowed from grilles set into the floor, flooding the confined space.

Dante, get out. Now!

"I know, I know, evasive action," the thief replied, already running for the exit. The door was closing but Dante squeezed through the rapidly diminishing gap, just getting his trailing arm and leg out before the vault was sealed once more. "Phew!"

Phew indeed. Now you've just got to get past all the Berez Enforcers, cybernetically enhanced attack dogs and the laser defence grid again. But this time, they're expecting you.

Dante was already sprinting away from the vault, retracing his earlier steps. "Got any good news for me Crest?"

All this vigorous exercise might help you stave off incipient middle age spread for another day or two.

"Thanks!" Dante replied as he ran round a corner to find three Berez Enforcers blocking his escape route. "I'll bear that in mind!"

Spatchcock shrugged helplessly when the Imperial Mint's alarms started rending the air. "And it was going so well," he said with a heavy sigh.

"What should we do?" Flintlock asked querulously.

"You heard him – stay here and keep the motor running." Spatchcock turned to glance at the vehicle parked nearby. "But it beats me why he wants a limousine as the getaway car. Hardly inconspicuous, is it?"

Dante ducked, dived, dodged and wove his way past more than a dozen Enforcers, outran a pack of attack dogs and somehow eluded everything else the mint's security contingent threw at him, aided and abetted by the Crest's imminent threat warnings and motion sensors. Trapped between two oncoming squads of Enforcers, Dante had taken refuge behind the nearest doorway, ignoring the Crest's protestations.

No, don't go in there, it's–

"Trust me Crest, I know what I'm doing!"

Dante was surrounded by mops, brooms, buckets and shelves laden with cleansers, bleaches and disinfectants. "I'm guessing there's only one way in or out of here?"

Genius, pure genius. .With such intelligence it's a wonder you need my help at all.

"Sarcasm is the lowest form of wit, Crest."

Now who's spouting quotations?

"Save it. I need an escape route, not smart-ass remarks!"

You could say you popped in to do a little late night mopping?

"Hmm... I've got a better idea." Dante opened the cupboard door and stepped out, smiling at the seventeen Enforcers crowding the corridor. As one they turned and aimed their pulse rifles at the intruder.

You call coming out of the closet a plan? the Crest spluttered.

"Gentlemen, I believe you've been looking for me," Dante announced grandly. "Congratulations – here I am!"

The Enforcers looked at each other quizzically, nonplussed by this development.

Dante bowed grandly before pulling a rectangle of card from inside his waistband. "Allow me to introduce myself properly. As you can see from my business card, I am Quentin Durward, Imperial Security Consultant."

One of the Enforcers snatched the card and examined it closely.

"All of you have been taking part in an exercise to test the security systems of this building and may I offer my thanks for your part in this. A most able and commendable display by all concerned," Dante continued, smiling broadly at the scowling Enforcers.

I don't think they're swallowing your story, the Crest whispered.

Dante ignored the voice inside his head. "It just remains for me to say something I have always wanted to utter: take me to your leader!"

The alien guard holding the business card dropped it on the floor and ground the card beneath his feet.

Dante's smile faltered slightly. "Is that a refusal?"

The Enforcer pulled back his weapon and swiftly smashed its butt into Dante's forehead. The thief staggered backwards into the broom cupboard, blood coursing from the wound below his hairline, eyelids fluttering weakly.

"That's no way to treat an accredited consultant to the… to the…"

Blackness closed in around Dante and he never finished the sentence.

"Spatch, it's been three hours. Surely he can't expect us to wait here much longer?" Flintlock was standing beside the limousine, his legs crossed, a pained expression on his face.

"How long have we known Dante?"

"Since the war."

"And has he ever let us down?"

"Not yet," Flintlock conceded.

"So we can wait a little longer for him, can't we?"

"I suppose."

Spatchcock noticed the Englishman's unhappy posture. "What's the matter with you? You look like you've been sampling my purge juice."

"If you must know, I need to relieve my bladder."

"You mean you want to take a piss."

"Must you be so crude about it?"

"You want to piss? Then piss. I couldn't care less," Spatchcock said.

"Out here, in the open? That's hardly seemly."

"Bugger that. I pissed my pants an hour ago."

Flintlock's face crumpled with distaste. "I wondered what the smell was."

The hum of an approaching vehicle cut short the exchange. Spatchcock watched intently as a stately silver flyer stopped outside the mint. Two Enforcers used electronic overrides to create a corridor in the laser grid and the flyer moved inside the perimeter. Once parked, a trio of middle-aged men in collar-less jackets emerged and strode into the building.

"I recognise one of them," Flintlock said, the call of his bladder forgotten for the moment. "Eugene Jamieson. He used to run the Bank of Britannia. Refused to extend my credit after an unfortunate flutter at Royal Ascot went awry one year. The arrogant sod!"

"Could be governors of the Imperial Mint. They look like merchant bankers. But what are they doing here, at this time of night?" Spatchcock wondered.

Dante opened his eyes to find three concerned men in suits peering at him. "Mr Durward? Are you alright?" one of them asked, his extra chins wobbling slowly.

"I've felt better, I must admit." He tried to stand but the pain stabbing through his skull persuaded him against such movement. Instead Dante sunk back into the plush, upholstered chair. He was sat in the centre of a large, richly furnished office. Portraits of stern-faced men lined the walls, each adorned with a gold plaque noting the past contributions to the Imperial Mint. "What happened exactly?"

The fattest of the three men stepped forward, his hands held open in apology. "I regret to say one of our alien guards was overly enthusiastic in the application of their duties. You received a blow to the head and were rendered unconscious. It was only after the members of the board were contacted about the apparent intrusion at the mint that this mistake was uncovered. I called the number on your business card and was reassured of your bona fides by the President of Imperial Security Consultancy, Lord Spatchcock."

Somebody had been doing some fast-talking, Dante realised. "Very well. In the circumstances, I'm sure my firm shall be willing to set aside any legal action that might otherwise follow from such a violent and painful incident."

"That would be most kind of you," the obese man replied. "Most kind."

Dante held a hand to the throbbing contusion on his forehead. "Forgive my asking, but the blow seems to have clouded my memory a little. What was your name, sir?"

"Sharapov, Sergei Sharapov. I am Governor of the Mint. And these are two of my directors, Boris Onegin and Eugene Jamieson." Sharapov's offsiders nodded at Dante, who acknowledged their presence.

"Well, gentleman, my report on the mint's security systems is mostly positive. Your laser defence grid can be penetrated, by only by an exceptional athlete such as myself," Dante said with a wry smile. "The locking mechanism on your external windows needs improving, but that should not cost you more than half a million roubles. The main area of concern is your so-called Vault of Doom. For such a fabled and supposedly unbreakable safe, it was all too easy for me to gain access to the valuables stored within."

Onegin stepped closer to Dante. "If I might ask, how is it you were able to defeat the vault when so many others have failed?"

"You may ask, but I must decline to reveal my methods. Trade secrets, you understand, must remain secrets, of course. Even when I deliberately triggered the final alarm sensor within the vault—"

Ha!

Dante did his best to ignore this outburst from the Crest. "Even when I deliberately triggered it, I was still able to escape the chamber – removing this with me." He reached into the waistband of his trousers and extracted the slim wooden case taken from box 027. "I doubt you would wish the printing plates for the million rouble note to fall into the wrong hands."

Sharapov's eyes widened with horror. "No, indeed not! Thank the Tsar you were able to uncover these flaws in our security perimeter, Mr Durward!"

"Don't thank me," Dante replied. "All part of the service. Of course, if you felt the urge to add a little extra to my fee as a bonus, I would be most grateful for any such consideration."

"Of course, of course!" Sharapov glanced at his colleagues, who nodded hurriedly. "An extra ten per cent on top of your fee?"

Dante coughed.

"Fifteen per cent, I meant fifteen per cent," Sharapov continued. "Sorry, slip of the tongue there. A fifteen per cent bonus."

Dante smiled. "Most generous. You may be assured of utter discretion. It would not do if the real Gentleman Thief or those of his ilk should learn of the vulnerabilities in your defences."

"I wanted to ask why you wore such curious garb," Onegin said.

"You haven't heard of the Gentleman Thief?" Dante asked. "The most famous cutpurse and cat burglar in all the Empire?"

The three men shook their heads.

"Thank heavens I arrived when I did! He would have robbed you blind. Imagine the consequences if that happened. Imagine facing the Tsar himself and trying to explain such a calamity!"

The trio swallowed simultaneously, their discomfit all too evident. Having had sufficient time to recover, Dante stood. "Well, if you'll just make out a banker's draft to the Imperial Security Consultancy, I'll be on my way. With any luck my limousine will be waiting to collect me outside."

Flintlock pulled the peaked cap down over his eyes, not wanting to be recognised by Jamieson. Fortunately the three men from the Imperial Mint were too busy ushering Dante to his limousine to notice the identity of the uniformed chauffeur holding open the passenger door.

"Well, gentleman, it's been both a privilege and an honour to do business with you. One of my associates will be back sometime in the next year to carry out a spot check, as a way of ensuring the mint undertakes the necessary upgrades and keeping your security forces on their toes."

"Excellent," the Governor replied. "I hope our next intruder is far less successful than you were, Mr Durward!"

"Absolutely. Thank you again for the banker's draft and the bonus. All that remains is for me to bid you farewell." Dante began climbing into the limousine but a concerned whimper from the Governor made him straighten up again.

"Sorry, Mr Durward, but you still have the plates in your possession!"

Dante smiled. "Dear, oh dear, what a forgetful fool I am! You wouldn't want me wandering off with those now, would you? Ha, ha, ha!"

The three men from the mint laughed along with him, their voices cracked with nervous hysteria. Dante produced the slim wooden case and handed it over to the governor.

"Here you are, Make sure it stays safely locked away from now on."

"I will, don't worry about that, I will!"

"Good. Then my work here is done. Good day to you all." Dante entered the vehicle, Flintlock shutting the door politely after him before hurrying round to the driver's side. Within moments the limousine was rolling away, leaving the three directors to heave a relieved sigh.

The Governor looked at his colleagues. "That was too close. My life wouldn't be worth living if the–" He stopped abruptly, colour draining from his face. "I–I–"

"Sergei? What is it? What's wrong?" Onegin asked. He followed the Governor's gaze down to the wooden case. Sharapov had opened the box to find the printing plates were missing. Instead a rectangle of card was nestling on the vermilion velvet lining, a single line of text visible on it: "Congratulations, you have just been robbed by Nikolai Dante, the Gentleman Thief."

"How will I ever report this to the Tsar?" Sharapov spluttered. "I let Nikolai Dante walk out of the Imperial Mint with our most valuable asset?"

Onegin read the card again. "This can't be happening. It can't!"

Jamieson wrung his hands in desperation. "Perhaps we can still get offworld before the loss is discovered?"

Sharapov shook his head helplessly. "It's too late. We're already dead men." He turned and began walking towards the mint's laser defence grid.

"Sergei! What are you doing?" Jamieson shouted.

But the Governor did not reply. He kept walking, never uttering another word, not even when the lasers began slicing his body apart.

"You realise you've condemned those men to death, don't you?" Spatchcock asked. He was sat in the front passenger seat of the limousine, his presence in the vehicle having been hidden by the tinted windows.

"The Tsar will order their executions, not me," Dante replied. "Besides, when you work for that bastard, you deserve what you get. Everyone knows the Tsar's price for failure."

"What about the banker's draft?" Flintlock looked at Dante in the rear-view mirror as he drove. "You can't be planning to cash it?"

That would be both foolish and suicidal, the Crest commented dryly. *Sounds just your style.*

Dante crumpled the draft into a ball and threw it to his accomplices. "You two can keep it as a souvenir. The only thing that piece of paper is useful for now would be wiping your backside."

Spatchcock smiled. "You better have it then, Flintlock, in case you get caught short again."

"You might have a mind permanently residing in the gutter, but some of us still aspire to higher things," the former nobleman said. "Where to now?"

"The black market at Tsyganov," Dante replied, removing two thin sheets of metal from inside his trousers. "I know a counterfeiter there who'll pay well for these. The mint will have changed the million-rouble note by tonight but the old ones will stay in circulation for a few weeks yet. The sooner we can sell these plates, the better the price we'll get."

THREE

"He that is feared cannot be loved"
– Russian proverb

The Imperial flyer re-entered the airspace above St Petersburg shortly before dawn, the majestic city sprawling below like some bejewelled, black velvet gown. But Jena paid the magnificent vista no heed. She had seen it countless times from such a vantage point and her thoughts were elsewhere, still mulling over what she had witnessed in the laboratories on Fabergé Island. The pilot had to clear his throat several times to get her attention.

"Yes, what is it?" she said testily.

"We're making our final approach to the Imperial Palace, ma'am. You asked to be kept informed."

"Very good. Take us in."

"Yes, ma'am." The pilot pressed his controls forward and the flyer surged towards the floating edifice in the sky.

The Imperial Palace was a remarkable melding of technology and aesthetics. Taking its inspiration from the legendary designs of Carl Fabergé, the palace was shaped like a huge white egg. A hundred metres in height, its exterior was divided into a multiplicity of segments. Each was studded with windows, tiny squares set into the vast circumference of the palace. A large circular portal was visible on one side of the structure, open to allow authorised flyers access. Raven Corps troops mounted on flying mechanical steeds encircled the palace, keeping watch for potential attacks. Once the sun was above the horizon, the palace would cast an imposing shadow across the city, just as the

Tsar's will could turn day into night for anyone unfortunate enough to invoke his wrath.

"Imperial Palace to approaching flyer, transmit entry codes."

Jena lent forward and thrust a studded ring on her right hand into a cavity on the flyer's control panel.

"Entry codes accepted. Welcome back, Lady Jena."

The flyer swept through the circular portal and found a docking berth inside. Jena was already disembarking by the time a captain of the Raven Corps ran into view. "Lady Jena! Your father wishes to see you. He's in the Chamber of Judgement. If you'll follow me–"

Jena brushed past the captain, not bothering to acknowledge his salute. "I know the way, thank you very much. Tell my father I'm going to shower and change first. I want to rid myself of Fabergé's taint before I do anything else."

"Er, yes... ma'am," the captain replied fearfully.

Thirty minutes later Jena strode into the Chamber of Judgement, an intimidating and cavernous space near the top of the palace. Ranks of seating were built into the walls, enabling invited guests to witness the Tsar passing sentence on those that had displeased him or broken one of the Empire's many draconian laws. The prisoners' walkway extended out over a sheer drop, while the officers of the court usually loomed overhead on hovering pedestals. For now the chamber was empty, bar the brooding figure sat on a floating throne.

The Tsar glared down at Jena, his arms folded across his chest. Barrel-chested and powerful of build, Vladimir Makarov was a fearsome figure in magisterial robes of silver. Greying hair swept imperiously back from his stern, remorseless features, while a black and grey flecked beard curled outwards from his chin. His face was a permanent snarl, black eyes burning with suppressed rage. "What took you so long?" he demanded. "You were told to come and see me immediately and on your return, yes?"

"I washed and changed first. I wanted to cleanse myself of what I have witnessed," Jena replied. She did a little twirl so her father could see the entire crushed crimson velvet trouser suit she was now wearing. "Perhaps you don't like the outfit? I thought you had no problems with the colour of blood, father."

"Jena, my love," the Tsar growled, "do not try my patience. You flouted my order deliberately! And you know how I dislike being disobeyed." He gestured at the remains of the captain sent to fetch Jena. The body had been flayed alive and now lay in a pool of blood and skin flaps.

"I think the entire Empire knows how you dislike disobedience."

"Then you would do well not to provoke me, child. Now – report!"

Jena outlined all she had seen and heard on Fabergé Island, excluding only her encounter with Di Grizov. That was of little consequence in her opinion and merely mentioning the name Nikolai Dante was likely to send the Tsar into a murderous rage. Instead she offered detailed descriptions of the experiments already completed and the extrapolated outcome of the doctor's ongoing project. Her father listened carefully, nodding as she made mention of the next stage in Fabergé's researches. Only after Jena had finished did the Tsar make any comment.

"Good. You have told me all I wanted to know. But I sense you have more you wish to say about the good doctor and his work, yes?"

Jena nodded, choosing her next words carefully, mindful of the bloody corpse not far from her feet. "I have significant doubts about the sanity of Doctor Fabergé. He is both deranged and potentially dangerous. Certainly he is bloated with his own self-importance, but that in itself is not a crime. However he appears to be developing unhealthy delusions of grandeur. Fabergé thinks that by playing God he can become like a god himself. I doubt he can be trusted in the medium to long term."

The Tsar nodded at this assessment. "Agreed. That was why I elevated the House of Fabergé to the status of the noble dynasty not long after the war. The doctor has a rampaging ego to rival even my own, but he will remain loyal to me long enough for my uses. After that he shall be expendable. If he dared challenge my rule, Fabergé would soon discover just how expendable he is."

"But what about his next experiment?" Jena asked. "Even you cannot condone such barbarity, an atrocity of that nature – can you?"

"Condone it? It was my idea," the Tsar replied, amusement evident in his deep, booming voice. "If Fabergé can deliver upon his promises, I shall have at my disposal a new weapon that strengthens my grip upon the Empire for decades, even generations to come. Since you are my sole surviving heir, I would have thought the Fabergé experiments were in your best interests too!"

"I could never be a party to such–"

"No one is asking you to be!" the Tsar thundered, his mood suddenly darkening. "For more than a decade the Romanovs held me at bay with their precious Weapons Crest technology. Now they have been swept aside, the survivors no more than a rabble hiding themselves in the corners of the Empire! The Crests they were once so proud of will be the playthings of a child next to the weapon Fabergé is developing. I will become all-powerful! None shall dare oppose me again!"

"None dare oppose you now, father!" Jena shouted back. "You won the war, you crushed all opposition. Why do you need this new weapon? What good can it possibly do?"

The Tsar shook his head sadly. "Weapons are never used to do good, my daughter. Weapons are about getting and retaining power – nothing more, nothing less. If you have not grasped that by now, you never will!"

"But you must see–"

"Enough!" The Tsar piloted his hovering throne down so he could step off it and onto the platform beside Jena. "I have tolerated your insolence and your pious attitude enough for today. You are dismissed!"

"But–"

The Tsar pulled back his left hand, ready to strike Jena across the face, but she did not flinch nor cower. After a moment he lowered his hand again, regarding his daughter thoughtfully. "I am Tsar of all the Russians, my child, and I will do as I see fit. Fabergé's experiments shall continue and by Easter Sunday I shall have my new weapon. Be thankful your involvement with its development ends here." He strode away, leaving Jena alone in the Chamber of Judgement.

She watched him depart, hatred etched on her features. "We'll see about that," Jena whispered under her breath.

At midday Jena was back at her bedchamber inside the Imperial Palace, when one of her ladies-in-waiting knocked on the door. Anastasia was twenty-one, a meek and plain-faced woman who had proven herself completely loyal to the Tsarina. "Lady Jena, I have a report marked for your eyes only."

"Leave it on the bed, I'll read it later."

"Very good, ma'am."

Jena waited until she was alone before hurrying to the bed and tearing open the envelope. She hated herself for the eagerness with which her eyes sped across the words, absorbing the latest information about a man she hated and loved in equal measure. As Tsarina she was allowed a personal staff of ladies-in-waiting, couturiers and maids to attend to her whims and pleasures. The Tsar's daughter was expected to have the finest gowns, always keeping one step ahead of other nobility.

Since the war Jena had been redirecting a fraction of the funding for her private staff to chart the movements of Dante. It was a compulsion, like an itch she couldn't help scratching, but she had to know where he was – even if she didn't allow others to say his name in her presence.

Apparently he was back in St Petersburg, the careless fool. He had been spotted near the black market at Tsyganov, involved in a heated transaction with a noted counterfeiter. A considerable sum of roubles had changed hands. Knowing Dante, he was now probably drinking himself into a stupor somewhere.

Nothing surprising there, except for the fool's willingness to put himself in harm's way. Devil may care or too stupid to know better? It was hard to tell with Nikolai. Despite herself, Jena wished she could see him again. The thought of being with him brought a flush to her face and quickened her breath. She shook her head at such folly. Now who was the fool – Dante or the woman who couldn't forget him?

Jena tossed the report to one side. There were more pressing problems than one rascal, no matter how much he invaded her thoughts and feelings. The parting threat from her father had been all too apparent. I'm his only heir, she thought, and that's the only reason I'm still alive today. No one else could challenge him the way I have and expect to survive. But if Fabergé succeeds in what he has planned, if his next experiment should deliver the weapon my father wants...

"He must be stopped," Jena muttered to herself. "But how?" She dared not intervene directly; such an act would sign her death warrant. To achieve her aim, she must move in such a way that Fabergé's failure could never be traced back to her. But the question still remained, how? I need a weapon of my own, a tool – someone I can send to do my dirty work, someone foolish enough to take on such a dangerous mission and yet brave enough to venture in where others would not dare.

"Where am I going to find such a person?" she wondered out loud. Another knock at the door interrupted her thoughts. "Yes?"

Anastasia re-entered, curtsying apologetically. "Sorry, Lady Jena, but you gave me a standing order that I destroy all reports about the whereabouts of you-know-who once you've had a chance to read them. If you have finished with the latest bulletin, I could–"

"Of course!" Jena could not help smiling, the irony of her solution too delicious not to be savoured. She picked up the report and handed it over. "Make sure you destroy all trace of it."

"Yes, ma'am." Anastasia curtsied again before turning to leave.

"Wait, there's something else," Jena added.

"Yes, ma'am?"

"I need you to deliver a message."

Famous Flora's Massage Parlour was among the Empire's most beloved houses of ill repute. While it lacked the House of Sin's legendary status or the breadth of perversity on offer at World of Leather, Famous Flora's was still a five star brothel with something to tickle the fancy of any client. Dante stood outside the parlour's entrance, gazing in disbelief at the doorway surrounded by a neon replica of female genitalia.

"Are you sure this is where you want to spend your cut from the heist?"

"Loathe as I am to admit this, it's been quite some time since I've been able to indulge myself with a lady," Flintlock replied. "Alas, too long spent in the company of Spatch here has rather blunted my appeal with the fairer sex. The finest of colognes can only mask so much."

"Yeah," Spatchcock said, grinning broadly. "They certainly don't cover the stench of dung when you're talking!"

"I resent that remark, and its implications!" Flintlock snapped.

"Resent all you want, I couldn't give a sh–"

"That's enough," Dante interjected. "You two starting a fight outside a cat-house will only attract unwanted attention. Let's get inside."

The trio entered the building, its doors closing with a wet slurp behind them. Ahead a steep staircase led up to the

reception area where a bored woman sat watching a soap
opera on the ImperialNet. "Six hundred roubles," she
announced, not bothering to look at the new arrivals.
"Each."

"Six hundred? That's outrageous," Flintlock spluttered.
"I'll have you know I'm a personal friend of Flora herself.
Ask her to come out here and I'm sure–"

"Six hundred. Each," the receptionist repeated. One of
her nostrils twitched as the first waft of Spatchcock's
unique personal odour began to insinuate itself into her
senses. Dante recognised the signs and quickly handed over
two thousand roubles.

"Keep the change," he offered, pushing the still protesting
Flintlock onwards. Spatchcock followed happily behind,
pausing to leer at the receptionist's cleavage. Dante grabbed
the grubby little poisoner and dragged him towards the
brothel's inner sanctum. The threesome pushed through a
set of double doors and beheld the waiting room.

A vast cathedral devoted to fornication spread itself
before them, lushly furnished in gold and crimson.
Around the walls hung erotic masterpieces, both painted
and photographed, depicting a myriad of human bodies
cavorting in daring and unlikely positions. Tall, phallic
cabinets of glass held displays of sexual aids and
appendages, some of such a size they made the eyes
water involuntarily. Dotted around the chamber were
dozens of seats occupied by the parlour's customers.
Most were men but a few women also waited for the next
parade.

"I've heard about this place but I've never been inside it,"
Spatchcock admitted. "Is it true what they say about the
girls here?"

"Yes," Dante admitted, "and the men too – they will do
anything you desire, as long as no one dies or is permanently injured."

"Nice," Spatchcock grinned, rubbing his hands together
gleefully.

"You should count yourself lucky you even got in here," Flintlock said pompously. "One more whiff of you and I believe that receptionist would have had the lot of us thrown out on our ears."

"Unlikely," Dante commented. "You may have been bluffing about being a personal friend of Flora, but I do know her. I doubt she would have let me be ejected without getting her hands on the contents of my pants first."

"Only if your pants contain an unfeasibly large sum of money," a husky voice replied from behind the trio. The three men turned to find a triple-breasted woman clad in black lingerie regarding them. She was tall, tanned and utterly bald but for a thick black beard.

"Flora!" Dante gasped in surprise. "Since when did you become one of the Devil's Martyrs?" All disciples of that religion were required to sport beards as a sign of devotion, even the women. The Devil's Martyrs were renowned for their wild sexual excesses.

The brothel owner stroked her beard. "Of course, you haven't seen me since before the war. I joined the House of Rasputin once I saw which way the fighting was going. Pledging allegiance to an official Imperial cult gave me protection from the Tsar's pogroms."

"And the extra breast?" Flintlock asked, getting an elbow in the ribs from Dante for his impertinence.

"That's why she's famous," Spatchcock hissed under his breath. "Famous Flora, the only human with three natural breasts!"

Dante smoothed down the bristles of his own goatee. "Hmm, I think the beard suits you. There's not many women that can carry it off, but on you–"

"Enough flattery," Flora said. "Why are you here? I don't know if you should even be allowed in the building."

"My friends would like to partake of your establishment's services."

"I hope your friends have deep pockets. We have a very rich client base and prices to match these days."

Dante smiled. "I'm sure they can meet any tariffs you care to charge."

"Very well," Flora agreed. "The parade is about to begin. You'd better take your seats."

Spatchcock watched the owner depart, licking his lips lasciviously. "Oh, three for the price of two – that's what I call value for money! But I'm not so sure about the beard. Never had it away with a woman whose got a better growth than me, not sure I'd like that."

"You should try it," Dante suggested. "The stubble rash can be a bit painful but there's nothing quite like the feeling of a beard brushing against the insides of your thighs, take my word for it."

"You mean... you and her?"

"No, Flora didn't have the beard when I knew her best. But I did once spend a night with Lady Eudoxia Looshin."

"And?" Flintlock asked excitedly. "Was she as good as her reputation?"

"Let's just say that's one night I won't forget in a hurry," Dante replied. "Now, be quiet, both of you – the parade is starting." The trio found an unoccupied chaise lounge and perched on its plush upholstery. The lights in the room began to dim, half a dozen crystal chandeliers rising into the vaulted ceiling. A catwalk slowly descended, nearly thirty men and women in various costumes and states of undress posing along it. Once the catwalk was locked into position at head height, a set of stairs swung down to the floor, allowing the sex workers to descend.

Flora herself reappeared above the scene, gracefully swinging on a trapeze while picked out by a follow spot. "Good afternoon, ladies and gentlemen. Welcome to my parlour of delights, where you can have whatever you desire – for the right price. Here you will find beauties and beasts, male and female, submissive and dominant, butch and bitch alike. Here you will be teased and taunted, tempted and punished, given pain and pleasure – all in whatever measures you wish. We make no judgements, keep no records and tell no lies at Famous Flora's. We merely wish to fulfil you, in every way possible. Let the fun commence!"

The first person on offer began descending from the catwalk. "We begin today's selection of delights with Hattie," Flora announced, "a former customer from Britannia who so enjoyed her time inside this establishment she decided to remain here permanently." She was a rotund woman in the uniform of a British matron, her mighty bosom hardly held in check by the navy blue latex costume. She strutted among the patrons, one hand smacking against the ample cheeks of her behind. "Hattie loves to punish naughty boys, putting them across her knee and administering six of the best. It's up to you whether you want to receive the spanking with your trousers on or off. Ladies and gentlemen, a big hand for Hattie!"

The customers responded with enthusiastic applause, several already waving large wads of cash in the air, eager to get their hands on her. Flora tutted theatrically from her swinging perch overhead.

"My, my, we do have some eager beavers waiting to be admonished! Don't let your excitement get the better of you, boys, otherwise Hattie will make you clean up the mess personally." That only flushed the faces of those waving their wads further, Flintlock among them.

"Oh, matron!" he cried out. "I've been a naughty boy and I need to be punished!" Flintlock began rising from his seat but a hand pulled him back.

"Restraint," Dante urged. "There's plenty more where she came from."

"Really? I think she brought most of it with her," Spatchcock chipped in.

"You're a fine one to preach," Flintlock told Dante. "You've never practised restraint one day of your life."

"There's a first time for everything."

"Our next offering is Maria," Flora continued, "the youngest of our talents. Just eighteen today, she is looking for a strong authority figure, someone who can teach her how to behave." A pretty, petite woman in a schoolgirl's uniform descended from the catwalk, choosing her steps carefully. "Maria is new here and needs to be taken in hand, if you know what I mean."

"I'll bet she does," Spatchcock leered. "I know just where to put 'em, too."

The parade of sex workers continued – muscled men with gleaming torsos, rampant women in an array of outfits, dwarves, aliens, even robots, all were on offer to anyone with the right number of roubles. Flintlock eventually decided to spend most of his cash on two women – the hefty charms of Hattie and a French maid known as Yvette. Spatchcock left to pursue a tempting young woman called Anya who specialised in naked mud wrestling. "Sounds just my kind of girl," the grubby ex-con announced. "Naked, dirty and ready for a roll in the mud."

But Dante could not get excited by any of the pleasures on offer, instead retiring to a well stocked bar in a corner of the sex cathedral. There he ordered a large bottle of Imperial Blue vodka and began drinking it like water. Once the parade was finished and all the staff occupied with clients, Flora joined him at the bar. "Drinking alone, Nikolai? Not a very healthy pass-time."

"Perhaps I've had my fill of whores," he said, before remembering what Flora did for a living. "Sorry – nothing personal."

"No, that's fine. If you want to drink here at our inflated prices, you'll make my accountant a very happy woman." Flora gestured at the seat beside him. "Mind if I join you?"

Dante shrugged and called for another glass, then poured a generous slug of vodka into it. "Here's to money, the root of all evil." He downed the contents of his glass in a single gulp before pouring another. Flora watched him closely, her face betraying her concern.

"Since when did you hate money, Nikolai? When we were both scraping a living in the back streets of St Petersburg you couldn't get enough roubles to make you happy. Now you're throwing it away like there's no tomorrow."

"Maybe there isn't," Dante replied, his voice beginning to slur a little. "The Tsar's put a bounty on my head that could finance Rudinshtein for a year."

"I know," Flora said. "You should be careful in here, some of my clients might be tempted to try and claim the reward."

"I'm surprised you haven't called the Raven Corps yourself."

"Those bullies would cost me more in damages and lost custom than I would gain by turning you in. Besides, we go back a long way."

Dante pointed a finger at Flora. "You bet your ass!"

She reached out a hand to touch him. "When did you get so bitter? I thought Nikolai Dante was all devil-may-care and honour be damned."

"Maybe I've started to grow up."

"Or maybe you're just feeling sorry for yourself?"

He shrugged in reply. "I never had two roubles to rub together before I became one of the Romanovs. Now I can steal a small fortune in one morning and it still doesn't make me happy. Why not? What's wrong with me?"

"Perhaps you realise there's more to life than just money?"

"Like what?"

"Love? Being happy? Having friends?"

Dante guzzled another tumbler of vodka. "And what would you know about that, Flora?"

The brothel owner smiled. "More than you, I suspect. I may put on the act of a lascivious old whore, but when I get home I know my partner is waiting for me. We can be together, just be, and there's nobody to judge us or trouble us."

"Sounds delightful."

Flora shook her head. "What do you believe in, Dante? What are you for? I followed your progress during the war

– you were fighting for something then, something bigger than you, something important. What are you doing now?"

"I'm enjoying myself!"

"So I can see – sat in a whorehouse, pockets bulging with money and trying to drink yourself stupid to blot out whatever you don't want to think about. I'm glad all our customers don't enjoy themselves this much, my staff would be out of work." Flora stood up, leaving a last comment for Dante to contemplate. "You're like a shark, Nikolai. You've got to keep moving forwards, or else you die. It's time to move forwards again."

She strode away, leaving him peering at the last measure of vodka in his bottle. He held it up as a mock salute to the departing woman before draining the contents.

For the owner of a house of ill repute, Famous Flora speaks a lot of sense, the Crest said.

"Oh no, not you too," Dante winced. "I knew you couldn't keep quiet long."

I'm just saying there is more than a little truth in what she observed. You are flailing around, Dante. Why did you rob the Imperial Mint this morning?

"Because it was there."

Bravo! Why not hit yourself on the head with that vodka bottle? It's there too and so is your skull. Why not bring the two together?

"Because that would be stupid."

That's never stopped you before.

"Have you quite finished? I've already had my lecture for the day from Flora, I don't need you joining in."

That's unfortunate, as I have more to say, the Crest replied. *You need a cause, something to get you out of this slough of self-pity and self-regard.*

Dante shook the empty bottle. "I wonder how much vodka I have to drink to incapacitate you, Crest?"

More than your body could sustain. You'll pass out long before I do.

"Pity." Dante threw the bottle over his shoulder, listening with satisfaction as it smashed in the background. "Did I hit anyone?"

No, but there is a woman approaching. She doesn't look happy.

"Flora?"

Not exactly, the Crest replied.

"Excuse me," a soft voice said, "but are you Nikolai Dante?"

"Who wants to know?" Dante asked, rotating round on his bar stool. He found himself facing an unremarkable, plain-faced woman. She was wearing a heavy black cloak and hood that hid her body and even the colour of her hair.

"My name isn't important," she replied nervously.

"Maybe not, but you'll have to display your wares a little better if you want to get any business in this place. Famous Flora's is many things, but subtle is not one of them." Dante was surprised to see her burst into tears. "Sorry – was it something I said?"

Why would she possibly think that? the Crest interjected archly.

"Be quiet," Dante hissed under his breath.

"I'm sorry," the woman said. "I'm trying not to cry too loudly."

"No, not you. I was talking to my..." Dante checked himself. "I was talking to myself. Bit of a one-sided conversation, to be honest."

I'll say, the Crest added.

Dante bit his lip rather than rise to the bait a second time. He stood up and ushered the young woman to a nearby seat. She produced a handkerchief from inside her cloak and dabbed away the tears.

"You must think me very strange, accosting you in this place," she said.

"I've been accosted in worse places."

"It's my Uncle James," the woman continued. "He's dying."

"I'm... sorry to hear that."

"He's dying and I can't get in to see him. I thought maybe you might be able to reach him, or at least get him a message. I know it's dangerous, but I didn't know whom else to turn to. My uncle always said you would attempt the impossible, no matter how foolhardy the venture."

Sounds like he knows you well, the Crest ventured.

Dante grimaced but chose to ignore the telepathic commentary, knowing the Crest would fall silent if he didn't respond to its jibes. "Your Uncle James – could you tell me his full name?"

The woman nodded, tears starting to flow again. "Di Grizov, James Di Grizov. Some people called him Jim."

Dante sat back as if punched in the chest. More than a decade has passed since he last saw his mentor, the lift doors at the Casino Royale closing between them. Di Grizov had beaten him, stolen the Fabergé egg and left him to face the music. But despite all that, Dante found he did not bear his former mentor a grudge – life was too short for that. "You say he's dying? Where is he? I'd like to see him before the end, for old time's sake."

"He's in a gulag, a work camp. I doubt he'll last another week."

"Where?"

"Near the Murmansk Alienation Zone. It's the only gulag in that region. They don't allow visitors and none of the prisoners ever leave the compound alive. I only discovered my uncle was being held there by chance. He bribed one of the guards to carry out a message for me."

Dante smiled. "I'm surprised Jim hasn't escaped. I've never known any cell or jail that could hold him."

"Maybe, when he was younger. Before they took his legs."

"His legs?"

"Amputated, to stop him escaping." The woman was sobbing gently now, unable to hold back her grief any more. "The guard laughed when he told me."

Dante could feel a red mist of anger rising. "Is this guard still in St Petersburg? I'd like to have a word with him."

"No, he's gone back to the gulag. The next shuttle to the Murmansk region leaves at midnight tonight. I was going to catch it, but knew I could never hope to reach my uncle in time. Then I remembered you..."

"Alright," Dante said softly, slipping a comforting arm around the young woman's shoulders. "It's going to be alright. I'll go. I'll find your uncle. If I can, I'll get him out of the gulag. If I can't, then I'll take your message to him. What do you want me to say?"

She turned and looked at Dante intently, the tears gone from her eyes now. "Before he was caught, my uncle had hidden his money in a secret location – said it was his retirement fund. If anything ever happened to him, I was to have it. He had a codename for his hiding place. You need to find out where that money is. Ask him you to tell you about the hiding place."

"You trust me with that knowledge?"

"My uncle said you were among the few men he had ever trusted. I have to show the same faith in you."

Dante nodded. "What's the codename?"

"Ask him to tell you about the Strangelove Gambit." The young woman noticed Spatchcock approaching and rose from her seat. "I have to go now. Remember what I told you, but don't share it with anyone else. Goodbye!" She hurried away, disappearing among the crowd of customers and sex workers mingled in the vast chamber.

Dante started after her. "If I do get a message for you from Jim, how will I contact you? I don't even know your name!"

But the woman was gone, leaving a confused Dante behind. He noticed her discarded handkerchief on the floor and picked it up. A three-letter monogram was sewn into one corner of the fabric: AdG. "Something Di Grizov," Dante speculated. "Alice? Alicia? Anastasia?" None of the names rang any bells in his vodka-muddled mind. "I can't even remember Jim saying he had any family, let alone a niece."

"What are you muttering about?" Spatchcock demanded.

"A mysterious encounter," Dante replied.

"I should be so lucky," the other man said with a scowl. "I couldn't find anyone willing to enjoy a little non-stop erotic action with me, despite offering all my cut."

"Not even Anya, the naked mud wrestler? I'd have thought your down and dirty charms would be right up her alley."

Spatchcock shook his head. "Claimed she was washing her hair tonight. Since when do whores take the night off to wash their hair?"

"Maybe you should have tried washing yours before you came in," Dante offered, trying not to inhale the odours wafting from his partner in crime. "There's a limit to what anyone will do for money."

Spatchcock nodded at the wisdom of this. "You found some company."

"No, I... Oh, that woman? She had a message for me."

"Yeah? How did she know you'd be here?"

"That's a good question," Dante conceded. "How *did* she know?"

More to the point, how many other people know? the Crest asked. *Considering the bounty on your head and the nature of this establishment's clientele, you might be well advised to take your leave. A close encounter with the Raven Corps would not make getting out of St Petersburg any easier.*

"Good advice, Crest. Spatch, where's Flintlock?"

The foul-smelling felon chewed his bottom lip thoughtfully. "I think he's either in the schoolroom or the parlour. He paid for a two hour session, so his lordship's still got another twenty minutes left."

"Well, he'll have to finish whatever he's doing in the next two minutes," Dante decided. "You take the parlour, I'll try the school room."

The two men consulted a signpost for directions to each of the massage parlour's pleasure suites before splitting up.

Dante found the schoolroom only after wrongly bursting into the baby's nursery. The sight of three grown men in diapers being nursed was enough to remove any lingering effects of his vodka binge. "And you call me a big baby!"

At least I don't have to burp you, the Crest conceded. *The schoolroom is directly ahead. May I suggest discretion as the better part of valour this time?*

"Good idea." Dante knocked circumspectly on the door.

"Yes, who is it?" an imperious female voice inquired.

"I'm looking for a friend of mine, I think he might be in there."

"I'm sorry, young man, but I refuse to carry on a conversation with a door. If you wish to speak with myself or any of the students, you must ask permission to enter like any other pupil."

"Alright, can I come inside?"

"No, no, not like that! Ask permission properly!"

"Crest?" Dante asked. "Any suggestions?"

You're on your own here. My etiquette training does not extend to the required form of address for a brothel's schoolmistress.

"Thanks, that's a great help."

"Well?" the woman demanded. "Do you wish to come in or not?"

"Er, please miss, may I enter the classroom," Dante ventured.

"You may."

Dante twisted the handle and opened the door enough to see inside. It was an exact replica of a schoolroom, complete with desks and chairs for half a dozen pupils, a blackboard on the far wall and a chart detailing the students' recent achievements. Four grown men dressed as school boys were cowering in their seats while a fifth was bent over double in front of the blackboard, his shorts round his ankles. A sour-faced woman of fifty clad in only an academic gown and mortarboard was standing to one side, wielding a prodigious cane.

"Well, young man – is your friend in here?" she demanded.

Dante glanced round the five students but could not see Flintlock among them. Still, he wouldn't put it past the exiled aristocrat to favour such a sexual preference. Dante's few visits to Britannia had convinced him the nation was home to all manner of perversities. Perhaps it had something to do with the weather, being stuck inside all day because of the rain, with nothing better to do than let your imagination run riot.

"No, he's not. Well, sorry to disturb you. I'll just–"

"You'll just what?" the teacher shrieked furiously, several parts of her anatomy wobbling in sympathy with her rage. "You'll just come here and take your punishment for interrupting my class!"

"But I–"

"Now!"

"No, you don't understand," Dante insisted. "I–"

I think you better do what she says, the Crest said gleefully. *This is one teacher who doesn't appear likely to take no for an answer.*

"I should have brought her an apple," Dante muttered under his breath.

"What was that, you insolent little boy?" The teacher was advancing towards Dante now, the cane twitching in her right hand. "I'll show you the meaning of discipline!"

It was Spatchcock who found Flintlock first. The former Lord of Fitzrovia was lying across the ample lap of Hattie the matron, receiving a trousers down spanking on his bare, bony behind. At the same time, Flintlock was being served tea and hot buttered crumpets. She was leaning over to pour another cup, her French maid's uniform riding up to reveal her stocking tops.

"Oh, yes, that's the way to do it," Flintlock purred. In between munches of his crumpet Flintlock gave little yelps of ecstasy as Hattie smacked his buttocks with a wooden hairbrush, the force of each blow wobbling her bosom.

"You've been a very naughty boy, haven't you, Flinty?" she cooed.

"If you say so matron," he replied happily.

"And you know what happens to naughty boys, don't you?"

"They get sent to bed without any supper."

"That's right."

"Will you come to bed with me, matron?" Flintlock began twisting round, trying to catch her eye. "I know a game we can play there. You pull down the top half of your uniform and I put my–"

"Enough!" Dante burst into the room, pushing Spatchcock ahead of him. "I've had quite enough of this place for one day. It's time we were going."

Hattie looked mournfully at the new arrivals. "Oh, do you have to? We were just getting to the good bit." Yvette nodded her agreement eagerly.

Dante held up a hand, not wanting to hear anymore. "Please, ladies, I beg you – share no details with us, lest we learn to think even less of our associate than we already do. All three of us must be leaving, and quickly."

"Why the rush?" Flintlock demanded, trying to pull his trousers up from round his ankles. "I still have at least half an hour of my session to go!"

Dante pointed down the corridor from which he had suddenly appeared. "Maybe you wish to continue your session with her?"

Flintlock followed Dante's gesture and saw the middle-aged schoolteacher approaching at speed, her academic gown billowing outwards as she ran towards them. The sight was neither pleasant nor erotic, and quickly removed any remaining arousal from Flintlock's body. "I see what you mean. Well ladies, please accept my apologies, but it's often better to save something for later."

Dante glanced round the parlour. "Is there another way out of here? I don't fancy taking on the prime of Miss Jean Whiplash."

Yvette pointed at a bookcase set into one wall. "You can leave through the secret tunnel of love," she said. "Just pull out the correct volume and the bookcase will slide aside for you."

Dante strode to the bookcase and began scanning the titles of the dusty tomes: *Another Week in the Private House*, *Confessions of an Imperial Courtesan*, *The Wench Isn't Dead* and hundreds of similar volumes. "Which book? Which one operates the mechanism?"

Yvette smiled coquettishly. "I'll only tell you if you make me, master."

Dante rolled his eyes. "I haven't got time for any more slap and tickle. Crest, can you identify which spine opens the bookcase?"

A very appropriate title, in the circumstances, it replied. *The Pervert's Guide to Secret Tunnels and Hidden Crevices.*

Spatchcock had joined Dante at the bookcase. "I see it!" He pulled the thick volume towards himself and the shelving slid sideways to reveal a corridor. Dante shoved his pungent companion through the gap and turned back to see what was delaying Flintlock. He was jumping around the room, his trousers still stuck at half-mast, while the seminaked schoolteacher was whipping him with her cane.

"Diavolo! Haven't you had your money's worth yet?" Dante asked despairingly. He bundled Flintlock into the hidden corridor, before bowing to the three sex workers. "Sorry to leave so soon ladies, but you know what men are like – our priorities always come first. Perhaps another time?" Dante ducked behind the closing bookcase, narrowly avoiding several hurled objects.

Spatchcock winked at his former commander. "You sure know how to show the ladies a good time."

"Just get moving," Dante snapped, pushing his two associates forwards. "We've got a long journey ahead of us and no time to lose."

"Where are we going?" Flintlock asked.

"To see an old friend."

FOUR

"There are many woes, but only one death"
– Russian proverb

Di Grizov had always been proud of his hands. They could crack any safe, disable the trickiest of alarms, and even undo the stays of the most sanctimonious dowager if a job required it. His fingernails were always immaculate, the palms smooth and warm, his grip firm and resolute. The hands of a grifter must never betray his origins or intentions, he had been fond of telling his apprentices over the years; they must reassure and satisfy all those they come into contact with. Di Grizov looked at his hands now and winced. He would have wept, if he'd any tears left to shed.

Just four days in the Murmansk Gulag had broken what little spirit was left in Di Grizov's body. Four days of hell on Earth, tearing at the walls of a mine with his bare hands, trying to claw out seams of glistening ore. With his legs gone, the grifter had been given a low trolley on wheels as his means of transportation, forcing him to propel it around the compound with his hands. Pleas for a pair of gloves were mocked or ignored. The gulag's commander, Josef Shitov, had laughed heartily at Di Grizov's request. A bear of a man, the veins on Shitov's shaven head bulged as he stood over the new prisoner.

"Where do you think you are, a holiday camp?" Shitov lovingly stroked his thick, black moustache while glaring at Di Grizov. "You came here to work! You eat when I say, you sleep when I say and you die when I say – understand?"

"But I need—"

"Need? All you need is to learn your place here, worm. This is my domain, and I shall do with you as I see fit." Shitov looked down and noticed a smudge on the gleaming surface of his boots. "For your first lesson, I want you to clean my boots. With your tongue."

That was four days ago. Four days of torture, ignominy and despair. Di Grizov would have killed himself long before now, if any simple method had been available to him. He even contemplated biting through the veins on his wrists in the hope of bleeding to death, but couldn't face that. Besides, he knew this torment couldn't last much longer. The mines were radioactive, having been used in the past as a storage facility for nuclear waste. Few prisoners lasted more than a month before the tumours and cancers took their lives.

Di Grizov studied his hands. The fingernails were broken and ragged-edged, the skin split open in several places, blisters mingled with each callous on the palms. They looked like a humble worker's hands now, with the hardened appearance of a lifetime spent in hard physical labour. Four days of hell had achieved that. What would they be like after four more days? But I'll be dead before that happens, the grifter thought. He welcomed the end. There probably was no life beyond this one, but oblivion had to be better than this place.

His grim contemplations were halted by the sound of sirens wailing outside. Di Grizov pushed his trolley to the nearest window and looked out of the barracks. The sun had long since set but the sky remained a pale blue overhead, thanks to the shortened nights of a northern summer, a full moon adding further illumination. Guards were rushing back and forth across the bleak, snow-strewn compound, shouting to each other and cursing in the local dialect. In centuries past the Murmansk region had been devoted to the sea and naval warfare. Now the remaining local people found work in the gulag, taking out their frustrations on the inmates.

It was good to see a little panic in the dead eyes of these slab-faced sadists, Di Grizov thought. But what could induce such a reaction? Perhaps one of the prisoners was trying to escape. Few had the strength or will to break out of this death camp, and those that did rarely made it past the first fence. The guards were particularly enthusiastic about hunting down would-be escapees, thanks to a generous reward on offer from Shitov. Nobody had every successfully broken out of the Murmansk Gulag and he was determined to maintain that record, promising a week's extra pay as a bonus for whoever succeeded in bringing down any prisoner trying to escape.

Di Grizov strained forwards and pressed an ear against the frozen glass of the nearest window, trying to catch what was being said outside. Shitov himself appeared to direct operations, trying to bring calm to the panicked ranks. "You fools! Stop and listen – let this enemy come to us. Let them walk between our pincers. Then we shall close in around them and feast on their folly!"

The grifter sat back in his trolley. Let the enemy come to us? If I didn't know better, I'd think somebody was trying to break *into* the gulag. But what kind of idiot would be stupid enough to attempt that?

Dante watched the high security compound sprawled below. A dozen wooden huts were arranged in rows of four, surrounded by guardhouses and a few rudimentary buildings – probably the kitchens and toilet block. At the far end stood several more elaborate structures. Three were large, superior versions of the wooden huts, but with smoke billowing from chimneys and interior lighting visible through the windows. Probably the guards' quarters, Dante reasoned. The elegant, almost palatial home beside them no doubt belonged to the gulag commander. Tall watchtowers stood in all four corners of the compound, the guards inside them sweeping mighty arc lights back and forth.

Beyond the gulag Dante could see a distant orange glow on the horizon. No doubt the light pollution was spilling from the Murmansk Alienation Zone, less than fifty miles away. The zone was an environmental disaster that had started more than five hundred years ago when some long-forgotten regime chose to abandon its fleet of war machines to the Arctic ravages of the Barents Sea. In the intervening centuries this military graveyard had welcomed more relics, its wrecks supposedly haunted by an armada of ghosts from the past. Few visited the alienation zone willingly.

Dante had been there only once, six years earlier, on a journey that changed his life forever. Captured by the Raven Corps, Dante was surprised to be despatched to Murmansk, along with the Tsar's daughter Jena. There they had encountered a two-headed robotic eagle, a Romanov Bird of Prey. The creature decided Dante was genetically suitable and initiated the bonding sequence that fused the Crest to his body.

Only later did Dante discover the Tsar had deliberately sent him to the alienation zone, knowing the thief was a bastard of the Romanov bloodline. The Tsar planned to have him dissected, allowing access to the Crest's secrets and neutering the Romanovs' greatest weapon. But Dante had escaped that fate and joined the house of his father instead. Six years on almost all the other Romanovs were dead. So much for the past.

Kopeck for your thoughts, the Crest said.

"I doubt they're worth that much to you," Dante replied.

Perhaps not, but it's hard to get change on a kopeck.

Dante couldn't help smiling. "I was just remembering when we first bonded. We've come a long way since then, Crest."

And yet you still refuse to listen to reason. Attacking a gulag single-handed is an act of suicide.

"I'm not single-handed. Spatchcock and Flintlock are busy creating a diversion on the far side of the compound."

Why you trust those two knaves I'll never know.

"Sometimes you have to let your heart do the thinking, Crest."

Well, it makes a change from your groin being in charge.

Dante sighed. "Have you finished hacking the gulag's security systems?"

Yes, they were so primitive. I've been triple-checking to see if something more sophisticated was lurking behind them.

"And was there?"

No. As a suitable task for my talents, it was like asking a watchmaker to repair a hammer. The defence grid should collapse right about... now.

In the valley below a cacophony of sirens and alarms suddenly fell silent. The generators maintaining the laser shield clattered to a halt and power drained away from the arc lights in the watchtowers. The gulag was defenceless, but for its cadre of armed guards and their commander.

"Time to stealth 'em up." Dante pulled the hood of his white cloak closer round his face before creeping down the snow-covered slope towards the outer perimeter. "Once we're inside the boundary line I'll need explicit instructions, Crest. I won't have time to search every building for Jim."

Spatchcock was loading sticky green pellets into his sidearm while Flintlock tended the bonfire. The pair had constructed a tower of dead wood from the snowy wasteland around the northern edge of the gulag and lit it on a signal from Dante. The cowardly Flintlock observed the nearest watchtower nervously, ready to scramble for cover at the first sign of danger. "Why do we always end up as the diversion? Why can't Nikolai risk his neck instead of us?"

"You want to swap places with him? Chance your arm breaking into a gulag guarded by two dozen thugs with enough guns to start a small war?"

"No, but I thought..." Flintlock shrugged helplessly. "Isn't there a less dangerous way for us to get their attention?"

"If there is, it's too late," Spatchcock replied, pointing a finger towards the gulag's perimeter. "Here they come!"

A dozen guards were marching towards the bonfire, all bearing pulse rifles and grim expressions. By the time they reached the blaze, the two arsonists had retreated to an abandoned hut nearby. Spatchcock clambered onto the roof and took aim with his sidearm. Flintlock was cowering at ground level, peering round a corner at the confused guards. His hands were shaking so much it was proving difficult to load a green pellet into his weapon.

"Why do I have to use the slingshot?" Flintlock protested.

"Stop whining and start firing," Spatchcock snapped. Ahead of him, half the guards had finished examining the bonfire and were fanning out, in search of the culprits. "They're coming into range... now!" Spatchcock shot first, the green pellet splattering as it hit the chest of the nearest enemy.

The guard looked down at his uniform in dismay, scowling at the viscous emerald substance slowly dribbling down his chest. He dipped a gloved finger into the liquid, peered at it and then brought it close to his nose for a sniff.

"That's it..." Spatchcock urged. "Get a good whiff of that."

The guard inhaled sharply. Disgust crossed his features, rapidly followed by horror. His cheeks billowed outwards for a moment, before projectile vomit spat forth from his mouth and both nostrils. At the same time a splattering sound could be heard from the guard's trousers, their seat suddenly becoming heavier. The unfortunate man crumpled to his knees, one hand trying to stop the spray from his mouth while another clutched at his rear.

"Gotcha!" Spatchcock snarled happily. "Purge juice one, guards nil."

"You mean that vile concoction of yours works?" Flintlock spluttered.

"Course it does – now get firing! We hit enough of those goons, the rest won't want to come any closer."

Slipping into the gulag proved simplicity itself once the Crest had disabled most of the security systems. The rest of the safeguards had been designed to stop prisoners breaking out, not prevent anyone from breaking in. Dante moved among the shadows, avoiding most of the guards and bluffing his way past the rest. Panic was in charge of the situation for now, but Dante knew that could not last forever. He found Di Grizov at the third attempt, discovering his old mentor inside a frozen wooden hut. Dante found it hard to believe the broken, shrivelled man on the trolley was once the Empire's greatest escapologist.

"Jim? Is that you?"

"Nikolai? What are you doing here?"

Dante closed the door and hurried to the grifter's side. "I've come to get you out of here. Your niece sent me."

"My niece? I don't have a niece. I don't have any family, at least none still alive. I was an only child."

"But then who was...?" Dante frowned. "I met a young woman. She said you bribed a guard to carry a message for her out of the gulag."

Di Grizov laughed bitterly. "Chance would be a fine thing, Nikolai. The bastards in this place wouldn't piss on you if you were burning alive."

"I don't understand – she knew you'd lost your legs. She said they'd been amputated to stop you escaping."

"Yes, but not here. That happened somewhere else."

Dante shook his head. "It doesn't matter how I found you. The important thing now is getting you out."

Di Grizov shook his head. "It's too late for me, Nikolai. I'm dying. You could be killed trying to save me and for what? I'll only live a few more days, a week at least. Get away from here, save yourself."

"No! I came here to help you, Jim–"

"You have already," the grifter replied. "You've given me a chance to say something that's been nagging at me for twelve years – I'm sorry."

"I don't–"

"Hush." Di Grizov pressed his broken, battered hands against Dante's mouth, silencing him. "I'm sorry I tricked you at the Casino Royale, how I treated you. You deserved better from me."

"It's okay, Jim. Leaving me there, it taught me a lot. I learned how to get myself out of danger, how to make the most out of an impossible situation. Trust me, they've been useful skills in the last few years."

"I know. I've been following your career. Quite a dash you've cut through the ranks of high society."

Dante smiled. "But I never forgot where I came from, and that's thanks to you. You taught me to always remember my origins, stand on my own two feet."

"Well, that's more than I can do now…" Di Grizov rested a hand on the stumps were his legs had been. "Tell me more about this woman who contacted you. Maybe I'll remember her."

Dante quickly outlined his encounter at the bar in Famous Flora's. "She said you had a retirement fund. I'm supposed to mention the codename for it and you'll tell me where to find the money."

The grifter raised an eyebrow. "I don't have a rouble to my name. My life's been one disaster after another, ever since the day I stole that damned egg. I spent all my savings staying out of the gulags – and look where it's got me."

Outside the hut a burly voice was cursing the guards, urging them to begin a thorough search of the buildings. "Friend of yours?" Dante asked.

"Josef Shitov, the barbarous bastard that runs this place."

"We're running out of time, Jim – we should get out while we still can."

"I told you, I'm not leaving," the grifter maintained. "I'll die here. It's as bad a place as any to end my days." His brow furrowed. "I thought I knew who might have sent you here, but the woman you described doesn't match her. You mentioned a codename – what was it?"

"The Strangelove Gambit."

Di Grizov's face hardened. "It's not a codename, Nikolai. It's a warning," he snorted with disgust.

"A warning? About what?"

"My legs were amputated before I was brought here. The man who took them was Karl Fabergé."

"The doctor you stole the egg from?"

Di Grizov nodded. "Fabergé has prospered since our first encounter. He has a private island off the Black Sea coastline, complete with its own castle. The island is home to an exclusive school called by the Fabergé Institute, but that's a front for his real work."

Dante could hear guards stomping around inside the nearest wooden hut, tipping over tables and bunks. In less than a minute the sentries would be searching this barrack. Dante reached one arm under his former mentor's stumps and another round his back.

"Nikolai, what are you doing? I said I don't want to be rescued. I just want to die!" Di Grizov protested.

"Maybe. But I don't like taking no for an answer," Dante replied, lifting the grifter from his trolley. "You of all people should know that about me."

Spatchcock watched with satisfaction as the guards retched their guts out on the snow. Judging by the chorus of wet farts bursting from their trousers, the purge juice had also debilitated them at the other end. "Mission accomplished!" he announced happily, climbing down from the roof.

Flintlock had tied a scarf round the lower half of his face, masking his mouth and nostrils from the vile stench being emitted by the stricken guards.

Spatchcock was checking his pockets. "You got any more pellets left?"

Flintlock held up two unused doses of purge juice. "Take them, please."

"My pleasure." The proud poisoner slotted both pellets into his sidearm, while keeping an eye on the gulag's perimeter. "Hmm, I think it's time we were moving on. Looks like our friends have got company."

Flintlock saw another dozen sentries approaching, hidden behind riot shields. "As Dante often says, discretion is the better part of valour, Spatch." The blond-haired Briton took to his heels.

"Like you'd know anything about valour," Spatchcock muttered.

Josef Shitov strode into the last of the workers' barracks. Most of the prisoners had been in the re-education hall when the attack began, undergoing their nightly indoctrination and loyalty-building session. A handful of inmates were excused attendance at these sessions, due to ill health or death – no other reasons were considered acceptable. As a consequence, searching the camp proved straightforward, yet none of the guards had found any evidence of an intruder within the perimeter.

Shitov snapped his fingers, summoning forward the guard assigned to this particular hut. "Kirilenko! How many workers from this barrack were not attending tonight's re-education?"

The heavy-set, slow-spoken sentry saluted briskly before replying. "Just one, Comrade Di Grizov."

"Ah, our most recent arrival. And where is he now?"

Kirilenko looked around helplessly. "I... I do not know, commander."

"Comrade Di Grizov has no legs, is that not true?"

"That is true, commander."

"Then how do you suggest he might have escaped from this building?"

"He has a trolley with wheels, commander. He probably used that."

Shitov turned his head to sneer at the guard. "He probably used a trolley with wheels to cross a compound buried in snow? Was this a magic trolley, Kirilenko? Did it possess the power to levitate, perhaps?"

"No, commander!"

"No, commander," Shitov echoed mockingly. "More to the point, this helpless cripple did not even take his wheels with him!" The commander gestured at the discarded trolley. "Perhaps he has magic of his own. Can Comrade Di Grizov perform magic, Kirilenko?"

"I do not believe so, commander," the sentry replied, his voice trembling.

"Dolt!" Shitov lashed out, his clenched fist smashing into Kirilenko's solar plexus, crumpling the guard as if he were tissue paper. "Search the compound! Find Di Grizov – and find whoever is helping him! Now!"

"You always had a taste for the low life, Nikolai, but this may be going too far. Even for you," Di Grizov said wryly. The two men were crouched inside the gulag's latrine block, hidden behind a row of wooden seats. Icicles of frozen urine hung from the rims. "I'd like to die with some shred of dignity, please?"

"We're not dead yet," Dante replied. "You were telling me about what Fabergé is doing on his private island."

"Secret experiments, fully authorised and funded by the Tsar. I was used as a guinea pig for some of the tests. I heard enough about what Fabergé was planning to scare the hell out of me. He's developing a new weapon, something that will strengthen tenfold the Tsar's stranglehold on the Empire. It's due to be put into effect on Easter Sunday, with the Tsar there to witness it. The Strangelove Gambit: that's what Fabergé is calling his new weapon."

"How many people know about it, Jim?"

"A handful on the island, plus the Tsar and his closest advisors. Beyond that, nobody else, I think. Apparently it's going to be a surprise worthy of the original Fabergé eggs."

Dante shook his head. "So how did the woman claiming to be your niece know of the Strangelove Gambit?"

"Smells like a trap," Di Grizov surmised, "and that's saying something in this block." He studied Dante's expression. "I know that look, Nikolai. You're thinking of taking on Doctor Fabergé."

"Maybe."

"Don't. He spent a dozen years hunting me down because I stole that egg from him. He knows you were my partner at the Casino Royale. If he ever gets his hands on you, I suggest that you commit suicide while you still can." Di Grizov looked down at his ruined hands and the stumps where his legs used to be. "Don't end up like me, Nikolai."

"I won't, I promise you that. I'll make Fabergé will pay for what he did."

Dante – I'm detecting a large group of guards closing in on this location, the Crest said. *Now would be a good time to leave.*

"We may have to shoot our way out of here," Dante murmured. He adjusted the rifle slung over his shoulder, then picked up Di Grizov again.

"Since when do you carry a gun?"

"It was a gift. Besides, this is a very special gun." Dante moved to the end of the latrine block and peered through a frost-coated window. "They're almost upon us. I wonder how they knew we were in here?"

Your tracks in the snow. Carrying Di Grizov made you heavier, so you left a clear set of footprints leading right to this building.

Dante looked around the sparse wooden hut. "I'm guessing there's no secret tunnels or hidden trapdoors in this place, right?"

His old mentor smiled weakly. "Sorry."

Commander Shitov kicked in the door of the latrine block, his pistol raised and ready to fire. "Normally I have to wait weeks, even months for fresh workers. You are the first to ever report here voluntarily. Tell me your name before I have my men induct you to the Murmansk Gulag."

"Dante – Nikolai Dante."

Shitov's face could not help betraying his surprise. "*The* Nikolai Dante?"

"In the flesh."

"How wonderful," the commander replied, firing his pistol.

Dante felt something spraying him with liquid, a scarlet aerosol staining the white of his cloak. The body in his arms jerked once, then lay still. "Jim? Jim, are you alright?" He watched the light leave Di Grizov's eyes, the wound caused by Shitov's bullet all too evident. Dante slowly dropped to one knee and laid the body on the floor. "What's your name, commander?"

"Shitov, Josef Shitov." The gulag's ruler sneered at Dante, his pistol aimed at the intruder's head, ready to fire again. "Why do you ask?"

"I want to know whose grave to piss on after they bury what's left of you." Dante reached forward and closed Di Grizov's eyes, resting his hands on the dead man's face. Purple and silver ripples began running along the veins of his arms, hurrying towards the fingertips.

"You're in no position to make threats, fugitive. True, the reward for your delivery to the Tsar while still alive is considerable, but I think it'll be safer if I gun you down in here like a dog and then deliver your corpse instead."

Dante's fingers began to lengthen, biocircuitry extruding itself from his hands, shooting forwards in the shape of blades. "You're welcome to try; but better men than you have failed, commander. What makes you think you'll do any better?"

"Because I have you right where I–" Shitov's words died in his throat, cut short by the bio-blades slicing through his windpipe. Dante flicked his hands in opposite directions, neatly severing the commander's head. It fell to the floor with a dull *thud*, bouncing once on the wooden boards.

Dante, there are still more than thirty armed guards outside. You'll never make it past them all unscathed, the Crest warned.

"I never said I was going to leave them unscathed," Dante snarled. He retracted the biocircuitry into his hands and slung the rifle from his back while walking towards the door. A grim smile crossed his face. Dante kicked Shitov's head out into the snow. "My name is Nikolai Dante and I am the most wanted man in the Empire!" he shouted to the surrounding guards. "I have just murdered your commander. Anyone who doesn't wish to join him in the next life, you have one minute to leave this place!"

A unique strategy, the Crest commented. *I can't think of many cases where a single man in a hopeless position surrounded by dozens of enemies has negotiated the surrender of his adversary.*

"Call it the Dante Manoeuvre. I'm inventing it today."

Let's hope you stay alive long enough to make it work.

Dante peered out the doorway. The guards were still trying to reach a decision. "Perhaps you need some persuading," Dante yelled. "Let me introduce you to the Huntsman 5000, a rifle designed by the same people who created the Romanov Weapons Crest. This rifle makes its own ammunition and replenishes automatically, so never needs loading. When targeted and fired, the rounds instantaneously adapt into the most effective means of terminating the enemy – whoever or whatever they may be. That probably sounds more like magic than a real weapon to you. But I can assure you it does everything I have just described."

"Prove it!" one of the sentries shouted back.

"I thought you'd never ask." Dante stuck the rifle around the door and began pulling the trigger. A fusillade of bullets flew out, shredding the bodies of those closest to the latrine block. Dante stopped firing, letting the sound of shooting fade in the air, leaving just the whimpers of pain and agony from those still alive. "Any questions?"

. . .

Spatchcock and Flintlock were waiting beside their flyer when Dante emerged from the forest, carrying a heavy bundle wrapped in his white cloak. Blood was seeping through the material, but Dante himself appeared unharmed. "We heard shooting," Spatchcock ventured. "You alright?"

"I'm not physically harmed, if that's what you mean." Dante lowered the body to the snow-covered ground. "I thought I saw a laser cutter in the flyer. Flintlock, can you check? I'll need it to dig a grave in this frozen soil."

Spatchcock grimaced. "Your friend didn't make it."

"No. I couldn't leave him in that place, he deserved better."

"And the other prisoners?"

"I told them they were free. It's up to them what they choose to do next. One thing the war taught me well – we can't save everyone, not all the time."

"What about the guards?"

"Most saw sense. As for the others... they'll never see anything again." Dante sighed, looking down at his bloody hands. "Once we've buried Jim, we've another visit to make."

"Where to next?" Flintlock said as he emerged from the flyer, clutching the laser cutter. Dante took it and began marking out a grave in the snow.

"The Black Sea, to see an old acquaintance."

"If you don't mind my saying so, this visit with one friend didn't go very well," Flintlock ventured. "Why risk another?"

Dante tossed the cutter back to him. "Doctor Karl Fabergé is no friend of mine. We have an old score to settle." He looked down at Di Grizov's corpse. "And a new one as well."

FIVE

"Fear never stormed a citadel"
– Russian proverb

Five days after burying his mentor, Dante sat looking out across the Black Sea. The journey from Murmansk in the north had been long and arduous, thanks to the necessity of avoiding contact with the many Raven Corps checkpoints. Dante and his travelling companions had skirted the edge of St Petersburg, jagged sideways to Kirov and crisscrossed the Volga several times to make sure they were not being followed. Finally they chose a vantage point for watching Fabergé Island and settled down to wait.

Dante had visited this region once before, while staying at the Hotel Yalta, but twenty-seven straight days of partying, drinking and debauchery had left little time for sightseeing. Now, sat on a high cliff overlooking the Black Sea's glittering waters, Dante could understand why so many of the noble dynasties retained palatial mansions along this coastline. You could watch the sea for hours without getting bored; it also supported hundreds of fishermen alongside swarms of tourists.

But the waters around Fabergé Island were different. Dante had been watching the isle and its environs for hours yet seen almost no activity. No birds flew within a mile of the small rocky outcrop that rose from the water like a fist. Fishing vessels took a wide berth around the island, careful not to steer close to its vicinity. Even the shimmering schools of fish that sometimes broke the water's surface elsewhere avoided Fabergé's private residence, as if afraid of what lurked there.

Two people approaching, the Crest warned, *one from the north, the other from the south – a pincer movement.*

"I hear them," Dante murmured. Bio-blades extended from his hands, forming themselves into the shape of long swords. Dante rolled over backwards and sprang nimbly to his feet, ready for combat. Spatchcock and Flintlock stumbled out of the undergrowth from opposite directions to find razor-sharp blades at their throats.

"I say!" Flintlock protested. "Must you always do that whenever I arrive unannounced? It's dashed disconcerting."

Dante retracted his blades and went back to studying his target. Fabergé Island was some three miles offshore, beyond the range of all but the best swimmers and far enough from land to make any approaching craft obvious. "Well Spatch, what have the locals got to say about the good doctor?"

The foul-smelling forger sat beside Dante and consulted a handful of notes scrawled across the back of his left hand. "Nobody likes Fabergé much, or his staff. All provisions are flown in from outside the region. The island is home to some sort of educational institute but nobody living round here has been allowed to enrol. Apparently the fees for students are astronomical, without exception. The island has its own shuttle that makes one return trip a day to the mainland, collecting supplies, dropping off students, that sort of thing. Security is tighter than a gnat's ass. Nobody gets on or off that rock without Fabergé's express permission." Spatchcock stared out to sea. "It'll be a challenge, that's for sure."

Dante turned to his other partner in crime. "What about the island itself?"

Flintlock shrugged off his jacket. "Apparently the waters around it are empty. No marine life, no nesting birds and no ships. I listened to some of the local fishermen moaning in a tavern by the docks. It could have been the ale talking, but they believe that sea monsters and terrible creatures from the deep surround the island. Nobody I approached was willing to take a boat within a mile of Fabergé Island. You could offer them all the money in the world but I doubt they'd accept it. Everyone is scared of the doctor, and more scared of what happens on that island."

"I am becoming more and more curious," Dante murmured. "Crest, what has your analysis found? Can we launch a covert mission to the island?"

Not a successful one. Fabergé has a state of the art security system built into the rock – motion sensors, laser defence grids, mines set into the grounds outside the castle walls. It's a fortress. The only safe place outside the castle's walls is the landing pad. There's a narrow walkway between the two that is made safe when the daily shuttle leaves and arrives, but that's it.

Dante nodded grimly. He noticed the quizzical expressions on his companions' faces. "Sorry, sometimes I forget you can't hear the Crest talking. It confirms what we already suspected – the only way on or off that island is via the daily shuttle. If we want to pay Fabergé a visit, we have to do it on his terms." In the distance a bulky black and silver shape was rising above the stone turrets of the castle. "Here comes the shuttle now, right on time."

The trio watched as the only viable link to their target swooped over to the mainland, landing neatly on a flattened area below their own vantage point. A dozen locals were carrying heavy crates towards it from a nearby village. The shuttle door opened and a tall figure in a hooded cloak emerged, barking orders. Within moments the supplies were being swiftly loaded into one of the shuttle's compartments. Once their task for the day was completed, the locals retreated to the safety of nearby homes, muttering darkly amongst themselves. But the shuttle remained on the landing pad for several minutes.

"That's unusual," Dante noted. "Normally it doesn't stay a moment longer than necessary. The shuttle must be waiting for something or someone."

After remaining for another four minutes the cloaked figure climbed back into the shuttle and it rose swiftly into the air. The return journey to the island was quickly completed. "Well, whoever or whatever it was, they missed today's flight," Flintlock observed.

"There!" Spatchcock jabbed a grubby finger at the pathway to the landing pad. A lone male figure was hurrying up the track, burdened by kit bags and military paraphernalia. Bushy brown hair framed his scowling features, a clipped military moustache prominent above the mouth. He reached the landing pad and dumped his gear, before cursing at the island in the distance.

"He'll have to wait until tomorrow – they won't send the shuttle back to collect him," Flintlock said with satisfaction. "Nothing like savouring the misfortune of others to make you feel better about yourself."

"Perhaps," Dante pondered. "But his misfortune also offers an opportunity. I think we should offer our condolences to the hapless traveller. I may have crossed swords with his kind before."

Captain Grigori Arbatov was furious. When he had been offered the job with the Fabergé Institute, one thing was stressed to him – there was only one way on or off the island. Miss the daily shuttle and he could expect to spend a cold night outside waiting for it to return the next day. Madame Wartski described the mainland's local residents as a surly lot who would offer little in the way of comfort or aide.

In fact, it was the locals who had conspired to make him late. Most of the road signs leading to the landing pad were defaced to the point of illegibility. When he asked a farmer for directions, they sent him the long way round the village. Arbatov had seen the shuttle preparing to leave the landing pad, but simply could not reach it in time, weighed down by all his luggage and equipment. Now he was stuck in a hostile environment with little prospect of finding a bed for the night. Hardly the best first impression to make on his new employer. Arbatov snarled another curse, not bothering to keep it under his breath. He was furious and he didn't care who knew about it.

"My, my, captain! What would your commanding officer say if he heard such language?" A sneering voice caught Arbatov's attention. A trio of men was approaching, climbing down the hillside towards him. They reached the scorched surface of the landing pad and moved to surround him, one taking a position on either side while the last remained facing the captain. He must be the leader, judging from his cocky arrogance.

"Who are you? What do you want?" Arbatov demanded.

The leader smiled. "There'll be time for introductions later. You're not going anywhere today, you missed the only shuttle." The leader was wearing an imperial red jacket with gold braid over a creased white dress shirt and skin-tight black trousers. Jet black hair was swept back to reveal a cunning face, his black moustache and goatee beard adding a devilish touch. Alarm bells were ringing at the back of Arbatov's mind, but he couldn't remember why. He sensed this man was dangerous, even if there was no weaponry in evidence.

Arbatov risked a quick glance at the other two. The man to his left was tall and blond, with a faded elegance and stately bearing somewhat at odds with the threadbare nature of his clothing. The creature to Arbatov's right was short, round-shouldered and smirking, a foul face accompanied by an odour of pickled eggs and fresh manure. Yes, there were even lice and ticks visibly moving on the creature's stained clothing. The trio were plainly brigands intent on relieving Arbatov of his valuables. Well, they were in for an unhappy surprise! Nobody got the better of Grigori Arbatov without suffering.

"I demand the satisfaction of your names," he said sternly.

The creature shuffled a little closer, scratching an open sore on its neck. "I'm Spatchcock, but you can call me Spatch if you like. You got any diseases?"

"Certainly not!"

"You want some?" Spatchcock cackled at his own joke, licking his lips to reveal a mouthful of decayed, rotting teeth.

Arbatov took a step back from the rancid creature and bumped into the blond bandit. "My name is Flintlock, Lord Peter Flintlock." The accent was pure Britannia. Arbatov recognised it from an interminable month he had spent stationed on that rain-soaked isle during the war.

"You're a long way from home, Lord Flintlock, and I do not care for the company you keep either."

Flintlock shrugged. "Beggars cannot be choosers."

Arbatov regarded the trio's leader. "And your name?"

The black haired brigand smiled broadly. "Let me hear yours first. I may have encountered your kin in the past and would like to know where I stand before giving you my name."

"Very well." Arbatov drew his sword and held it in front of his face, standing to attention. "I am Grigori Arbatov, one of the finest swords in all the Empire and, until recently, a captain in the Tsar's own Hussars. Now, tell me your name or there shall be trouble!"

The trio's leader gave a heavy sigh. "Dante. My name is Nikolai Dante."

Arbatov's nostrils flared angrily. "*The* Nikolai Dante?"

"Why do they always ask that?" Spatchcock enquired.

"Every time," Flintlock agreed. "It's not like there's dozens of people called Nikolai Dante wandering about, causing trouble wherever they go."

"The Nikolai Dante responsible for one of my family being flayed alive on orders from the Tsar?" Arbatov demanded. "The Nikolai Dante who unsportingly beat another member of my family when they demanded the satisfaction of a duel for that first ignominy? The Nikolai Dante who had another of my kin falsely arrested for embezzling at the Hotel Yalta? The Nikolai Dante who has killed, maimed, beaten, emasculated and humiliated more than a dozen of my relatives for no other reason than capriciousness?" He was shaking with fury, such was the rage building within him.

"Don't forget what he did to the Arbatov sisters," Spatchcock chipped in.

"Pink ball in the corner pocket, you might say," Flintlock added. "He snookered three of them during the war. I wouldn't be surprised if they've all given birth to his bastards by now."

"Enough," Dante snapped. "Yes, I'm that Nikolai Dante – bane of the Arbatovs, accursed by your family for all time. Satisfied?"

"Only when I have the pleasure of killing you and dragging your rotting carcass to my family's estate. There we will feast on your sweetmeats and have the skin from your loins made into a ball for dogs to play with. Prepare to die, you festering pustule upon the face of humanity!"

Arbatov drew back his sword, ready to charge at his mortal enemy. But Dante raised his hands in surrender, urging the enraged man to wait.

"Please, captain, I have no quarrel with you or your family, no matter how difficult you may find that to believe. In almost every instance you cited, my brushes with the Arbatovs have been a mixture of bizarre coincidence and an over-developed sense of vengeance on the part of your relatives. Even my, er, encounter with the three sisters, that was purely unintentional. To be honest, they threw themselves at me. I was injured at the time, found it hard to resist."

"That's not all he found that was hard," a rough voice snickered.

"Quiet, Spatch, you're not helping," Dante hissed. "I never meant to be the individual who deflowered those women. It was just a quirk of fate. Sorry."

"Sorry?" Arbatov spluttered. "You're sorry?"

Dante shrugged. "It was beyond my control."

"You say you're sorry and I'm to do what, simply accept that as the truth? Believe the word of one of the Empire's most wanton liars and thieves? Take his feeble apology as adequate compensation for six years of ignominy, humiliation and degradation heaped upon the noble family name of Arbatov?"

"Nikolai, I don't think he's quite on your side," Flintlock said quietly.

"I was getting that impression too," Dante commented.

"Even if I could kill you a thousand times it would not be enough to undo all the ills you have visited upon my family," Arbatov snarled. "Instead I shall kill you once and rejoice in being the man who brought about your destruction!" The captain flung himself at Dante, his sword flashing through the air.

But before he could reach his target, Arbatov's right foot got snagged in the handles of his largest kit bag. The captain threw both hands forwards to break his fall, forgetting one of them still clutched a long and deadly blade. It twisted in his grip, so the point was facing Arbatov as he plunged to the ground. The captain did not even have time to cry out before being run through by his own weapon, the blade puncturing his chest to emerge from his back. Momentum pushed the sword further inwards, all the way down to the hilt.

Dante looked down at the dying man. "What is it with these Arbatovs? Can't they just let sleeping dogs lie?"

The captain spat blood on the ground before replying. "Not where you're involved, fiend! We shall have our vengeance upon you yet, Nikolai Dante. We shall prove ourselves superior. We shall... shall..."

Spatchcock knelt beside the body, checking for life. "He's gone."

"Good. His ranting was proving rather tiresome," Flintlock added.

"Help me shift the body before it bleeds all over the landing pad," Dante said, grabbing one of Arbatov's arms. "Grigori may still be useful to us."

Once the corpse was buried in a shallow grave, Dante and his companions returned to the top of the cliff. The trio sorted through the dead man's possessions, looking for some clue why he wanted to catch the daily shuttle to Fabergé Island. Spatchcock opened a bag and found it full of fencing foils and facemasks. "Those who live by the sword…?"

Flintlock uncovered a cache of personal papers, including travel documents and instructions. "Seems Arbatov was joining the Fabergé Institute as a tutor in self defence, swordplay and two unspecified disciplines. There's a letter from a Madame Wartski, offering the captain a two-week probationary post. If that proves successful, the job becomes permanent."

"Not anymore," Dante noted wryly. "But those papers could give us a legitimate way on to the island."

Spatchcock frowned. "What kind of educational institute offers classes in self defence and swordplay? Who *are* Fabergé's students?"

"Perhaps the contents of this will give us a clue," Dante ventured as he opened the last of the kit bags. A selection of silk and lace lingerie tumbled out. "Or perhaps not. Who carries a bag filled with women's underwear?"

"Maybe the captain fancied himself a ladies man and kept a trophy from each of his conquests?" Flintlock suggested. "They are all different shapes and styles, so they probably come from different women."

"Or maybe he liked dressing up in frilly knickers?" Spatchcock replied with a broad smirk. "Takes all kinds, doesn't it Flintlock?"

"What are you trying to imply, Spatch?"

"I wasn't implying anything."

"I should hope not," Flintlock grumbled.

"I was inferring."

"No, no, no! The speaker implies, the listener infers."

"Whatever you say," Spatchcock said. "Don't get your knickers in a twist."

"There you go again! I will not be subject to these snide little remarks of yours. Just because I come from Britannia, does not mean I am some sort of sexual pervert to be taunted and teased for your pleasure!"

"Well, if it turns you on–"

"Enough!" Dante interjected. "Spatchcock, spare us the details of your sordid fantasies. Flintlock, stop rising to his bait. If you two can't work together you can stay here while I visit the island on my own." He examined the other paperwork. "Spatchcock, how are your forgery skills?"

"A mite rusty, but I can match anything you've got in your hand, given time and the right materials."

"We've got twenty-four hours till the shuttle returns, so you'd better get to work. Flintlock, forage for supplies in the village. We'll be staying here tonight and those look like rain clouds coming round the hills. Beg, steal or borrow food and shelter."

The two men nodded and began their tasks, while Dante continued studying the papers Arbatov had carried. "Crest, forged papers will only get us so far. I'll need credentials listed on the Imperial Net if I'm going to survive more than a few hours on the island."

You're not planning to become Grigori Arbatov, are you? I cannot work miracles, Dante, not without prior notice.

"No need for that. I'm reviving a favourite alias of mine. I need you to hack the Imperial Net and establish a fresh life story for him."

Using what – thin air? the Crest demanded.

Dante produced a slim silver rectangle from among Arbatov's things. Smaller than a cigarette case, it had the Imperial Net logo embossed on both sides. "How about a netski? Will that give you enough access?"

Part credit card, part communications device, and solar powered too. That'll do nicely, the Crest said happily. *Rest your fingers against either side of it and relax. I'll do the rest.*

By noon the next day the trio were ready. Sleep had proved elusive overnight, thanks to a torrential downpour. But strong sunshine in the morning soon helped restore their spirits. A distant, mournful bell chimed twelve. "What day is it?" Dante wondered. "We didn't hear that bell once yesterday."

"Sunday, isn't it?" Flintlock scratched his chest absent-mindedly. "The bells must be calling the faithful to worship."

It's Palm Sunday, the Crest told Dante. *Only one week until Fabergé's new weapon becomes active.*

"Religion is wasted on us," Spatchcock smiled. He slapped Flintlock's back. "Something wrong, your lordship? You don't seem comfortable today."

"No, you're right. I can't seem to stop scratching." Realisation dawned on the aristocratic face. "Spatch! What did you do to me in the night?"

"I was cold and wet, so I snuggled against you for warmth."

Flintlock ripped open his shirt to discover a profusion of tiny red bites on his chest, the marks made more livid by scratching. "Fleas! You've given me fleas, you disgusting little worm!"

Spatchcock shrugged, scratching himself under an armpit. "You were sharing your warmth with me. Seemed only fair to give you something back."

"Give it a rest for five minutes," Dante snapped. "I see our ride leaving the island."

In the distance the shuttle rose above the castle and began swooping across the water towards them. Dante led the others down to the landing area, carrying a selection of luggage culled from their own possessions and those of the late Grigori Arbatov. The trio were waiting for the shuttle when it arrived, its afterburners eradicating the last traces of blood from the launching pad.

A burly figure in a hooded cloak emerged from the vehicle. Dante stepped towards him, smiling and offering to shake hands. "Good afternoon, sir. My name is–"

"Address me as either Madame Wartski or simply as Madame, but never as sir!" The hood was pushed back to reveal a wart-strewn face, greying hair scraped back into a bun and a scowling countenance. If this person was not the ugliest woman alive, Dante had no urge to go in search of any alternatives.

"Of course, Madame! Excuse my folly, I could not see your face beneath the hood," Dante continued. "My name is–"

"Why were you not here yesterday, as previously agreed? Why did you not contact us and explain the reason for this unforgivable delay? And why are three of you waiting, instead of one?"

Dante stood his ground before the flurry of interrogation, doing his best to smile ingratiatingly at the horrendous harridan. "Alas, I was only contacted by Captain Arbatov late last night and thus it was impossible for me to be here yesterday."

"So you are not Captain Arbatov?"

"No, Madame Wartski. As I tried to say before, my name is–"

"Your name is of no consequence." Wartski turned back to the vehicle.

Dante grabbed her by the arm, his fingers failing to encompass even half of her fleshy limb's circumference. "Please, Madame Wartski, if you will just let me explain..."

Wartski called to the shuttle's pilot. "How long before we can take off?"

"Fifty-five seconds, Madame!"

She turned back to Dante. "You have that long."

"As I have been trying to say, my name is Quentin Durward and I am a close personal friend of Grigori Arbatov.

Alas, a fencing accident means he could not accept your gracious invitation to join the Fabergé Institute for the final days of this term, so he suggested I offer my services in his stead. Had I been able, I would have called ahead to explain. I wrongly assumed he had already done so and apologise for that error."

Dante produced a sheaf of papers, all of them artfully created by Spatchcock. "I believe you'll find these documents establish my bona fides. As for my travelling companions, they are servants and have been with me since I was a youth." He gestured for them to come forwards. "The shorter, Spatchcock, is a fine cook and would add distinction to your kitchen, while the taller is my factotum, Flintlock. The latter, sadly, is a mute and thus unable to speak." Spatchcock suppressed a snort of laughter.

"Madame Wartski, we're ready to go," the pilot called.

Wartski regarded the trio, her bottom lip curling outwards sourly. "I am not satisfied with these explanations, but your papers appear authentic. You may come to the island, Mr Durward, where I can better establish the truth."

"And my servants?"

"We have little need of their services."

"They work without payment. Mere lodgings and board will satisfy them."

Wartski scowled. "Very well. But be warned of this: should I have any reason to doubt your veracity or that of your servants, all three of you shall suffer the consequences equally. Is that clear?"

"As the blue of your eyes," Dante said sweetly.

Wartski leaned into his face, the rank stench of her breath invading his nostrils. "Flattery will get you nowhere with me, Mr Durward. I am interested only in what you can do for the institute."

"Of course, Madame Wartski. I would have it no other way." Dante snapped his fingers at Spatchcock and Flintlock. "You two! Fetch my things!" Ignoring the foul looks they were sending in his direction, Dante followed Wartski into the shuttle. The interior was luxuriously fitted, with four plush chairs for the passengers. But once Wartski had sat down only one of the seats remained, leaving nowhere for Spatchcock and Flintlock. "You'll have to travel in the cargo hold with my bags," he told them, suppressing a smile at their reactions. "And be quick about it! Madame Wartski has waited long enough on our behalf, let's not keep her here any longer!"

The flight to Fabergé Island took only minutes but Flintlock still found time to throw up thanks to airsickness and being confined in the cargo hold with Spatchcock. "A mute? Why did he say I'm a mute?"

"I can think of two reasons," Spatchcock replied. "Either he figured your Britannia accent would attract unwanted attention…"

"Or?"

"Or he didn't want to listen to your whining any longer – and I can't say I blame him. Now put a sock in it!"

"Why should I?" Flintlock protested.

Spatchcock indicated a security camera in the ceiling. "Your lips do a lot of flapping for somebody who's supposed to be mute. Best not to let anyone else see you talking, alright?"

"I– I–" Flintlock sighed in exasperation and clamped his mouth shut.

Spatchcock smiled blissfully. "Ahh, the sound of silence. Could anything be finer?" The sound of violent farting issued from his trousers, closely followed by a noxious stench. Flintlock pinched his nostrils shut and moved to the other side of the cabin, getting as far from the odour as possible.

"I'll take that as a yes," Spatchcock decided.

The shuttle circled Fabergé Island once so Wartski could point out the castle's exterior features to Dante. The imposing square structure covered more than two-thirds of the island's surface area. Each corner was adorned by a tower, standing twice the height of the adjoining building. "This entire complex was reconstructed stone by stone, after the doctor bought it from a Britannia noble family who had fallen on hard times. Most of the building is devoted to the institute's work, but the north tower is reserved for the doctor's private research."

"Sounds fascinating. What is Doctor Fabergé researching, if I may ask?"

"You may not," Wartski replied with a scowl. "The north tower is strictly out of bounds at all times. Anyone caught trespassing there will be dismissed or expelled immediately – without exception."

"I understand, of course. Rules are rules."

"And must be obeyed at all times."

"Precisely," Dante agreed. "I couldn't have put it better myself."

Dante, you've never obeyed a rule in your life!

The shuttle descended towards the island's landing pad. Dante peered out of his window, absorbing as much information as he could about the external facilities. "Well, I must say I am looking forward to working with your pupils," he said. "How many do you have here at present?"

"Most have already returned home early for the Easter holidays, as have many of our regular tutors," Wartski replied. "But the elite class is here for another week. We have a dozen students from around the Empire, most aged between eighteen and twenty-one." The shuttle finished landing procedures and Wartski pulled open the passenger door.

"And what's the split between male and female?"

Wartski stopped and looked at him. "Didn't Captain Arbatov tell you? The Fabergé Institute is a finishing school for young ladies from the richest and most important families in the Empire."

"Really?"

"Yes." Wartski started climbing down the shuttle steps. "I hope that isn't going to be a problem for you."

Dante shook his head slowly. "A finishing school for young ladies aged eighteen to twenty-one? No, I don't think that should present any difficulties…"

Except keeping your pants on long enough to take lessons, the Crest said. *This situation will only lead to one thing…*

"No difficulties at all," Dante concluded.

Trouble, trouble and more trouble!

SIX

"Deceit and cunning go together"
– Russian proverb

Wartski marched towards the castle entrance, her chunky legs stomping along the pathway. Dante followed close behind, his eyes roving across the exterior of the stonework. Flintlock and Spatchcock brought up the rear, struggling to carry the entire luggage between them. "Be careful not to venture off the path," Wartski warned them sternly. "The island may look benign but its external surface is embedded with pressure mines. Your first step off the correct path would also be your last."

"An impressive security system," Dante said. "But is it strictly necessary for a girls' finishing school?"

Wartski stopped outside the entrance and folded her arms. "Firstly, this is an educational institute for young ladies, not girls. Give our students the respect they deserve, Mr Durward. Secondly, there have been instances where predatory males thought they might be able to satisfy their carnal lusts with our pupils. The few who made it to the island alive did not leave it in the same condition. Thirdly, our director believes such security measures are necessary to protect his personal research. You would do well not to question the judgement of Doctor Fabergé."

"Of course. Your comments are noted and will be respected," Dante said.

Chance would be a fine thing.

Wartski pressed her palm against a block of frosted glass in the wall beside the entrance. A beam of light scanned the contours of her hand before the glass turned green. Double doors sighed open, revealing a vast reception chamber inside. "Once your bona fides have been confirmed, your palm print will be recorded and logged into our security system," she explained. "That will enable you to access all areas of the castle necessary to perform your duties. Your servants will also have to undergo such screening."

"Of course," Dante said, nodding vigorously. "We must be on our guard at all times. Heaven forbid anything that might impugn the name of Fabergé!"

Wartski raised an eyebrow at this outburst before gesturing for him to enter. "After you, Mr Durward."

Dante bowed deeply, then strolled into the reception chamber, followed by Flintlock and Spatchcock. Wartski was last inside, waving her hand across another palm reader within. The doors slammed shut with a boom of finality. Dante looked around the room, marvelling at its high ceiling and oak-panelled walls. A banner with the Fabergé family crest hung on one wall, close to an honours board marking the achievements of past pupils. The institute had only been open nine years but could already claim several prominent alumni. Top of the list were two names – Strangelove S, and Strangelove T.

Any relation to the Strangelove Gambit?

Wartski noted Dante's interest in the honours board. "Storm and Tempest were our first pupils, the stars of their year. You may remember their success at the Imperial Games?"

"Of course," Dante replied with a smile, the Crest filling his thoughts with facts and statistics from its files. "A remarkable pair!"

"I thought they both had a remarkable pair," Spatchcock muttered, jabbing an elbow into Flintlock's ribs and leering crudely. He wiped the smirk off his face before Wartski could see it.

She opened a side door with a gesture across another palm reader. "If you'll excuse me, I need to report your arrival to Doctor Fabergé and check the identification papers you supplied. Please wait here."

Dante nodded and smiled, watching her depart before turning to his companions. "Now, I want both of you to be on your best behaviour. Do nothing to embarrass the good name of Quentin Durward, is that clear?"

Spatchcock rolled his eyes and grinned. Flintlock began to speak, then stopped, clamping his mouth shut in frustration.

"Very good," Dante continued, his eyes searching the reception area for surveillance devices. "We must be on our guard at all times, to ensure we meet the high standards set by the Fabergé Institute."

Madame Wartski has begun searching the records for your fake identity, the Crest warned. *The false history I created should sustain itself through a routine scrutiny, but if she digs any deeper…*

Dante folded his arms and waited. "I wonder where the pupils are?"

"At mass," Wartski replied, emerging from the side door with his papers clutched in a chubby, wart-ridden hand. "Our director insists all the students observe the main feast days of the church calendar. Why feed the mind if the soul goes unnourished?"

"An admirable sentiment," Dante agreed, reaching for the documents. "I trust everything was in order?"

Wartski smiled broadly, an expression that ill suited her fearsome face. "We are honoured to have such a distinguished instructor join our faculty. Hopefully we will be able to make your time here a stay of some duration. Perhaps you would like a tour of our facilities?"

"That would be most kind. But I hardly think it appropriate for my servants to join us. If I might be so bold, may I suggest their fate be determined first?"

Wartski acknowledged the wisdom of this. "Very well. You two, take the first door on the right after you leave here. There is a staircase leading down to the kitchen where our resident chef and housekeeper Scullion will find a use for both of you. Once you've been assigned suitable tasks return here and carry your master's luggage to his quarters. I will leave directions. Do you understand?" Spatchcock and Flintlock nodded quickly. "Very good. Off you go and try not to antagonise Scullion. Her temper is short and her tentacles long."

The two men hurried to escape the matron's fearsome gaze. Dante could hear Spatchcock muttering to Flintlock as the pair left the reception chamber. "Her tentacles are long? Who is this Scullion, an octopus?"

Once they were gone Wartski began leading Dante around the castle, explaining the use of each room on their tour. The east tower and nearby rooms were devoted to dormitories and other student facilities, while the south tower and its environs were classrooms and training areas. "We teach all the key subjects our pupils might require for their lives as the leading ladies of the Empire," Wartski explained. "History, business communication, literature, philosophy, organisations behaviour, psychology, ecology, a dozen different languages, economics, etiquette, domestic science, music, ballroom dancing and flower arranging."

"A broad curriculum," Dante replied. "You offer an admirable range of knowledge to the young ladies."

Wartski threw open a door to reveal the top level of the south tower. The entire space was given over to a well-equipped gymnasium, the floor and walls heavily padded to prevent injury. "We expect you to give each of our pupils a strenuous workout, discover their strengths and weaknesses."

"It will be my pleasure," he replied. "Hopefully they will respond well to the personal touch and breadth of experience I can offer."

Take a care, the Crest warned. *The matron may have a face to curdle milk, but the woman is no fool.*

"I've been taking the classes myself since your predecessor left," Wartski continued. "Alas, I am not as nimble as I once was. The students are looking forward to having you really stretch them."

Dante merely nodded, not trusting himself to say anything out loud. His tour guide gestured at the west tower, the gymnasium's window. "That area of the castle is given over to the faculty: private quarters, ablution blocks, a study and library area, along with meetings rooms. The junior tutors have left for the term but our senior staff remain on site all year round. You'll meet them at dinner tonight, beginning promptly at seven."

A heavy chiming filled the air, closely followed by the sound of feminine giggling outside. "Ah, mass is over for today, the students are returning to their dormitory. Would you like to see them?" Wartski asked.

Dante looked down at a square courtyard in the centre of the castle. A dozen beautiful young women were hurrying across the cobbles, laughing and teasing each other. All were clad in demure gowns of blue and white, but even the severe cut of the cloth could not disguise their firm buttocks and jutting breasts. The women disappeared into a doorway at the foot of the east tower, the sound of their laughter like music in the air. "They look very fit," Dante said, trying to keep his voice neutral. "You've obviously done a good job of keeping them active."

"I wish I could claim the credit. Your predecessor, Mr Russell, drove the students hard. Sometimes I think he would have been happier teaching a class of young men, such was his passion for the more masculine athletic pursuits – wrestling, boxing and the like."

"I'm all for treating women like women," Dante avowed.

"Good, then you won't mind picking up some of the classes Mr Russell neglected, such as philosophy and literature studies."

Something tells me I'm going to be rather busy, the Crest commented.

"Two of my favourites!" Dante lied. "When do I start?"

"Classes resume tomorrow," Wartski replied. "I'll escort you to your quarters. No doubt you'll wish to freshen up before joining the other staff in the library for a pre-dinner drink?" She began striding from the gymnasium, not noticing Dante lingering at the window. He was studying the north tower opposite, its windows shrouded with black-tinted glass. "Mr Durward?" Wartski called, but got no response.

Dante! She's calling you!

"What? Oh, sorry!" Dante shouted, hurrying after his host. "Just planning my first class for tomorrow. It's always been an ambition of mine to work at a prestigious facility, especially one with such an admirable student body. I do believe I'll fit right in here."

In the kitchen Spatchcock and Flintlock were standing to attention as a green-skinned creature with at least a dozen tentacles studied them with disgust. An entire wall of the kitchen was given over to a pantry, while foul-smelling liquids bubbled away in cast iron vats. A sturdy wooden table filled the centre of the cooking room, lined with chairs on either side. Three doorways led away from the kitchen. One was the staircase down which Spatchcock and Flintlock had descended into Scullion's domain. The other two led to a drainage room and another, as yet unseen destination.

"My name is Scullion," the creature announced, "and no matter what Madame Wartski might think, I am responsible for keeping this institute running. I do this by taking responsibility for all its needs below stairs: the cooking, the cleaning, the laundry and any other ablutions required. Any questions?" Scullion jabbed Flintlock in the stomach with a tentacle, making him wince in pain.

"He's a mute," Spatchcock offered helpfully. "Can't speak a word."

"Thank you, I am aware of what the word mute means."

"Sorry. I just thought, what with you being an off-worlder–" Spatchcock was abruptly silenced as his head was clamped inside another of Scullion's tentacles, moist pink suckers adhering to his face. The squat, emerald-hued alien leaned closer to Spatchcock, its one red eye peering at him intently.

"I've had enough anti-alien abuse to last me a lifetime. On my home planet of Arcneva I was Gourmet Chef of the Cycle twice in a row. I do not need some snivelling weasel of a servant to tell me–" Scullion paused in mid-rant, sniffing the air with disdain. "What is that stench?"

Spatchcock peeled away the tentacle from his face to reply. "Sorry, that's probably me. Most people complain that I smell worse than an alien's arsehole." The words were out of his mouth before he realised what was being said. "I–"

Scullion slapped the tentacle back into place. "Silence! I wasn't talking to you. I was talking to this loathsome creature!" The alien jabbed Flintlock once more. He opened his mouth to protest, remembered his status as a mute and closed his mouth again with a snap. Scullion sniffed at Flintlock's armpits before reeling away, squealing in horror and quickly retracting its tentacles. "Most humans smell like wet pork to me, but you – you carry the foulest of stenches with you! What is your name?"

"He's called Flintlock," Spatchcock chipped in.

"From now on he shall be called Faeces," Scullion decided. "He shall be addressed only by that name in my presence. Do you understand?"

"Yes, er..."

"You can call me Scullion, or ma'am."

Spatchcock smiled. "Yes, ma'am."

The alien studied him carefully. "Can you cook?"

"I can always rustle something up," he admitted.

"Good. I will tutor you in the ways of Arcnevan cuisine, Spatchcock." Scullion slipped a tentacle round his shoulders and gave them a playful squeeze. "As for your friend Faeces..."

"He could clean out the drains," Spatchcock suggested with a smile.

"A task to match his title and his aroma! Excellent. I couldn't have thought of anything more appropriate myself." The alien pointed at a circular sewer covering in the adjoining drainage room. "You can start over there."

Flintlock hurried to the grille and lifted it up, his head snapping away from the odour of raw sewage wafting upwards. The former aristocrat gave Spatchcock a murderous glare, his fists clenching and unclenching. "I said get started, Faeces!" Scullion snapped. "You brought this on yourself, so don't blame you sweeter-smelling colleague. Try following his example in future and I might forgive you. Now get on with your allotted task!"

Dante was less than impressed with his private quarters. The spartan stone chamber contained a wardrobe, stiff-backed chair and single bed as furnishings. Wartski explained that Doctor Fabergé preferred his staff to spend as much time as possible among the other faculty members and students. "Bedrooms are for sleeping in, nothing more," she added with a growl of warning. "Your servants will be permitted to wait upon you here once a day, if their duties are completed, but no other visitors are allowed."

"Perfectly fair and reasonable," Dante replied out loud. How I am supposed to know my students better with this behemoth breathing down my neck, he thought to himself.

You would do better to concentrate on your mission, the Crest suggested. *The Strangelove Gambit, remember?*

"Captain Arbatov told me the institute was soon to be honoured with a visit by the Tsar," Dante said. "Is that true?"

Wartski frowned. "Yes, although I don't know how he can have told you that. It hasn't been announced in the court circular."

"Really? Well, when I see Arbatov next I will remonstrate with him for such a lapse. It does not do to gossip about such matters."

"No, it doesn't," Wartski agreed. "Why do you ask about the Tsar? Have you met him before?"

"Once or twice. We've crossed swords, you might say."

"He is due to visit us a week today. It should be a glorious occasion for the institute, helping promote our efforts to all the Empire. Doctor Fabergé cannot wait to show the Tsar what he has achieved here. Now, if you'll excuse me, I must attend to matters elsewhere in the castle."

Dante listened at his door to ensure Wartski was gone before sitting on the single bed. He bounced up and down on the thin straw mattress, wincing at the lack of give. "Not exactly the lap of luxury."

You can stop talking to yourself, I've finished scanning the room, the Crest interjected. *No obvious listening devices or surveillance cameras. If you are being watched, it's technology beyond my ability to detect. To be safe I've established a low level-jamming signal.*

"What about the palm readers?"

More problematic, the Crest admitted. *I should be able to override the scanning systems but no doubt Fabergé has other methods of securing other parts of his castle.*

"Like the north tower?"

Precisely. His private research is almost certainly the source of this new weapon. The institute's pupils are just a front to distract attention.

Dante smirked. "They're doing a pretty good job so far." He spread himself out on the mattress and closed his eyes. "Keep scanning Crest. The more we know about the castle and its contents, the easier it will be discovering what the Strangelove Gambit is all about."

And what will you be doing?

"Getting some rest. A night under canvas with Spatchcock and Flintlock is no way to get any beauty sleep."

True, but some of us need more than others.

"Call me when it's time for dinner."

I'm not an alarm clock, you know! the Crest protested. *Dante? Dante!* But the only response was the unpleasant grating sound of Dante's snoring.

· · ·

It was the smell that roused Dante from his slumber. "Diavolo, who killed the cat?" he muttered, sitting up on the thin mattress. "Flintlock? Is that you?"

"Yes, it's bloody me!" A tall figure was standing beside Dante's bed, smeared from head to toe with viscous slime. Whatever colour of clothing he had been wearing was now impossible to tell, replaced by shades of black and brown. The face and hair were just as bad, only the pale blue eyes and white teeth providing any break in the sewage-stained visage. Worst of all was the smell, a rank odour worse than any back street pissotière. Dante waved Flintlock back before standing, eager to keep some distance between them.

"What happened? Did you fall into a septic tank?"

"Not exactly," Flintlock snarled. "That bitch Scullion had me cleaning the drains while Spatchcock, the foulest smelling creature in the Empire, is cooking the soup for tonight's meal!"

Dante clamped his nostrils between the thumb and forefinger of his left hand. "I think your smell might beat Spatchcock's now." He opened the window in the hope of admitting some fresh air. "How come you got sewer duty?"

"Scullion is an alien from Arcneva," Flintlock replied grumpily.

A planet where the indigenous people consider offensive body odour an aphrodisiac, the Crest said. *No doubt Spatchcock's scent seemed like a fine perfume to her.*

Dante did his best to suppress a smile without much success. "I don't see what you've got to smirk at," Flintlock protested.

"No, you're absolutely right," Dante agreed. "What else can you tell me?"

"This mute act – how long do I have to keep it up?"

"A week at the most. Wartski confirmed the Tsar will be here for Easter Sunday, so we've got until then to find and stop this new weapon – whatever it is." Dante stood beneath the window, trying to catch the few wisps of air that crept into the room. "Where have you and Spatch been given access to so far?"

"The drains, the septic tank and the overflow pipes for me," Flintlock said testily. "Spatch hasn't got out of Scullion's clutches in the kitchen yet."

"We need to discover everything we can about what's happening here, especially in the north tower. Tell Spatch to grab every opportunity."

"And what about me?"

"Try not to catch anything fatal." Dante gestured towards the door. "I'm sorry, but you'll have to leave now. I need to get ready for my first faculty dinner."

"So? Perhaps I could help, I am meant to be your servant."

"No disrespect, but the longer you stay in here the worse I'll smell later."

Flintlock turned on his heels and flounced towards the door. "I've never been so insulted in my life," he muttered. "Forced to squeeze down a pipe filled with heaven only knows what then told to–"

"And go quietly, please," Dante called after him. "You're meant to be a mute, remember?"

Flintlock made an obscene finger gesture and departed, but the stench from his visit remained.

It was after seven when Dante found his way to the staff library. Inside the book-lined room five women and an elderly man were talking in hushed voices beneath a towering portrait of Doctor Fabergé. The painting neatly captured the cruel face and dismissive eyes of its subject, but added a haughty grandeur to the driven countenance. The staff gathered beneath the image of their director was not nearly so intimidating.

All of the women were middle-aged; their age reflected in the staid tweeds and checks of their clothing. Sensible shoes and thick woollen stockings, a few strings of second rate pearls, greying hair and crow's feet wrinkles were further evidence of their dry lives and interests. I doubt this lot start many orgies, Dante reflected ruefully.

Dante approached the only other male in the room, a crusty old man in brown corduroy trousers and an ancient blazer with leather patches over the elbows. A pair of half moon spectacles perched on his nose while red, rheumy eyes peered at the volumes on the shelves around him. Dante clapped a hand on the old man's back, sending a small cloud of dust into the air.

"Durward, Quentin Durward – I'm the new self defence instructor!" Dante announced cheerfully. "And what's your name, if I may be so bold?"

The old man coughed and wheezed before answering laboriously. "Mould. Professor Augustus Mould."

Dante suppressed a pun. "Fascinating. And how long have you been here?"

Mould looked at his watch, not noticing the sherry he was pouring over his brown brogues. "About twenty minutes, I think. Yes, twenty minutes."

"Really? I didn't realise the fun started so early here."

"Fun? What fun?"

"I, er..." Dante shrugged helplessly before muttering under his breath. "Crest? A little help here, please?"

Oh no, it replied gleefully. *He's all yours. Enjoy.*

"Wonderful," Dante said to Mould. "Well, a delight to meet you. Perhaps we'll get a chance to talk again later." But before he could move away the elderly professor had grabbed Dante's arm.

"Self defence, you said? Then you must be Russell's replacement."

"Yes, that's right."

"Odd chap, Russell. I think he'd have been happier at a finishing school for young men, if you know what I mean," Mould said, conspiratorially tapping the side of his nose. "Played for the other side, you might say."

"Did he? I wouldn't know. I've never met him."

"Never saw the point in that sort of thing."

"Sex?"

"Chasing other men around. Much fonder of the fairer sex, myself."

Dante looked at the crusty professor. "You were? I mean, you are?"

Mould nodded wistfully. "Used to be. Quite the catch I was once. Had to fight the young girls off with a stick. At least I believe that's the expression."

"I thought the Tsar had outlawed corporal punishment," Dante said.

But Mould was no longer listening to him. "I sleep through most of my lessons now. The students here, they're not interested in history or language. They just want fame and fortune, how to catch a husband..."

"Madame Wartski doesn't share your views."

The professor's face darkened. "Beware of her, young Durward. Beware of any woman with that many warts. She has them for a reason, you know."

Dante leaned closer to the professor. "And why is that?"

"Toads. That's all you need to know. Beware of the toads."

"Beware of the toads?"

Mould nodded sagely. "I'll say no more."

"I understand," Dante agreed. "Well, if you'll excuse me..." He turned away and walked face-first into a large pair of firm, proud breasts. "Bojemoi!" Dante stumbled back a step, blinking to clear his vision. He reached out a hand for support and found himself grasping another breast to his right. "Diavolo, I'm surrounded by them!"

"You must be–" a woman's voice began.

"The new self defence instructor," another woman said, completing the first's sentence. "Perhaps you could do with–"

"A refresher course yourself?" the first voice concluded.

Dante looked up to find two Amazons towering over him. Their mighty breasts were level with his eyes, providing a daunting introduction to their physical presence. Their strong, angular features stared down at Dante, a difference in hair colouring the only way of telling them apart. Both were clad in skin-tight bodysuits that left little to the imagination. "Are you offering to give me one?" Dante asked hopefully.

"We already have–" the red-haired woman began.

"A full teaching load," the brunette said.

"Oh," Dante said sadly. "What a shame."

"Mr Durward," a familiar voice called out. Wartski was marching towards the trio, holding two glasses of sherry before her. "I see you've met the Furies." She handed Dante one of the glasses. "Storm and Tempest joined the teaching staff this year and have proved a great success with the students."

The Strangelove twins, Dante realised. He had caught a little of the media hype surrounding these remarkable women. In the flesh they were even more impressive. Dante felt a stirring in his loins at the prospect of finding out how impressive. "Which one's which?"

The red-haired woman offered her right hand to him. "I'm Tempest."

Dante kissed the hand, adding his wickedest of grins. "Enchanted," he whispered before moving on to the other twin. "And you must be Storm. How delightful to make your acquaintance." She did not offer Dante a hand, folding her arms instead. "I'm told you two do everything together."

"Almost," Tempest replied. "We find two heads are better than one."

"Still, three needn't always be a crowd," Dante countered. "Perhaps we could get together and talk about it sometime."

"I doubt that will be possible before the end of term," Storm said brusquely before walking away. "Come along, sister." Dante watched them walk away, admiring the rippling muscles in their thighs and buttocks.

You're out of your depth, the Crest warned. *Those two would eat you for breakfast and leave nothing behind.*

"But what a way to go." Dante murmured. "What a way to go."

"Sorry, did you say something?" Wartski asked.

"Er, I was wondering which way to go – for dinner."

A chime sounded once, silencing the hubbub of voices in the library. Wartski nodded at the others. "Now you shall find out, Mr Durward. Dinner is served and Doctor Fabergé is dying to meet you." The hefty harridan strode away, leaving Dante to finish his sherry.

The evening meal was served in an oak-panelled dining hall next to the staff library. A long table ran the length of the room, but most of the seats went unoccupied with only the senior staff in attendance. Wartski stood near the head of the table, motioning for Dante to take the chair opposite her. Mould moved to beside Dante, while the other tutors choose seats nearby. But nobody sat down, all waiting patiently beside their chairs.

Finally a doorway opened and the Strangelove twins emerged from it, Doctor Fabergé followed them inside. He moved to the head of the table, fixed the gaze of each staff member and nodded to them individually. Lastly he acknowledged the presence of Dante, then sat down. The staff followed his example, the twins sitting opposite each other but farthest from Fabergé.

Murmurings of small talk began along the table while everyone waited for the first course to be served, giving Dante a chance to cast a furtive eye at Fabergé. Twelve years had passed since their last encounter, enough time for the doctor's hairline to recede further and more lines to appear on his face. But for these changes Fabergé was much as Dante remembered, proud of bearing and inquisitive of eye. He noticed the attentions of the new teacher and addressed them immediately.

"You must be our new self defence tutor, Mr Durward."

"That's correct, Doctor Fabergé," Dante replied.

"And why have you been looking at me so intently?"

A hush fell upon the table, the others waiting for the newcomer's reply.

"I was comparing your true appearance to the portrait I saw in the library."

"Indeed. And how would you rate the quality of that likeness?"

Dante smiled. "The artist captured your looks, but not your stature."

Fabergé regarded him carefully. "Well chosen words. I wonder how close they are to the truth?"

"As someone versed in the arts of self defence, I know that such skills are as much about brain as they are brawn. You can often talk your way out of trouble with less danger than you can fight your way out."

The doctor stroked his chin thoughtfully. "Have we met somewhere before, Mr Durward? Your face seems familiar, but I cannot recall from where."

Dante shook his head. "I have a common aspect but can say for certain you have never met Quentin Durward before."

"Perhaps I was mistaken..." Fabergé was interrupted by the arrival of Scullion, carrying eleven bowls of steaming soup in her many tentacles. "Ah, the starter. Let us eat, drink and be merry..."

The meal continued for three hours and twice as many courses, until Dante felt his belly bloating and trousers tightening. "I'm not sure I shall be able to lead my classes for long, if you feast like this every night."

Wartski waved away his concerns. "We only eat this well on Sunday evenings. Simpler fare is served during the week."

Fabergé had been watching Dante throughout the meal. "We live by an old proverb here, Mr Durward – eat the honey, but beware the sting."

Dante, be careful! the Crest warned. *He's trying to draw you into a battle of wits – and that's one fight you can never win. Just repeat what I say...*

Dante listened to the voice inside his head and then smiled at the institute's director. "I prefer a different saying: luck is a stick with two ends."

Fabergé laughed out loud at that. "Well said, Mr Durward, well said. Perhaps you've heard another adage: God made two evils, tax collectors and goats. Which one are you, I wonder?"

Dante nodded before replying. "Well, I'm not a god, if that's what you're wondering."

"Few of us are," Fabergé agreed. "But some aspire to match the achievements of the Almighty."

"Is that always wise?" Dante asked, pausing as if choosing his words carefully. "As the proverb has it, the spirit is God's, but the body is the Tsar's."

"Well, the Tsar is expected here in a week's time. You may debate morality and proverbs with him then," Fabergé said. "You have an interesting habit of waiting before you reply, Mr Durward. Why is that?"

I like to think before I speak, the Crest prompted Dante, who repeated the phrase out loud.

"An admirable quality, and one many of our pupils could do with learning. Perhaps you're the man to take them in hand?"

"I'm sure I'll soon have a firm grasp of their strengths and weaknesses."

"I hope so," Fabergé said before standing. Everyone else rose from their chairs, Dante swiftly following their example. "In the meantime I have more work to do if my research is to be complete in time for the Tsar's visit. I bid you all a good night's rest. Tempest, Storm – will you join me in the laboratory? We have a very busy week ahead."

Wartski and the others murmured their good nights, watching as Fabergé and the twins strode from the dining hall. Once the trio had departed everyone returned to the staff library, whether they had finished or not. "Once our master leaves his seat, the meal is over," Mould whispered in Dante's ear. "It always pays to eat as quickly as possible."

"That explains why we were the only ones talking." Dante wanted to ask the old professor a question but Mould was already scuttling towards the sweet sherry decanter, intent on refilling his glass. Instead Wartski gravitated to the new arrival's side, the aroma from her sweaty armpits indicating her presence.

"You'll have to forgive the professor. A brilliant tutor once, but past his prime; now slowly pickling himself to death."

"Why do you keep him on if that's the case?"

Wartski smiled. "Call it user loyalty."

Dante nodded, not wanting to think about what her remark implied. "Well, I think I've imbibed quite enough sherry for a month, let alone one night. I shall be returning to my room for the evening." He walked from the room, nodding a goodnight to the other teachers, but Wartski followed him out.

"Mr Durward, there is something I forgot to mention earlier. I advise locking yourself in each night. Your predecessor was prone to sleepwalking. Indeed, that's what caused his death."

"His death? I thought he went to another place of learning."

Wartski shook her head. "That's what we told the pupils and some of the other tutors. In fact Mr Russell was a frequent sleepwalker. He wandered into the north tower one night and was cut to pieces by the security defence lasers. Not a pleasant sight, not pleasant at all."

"I can imagine," Dante said grimly.

"So, as I said, best if you lock yourself in. We wouldn't want such an unhappy incident to happen to you too, would we?"

"Thank you for the warning. I'll be sure to remain on my guard." Dante walked back to his quarters, seething at the veiled threat. The unfortunate Russell had been murdered to preserve whatever secret Fabergé had locked inside the north tower, just as Di Grizov had been tortured to aid whatever barbaric research the doctor was undertaking.

Just be grateful Fabergé didn't remember you from the Casino Royale, the Crest said. *He would not hesitate to have you killed if he realised you helped Di Grizov steal the Steel Military Egg.*

"Tell me something I don't know," Dante muttered bitterly.

SEVEN

"How do I look, Crest?" Dante's luggage had appeared in his quarters while he was at dinner the night before, carried there by Flintlock if the vile smell on the handles was any indication. The next morning Dante took a hearty breakfast, showered and scrubbed in preparation for his first class, and was now admiring himself in a mirror borrowed from the late Captain Arbatov.

Like an unshaven monkey, the Crest replied archly.

"I can hardly remove my moustache and goatee, they're keeping my identity secret from Doctor Fabergé."

You asked, I answered. It's not my fault if the truth offends.

Dante sighed. "Let's not start the day by bickering, alright? If I'm going to teach these girls about swordplay and self defence, I'll need your help."

You've had enough women fend off your dubious charms, the Crest said, *I'd have thought you'd have plenty of experiences worth sharing.*

"Yeah, yeah, make all the jibes you want. When the time comes, your programming requires that you help me avoid death or ignominy."

Death, yes. But avoiding ignominy? Even I can't perform miracles.

"Just tell me when I'm going wrong and offer a few helpful hints, okay?"

I'll try.

"Thank you."

But you still look like an unshaven monkey.

"Bojemoi! Give me strength." Dante chose a quilted crimson jacket and matching fencing helmet from among Arbatov's clothes. The jacket was a tight fit across the shoulders, its seams straining to contain Dante's bulkier frame.

May I suggest you avoid the cooked breakfast from now on. I doubt that stitching will last the day if you eat much more.

"You're not my mother and you're not my wife, so stop nagging!"

Fine. Have it your own way.

"I will."

Good.

"Be like that!"

I will!

"Suits me!" Dante snapped.

Unlike that jacket....

Dante resisted the urge to push his fingers into both ears, knowing it would not shut out the insistent, superior voice of the Crest. "Think calm thoughts," he told himself. "Just think calm thoughts".

Natalia Sokorina was not only the youngest pupil at the Fabergé Institute, but also the brightest. Students were not normally accepted before the age of eighteen but Natalia won her place on merit, having already finished a university degree before her seventeenth birthday. She had never wanted to waste a year in such a place but her ambitious mother insisted. "I let you go to college on the condition you went to a finishing school afterwards. I mean, how can you ever hope to become a young lady if you spend every minute with your nose buried inside text books? How will you ever find a worthy husband? Your sisters all attended finishing schools and now you shall do the same."

Natalia knew her elder sisters had few ambitions beyond possessing the grandest home, richest husband and most handsome lover in the Empire. But arguing that such things were of little merit carried no weight with her mother, who had followed the same code rigorously and instilled it in most of her daughters. So Natalia had reluctantly agreed to a year's exile at a finishing school, selecting the Fabergé Institute because it at least had some record of academic excellence. True, the Strangelove twins were frightening in person, but not even Natalia could deny their many scientific achievements under Doctor Fabergé's tutelage.

Now the institute's youngest student was a week away from graduating from its mink-lined prison, seven days from escaping the gilded cage. She would be eighteen and free of her mother's authority, free to create a life for herself beyond a stifling world of flower arranging, gossip and business communication lessons – whatever the hell that was supposed to be. For all the attention Natalia had paid in that class, it could have been about how best to catch your boss's roving eye. Now that she came to think about it, that had been the essence of the second term's studies, with particular attention paid to how short skirts should be (the shorter the better for displaying perfectly sculpted thighs), why glossy red lipstick was important (apparently it sent a subliminal signal of sexual availability) and the advantages of wearing the best lingerie (it helped flaunt your assets, allegedly).

Natalia regarded herself in one of the dormitory's full-length mirrors. Plainly, she hadn't been paying much attention in any of those lessons. The other students were women, with fully developed bodies and practiced poise from a lifetime of elocution and deportment classes. Natalia was a late developer, her body still finding its adult shape. She had grown four inches since arriving on the island, this spurt accompanied by a widening of the hips and thickening of the thighs. Her breasts were the most embarrassing change, having swelled to create a pair of attention-seeking balloons. Even ancient Professor Mould had noticed them, making a comment about the baby of the class growing up at last. She'd wanted to climb into a hole and disappear as the others laughed at her embarrassment.

Despite the urgings of tutors to make the best of her looks, Natalia refused to wear make-up unless it was absolutely required. She kept her strawberry blonde hair back from her face in a simple ponytail and did nothing to hide the smattering of freckles across her cheeks. Even her clothes avoided the pouting glamour favoured by the other students, a modest skirt and shapeless top disguising her womanly attributes.

"Oh Natalia! You're not wearing that again, are you?" a voice protested from the doorway. A big-boned and boister-ous pupil called Helga was shaking her head in dismay, two plaits of blond hair pinned to the side of her head. The eldest daughter from the Germanic House of Hapsburg, Helga occupied the bed next to Natalia in the senior dormi-tory and frequently tried to talk the younger woman into more revealing clothing.

"And why not?" Natalia asked.

"Haven't you heard? We've got a new tutor – a man! He's quite a hunk, if you believe Carmen and Tracy. They saw him coming out of the west tower first thing this morning."

"If I believed everything Carmen and Tracy said, I'd be almost as silly as them," Natalia replied dryly. "You shouldn't listen to gossip. The tutor is probably a hundred and covered in cobwebs, like Professor Mould."

"But he's still a man!" Helga enthused, her cheeks flushed red. "I haven't seen a real man in weeks, not since poor Mr Russell left in such a hurry."

"Poor Mr Russell preferred the company of boys, not girls."

"But he was ever so handsome!"

Natalia rolled her eyes. Having a conversation with Helga was like trying to calm the ocean with words during a storm. "You were barking up the wrong tree then, Helga, and you're no doubt barking up the wrong tree now. Do you honestly think old Wartski would let a virile heterosexual man loose amongst the senior class? The other girls would eat him alive."

Helga began digging through the locker at the end of Natalia's bed, throwing the clothes on to the floor. "I don't care what you say! We're going to find you something decent to wear and make you look pretty, just this once. Thumbelina shall go to the ball!"

"I think you mean Cinderella."

"Whatever," Helga replied. "I never pay attention in literature appreciation class." Her face lit up as she emerged from the locker, clutching the smallest of black silk camisoles. "This is it, this is the one."

Natalia's horror was all too evident. "Forget it! My mother sent me that as a present. I'm not wearing so ridiculous a piece of underwear!"

Helga had an evil glint in her eye. "Who said it would be *under*wear?"

Dante was standing outside the gymnasium, clutching his fencing helmet and trying not to think about the knots his lower intestine was trying itself into. "They're just girls," he told himself. "There's nothing to be afraid of inside there."

They're young women, the Crest replied. *Young women filled with raging hormones who probably haven't set eyes on a virile male for weeks or even months. I hope you brought a whip and chair to keep them at bay.*

"They're just girls," Dante repeated to himself, ignoring the voice in his head. "You've had plenty of experience with them before."

Perhaps. But twelve at once?

"You can do this, nothing to be scared of. You're the man, the boss."

"Psyching yourself up?" a stern voice boomed from behind Dante. He spun round to find Wartski stomping towards him.

"Just preparing myself for the first class," Dante admitted. "I want to make a good impression, announce my presence with authority."

"Then I suggest you do up your fly first," the matron said, her gaze wandering down to his crotch. "What you've got on show there wouldn't intimidate a dormouse."

Dante hurriedly buttoned the front of his trousers. "If you'll excuse me, Madame Wartski, I have a class to attend. Good day!" He pulled open the gymnasium door and strode inside, slamming it shut behind him. What he found inside made Dante's heart skip a beat. "Bojemoi!"

A dozen young women were working on a variety of exercise equipment: climbing ropes, throwing medicine balls around, bouncing on trampolines and limbering up with stretching exercises on the padded floor. All but one were clad in the slightest of clothing, scraps of fabric stretched tautly across rippling thighs, firm buttocks and barely contained breasts. The exception was doing her best to hide at the back of the class, arms folded across herself, a bright red blush colouring her face.

Wartski's boasts about the institute drawing its students from across the Empire were plainly true. The twelve women displayed a variety of ethnic backgrounds, ranging from Latin states and the Orient to those of paler skinned Nordic and European origins. As one the women turned and looked at the new arrival, their gaze filled with an avid hunger and curiosity. Dante had an uncomfortable feeling the pupils were undressing him with their eyes and resisted the urge to protect his crotch with both hands.

"Now I know what a beautiful woman feels like alone in a room full of men," he whispered to himself.

Now you know what any woman feels like alone in a room full of men, the Crest commented.

Dante forced himself to smile and began walking among the students, observing them as they stretched and bounced and displayed themselves. He passed a few appreciative comments and did his best not to ogle the female forms being flaunted. Finally he reached the one pupil straining not to be noticed, a shy girl stood behind a vaulting horse. "And what's your name?"

"Natalia," she replied quietly. "Natalia Sokorina."

"Why aren't you warming up with the others?"

"I, er…" Natalia blushed an even deeper crimson than before. "I wore the wrong clothing for this lesson."

"Let me be the judge of that," Dante said politely and waved for her out from behind the vaulting horse. Natalia reluctantly walked around the equipment to reveal her garb: a mini skirt so short it would have been better employed as a cummerbund, and a black silk camisole that was almost transparent beneath the bright lights of the gymnasium. She kept both arms folded across her chest, hiding some of herself from embarrassment.

In the background Dante could hear the other pupils whispering comments and sniggering. "Yes, I'm not sure that's entirely practical for today's lesson. Why don't you go find something more… comfortable… and come back. I'll spend the next few minutes getting to know the rest of the class, so you won't miss anything important. Alright?"

Natalia smiled gratefully and hurried from the room, shooting one of the other pupils a pointed glare on the way past. The big, blonde recipient mouthed an apology but Natalia was already out the door, her exit accompanied by another burst of giggles from the others.

Dante strode to the front of the gymnasium and picked up a foil from a selection. "Everybody gather round please. I'd like to introduce myself. My name is Durward, Quentin Durward." He used the point of the foil to write his name in the air, remembering just in time not to spell out Dante. "You may call me Mr Durward, or sir. I will be your tutor in fencing, self-defence and several other disciplines for the remaining few days of term. If this short stint goes well, I will be invited back to the institute next year, so I will be doing my best for the few days we shall have together. But you also have something at stake here, as my report will influence the marks you receive upon graduation."

A beautiful Oriental student raised her hand.

Dante indicated she should stand. "What is your name?"

"Zhang, from the Black Dragon dynasty, sir."

"And your question?"

"We are the elite class. Surely that indicates we are among the best of the best. What can you add to that in just a few lessons?"

I think she's got you there, the Crest observed.

Dante smiled thinly. "Well, Zhang, our time here together may be limited but I can promise you it will be memorable. I hope to impart a little piece of my experience with each of you–"

I've never heard you call it your experience before, but at least you're being honest about the size.

"–so that you will have something to remember our time together by. I fought in the war and know what it is to stare death in the face. I pray you may never have to make the same choices I did on the battlefield, but I still wish to protect you from any danger that may threaten your life." Dante raised an eyebrow at the Oriental student. "Does that answer your question?"

Zhang shrugged and sat down again. Another pupil raised her hand, this time an olive-skinned young woman with cherry red lips, fiery eyes and a mass of curling black hair. "Mr Durward, what battles did you fight in?"

"Sorry, I didn't catch your name…"

"Carmen, from the House of Andorra."

"Very good. If you must know, I fought in several significant conflicts – on the front line in Tolsburg Province, at Sebastopol, the Battle of Vladigrad, at New Moscow, the Battle of the Baltic Sea, the Battle of Rudinshtein…" Dante's voice trailed away as he recalled the death and destruction he had witnessed, the comrades in arms he had lost.

"And what was it like, fighting for such a glorious cause? To vanquish the Romanov pretenders to the Imperial throne?"

"There are no true winners in such battles," Dante replied sadly. "War is about the taking and using of power to feed ambition. There is no honour in killing. You would do well to remember that."

"Oh." Carmen sank back to the floor, her enthusiasm fading. Silence fell upon the class, as the pupils looked at each other, unsure of themselves. The sombre moment was broken when Natalia returned, now clad in a more suitable leotard and tights. Dante smiled at her and clapped his hands.

"Well, let's see how far you have progressed with your fencing skills. Everybody up on their feet! Show me what you've got." That brought a fresh chorus of giggles from the students. "I meant show me what fencing skills you have got," Dante said with a sigh. "Take a foil and facemask each, put on a padded tunic to protect yourselves, and then pair off, one as the aggressor, the other defending themselves. Begin!"

The pupils were quick in position, each pairing trying to impress the new tutor as he moved between them. Dante had to be nimble on his feet to avoid getting caught in the action, swaying and ducking to escape the flash of a blade. Each slender, flexible sword was tipped by a button to protect the combatants, but an unwary spectator could still be badly injured if they ventured too close to those duelling. A powerful clash of swords between Carmen and Zhang forced Dante to leap out of their way, sending him hurtling backwards into the blonde who had tried to apologise to Natalia.

She spun round, foil raised and ready to strike, but stopped when Dante threw up in hands in protest. "Sorry, Mr Durward. Sorry!"

He took the sword from her grasp and examined the blade. "You should be more careful, Miss…?"

"Helga." She removed her facemask and brushed an errant strand of hair from her face. "I am Helga, from the House of Hapsburg."

Dante took her right hand and kissed the back of it. "Charmed, I'm sure."

Helga grinned with delight. "I will try to be more careful in future."

"Good. Now, show me how you defend while your partner attacks." Dante stepped aside to watch as Helga tried to fend off her aggressor. The other fighter was smaller and less powerful, but more than made up for that with deft footwork and quickness of hands. Twice she cut through Helga's hapless parries and landed a palpable hit.

"Very good!" Dante applauded the effort, delighted to discover the other combatant was the unfortunate Natalia. He called the rest of the students to a halt and made them watch the pair fight again. Natalia easily outdid Helga, earning the acclaim of the new tutor.

"Let this be a lesson to all of you," Dante said. "Skill and confidence can often undo a physically intimidating opponent."

A chiming bell echoed around the gymnasium. "That's the signal for the end of the lesson," Helga said helpfully.

"Very good. Well, hit the showers and move on to your next lesson. No doubt I'll be seeing you later in the day." Dante smiled and nodded to the pupils as they passed him on their way out, inwardly breathing a sigh of relief. Helga remained behind to ask him a question, peeling off her padded tunic.

"Mr Durward, I have always struggled in these more physical classes. My family, we can be big eaters and I lack the speed of Natalia and the others. I was wondering if you could offer me any further help?" She smiled at him coyly, one finger twirling the plaited braid hanging from one side of her head.

"I suppose that could be possible. I certainly want to be available for all my students," Dante said. "Do you have any free time later today?"

"No, but I could visit your private quarters tonight, after supper." Helga did her best to look coquettish, a twinkle in the corner of her eyes.

Be careful, Dante, the Crest warned. *You've no way of knowing whether this young woman is a spy for Doctor Fabergé, trying to lure you into a trap!*

Dante was suddenly aware of the perspiration forming in the deep valley between her breasts, unable to tear his eyes away from the rise and fall of her breathing. "I'm not sure students are allowed to visit tutors' private quarters."

"Why not?" Helga asked innocently. "When Madame Wartski was filling in after Mr Russell left the institute, she was always trying to persuade one of us girls to visit her room after dark. She said it was to see her collection of toads."

"I hope none of you did."

Helga stifled a giggle at the thought. "Nein! She is covered in warts and she couldn't keep her hands to herself – ugghhh! Repulsive!"

"Nevertheless, I do not believe it would be seemly for us to have a private session in my quarters..." Dante maintained, trying to tear his gaze away from Helga's hefty décolletage.

"Then perhaps we could meet here," she suggested. "No harm could come to us having extra tuition in a padded room, could it?"

"I suppose not."

"I mean, there's nothing hard in this room that could hurt me?" Helga whispered, leaning closer to Dante. One of her hands began sliding past the waistband of his trousers.

Dante, don't give in to her! the Crest urged. *Think of something, anything that might quell your desire – Algebra! Madame Wartski naked! The collected works of William Shakespeare!*

Helga's hand swivelled round to encircle his crotch. "Unless you think I could be wrong about that? Maybe there is something hard in here?"

Dante bit his top lip, trying to retain some scintilla of composure. "Perhaps we can continue this discussion later?"

Helga removed her hand. "I'll see you here after nine tonight." She hurried from the gymnasium, her rounded bottom bouncing inside the straining fabric of her leotard. Only when Helga had left did Dante let himself relax, slumping to the padded floor, sweat soaking the armpits of his fencing jacket.

"Fuoco," he muttered. "She knew what she was doing."

You're the one who needs the self defence class, the Crest observed. *She had total control over you, Dante!*

He smiled. "You could say she had me in the palm of her hand."

I was trying to avoid such obvious crudity.

"Yeah? Well, it's my speciality." Dante wiped the sweat from his brow. "Have I got time for a shower before my next lesson?"

No. You should be two flights down by now, beginning a tutorial in the ancient Oriental art of origami.

"I don't suppose that's Japanese for orgasm, by any chance?"

No. It's Japanese for paper folding. And if you're going to continue with the steady stream of smut I'll leave you to lead the class unaided.

"I told you, obvious crudity is my speciality. Besides, how hard can paper folding be – right?"

Having impressed Scullion with his skills as a bottle washer the previous night, Spatchcock had been promoted to cook's assistant after breakfast. So far that had involved cutting, peeling and preparing the less glamorous ingredients for lunch while avoiding a multitude of tentacles the verdant alien was intent upon sliding inside Spatchcock's clothing. He had responded by accidentally slicing one of the fleshy intrusions with his kitchen knife, bringing a howl of pain from the offworlder. "Be careful, you little oaf! These tentacles are precious objects, capable of rendering great culinary joy to many species!"

"Fine, just keep them away from me," Spatchcock muttered under his breath. It was a relief when he was given a break from preparation and escaped Scullion's attentions for a few minutes. A narrow metal walkway ran outside the castle walls across to the servant's quarters in the west tower. For a short section it passed above the waters of the Black Sea. Spatchcock stopped and leaned on the railing, staring out over the gently undulating waves.

The grimy ex-con blew air out through his mouth, his shoulders sagging. The prospect of spending the next week fending off Scullion's amorous advances held little appeal. He was used to being rejected by women, thanks to his repulsive appearance and virulent body odour. It felt strange and unsettling to be on the receiving end, even if the hunter was a green alien with more tentacles than inhibitions. *Maybe I should swap jobs with Flintlock*, Spatchcock thought to himself. *I'm the one who belongs in the sewers, not him.*

A sudden splash nearby caught his attention. Spatchcock leaned over the railing, trying to focus on a shimmering silver shape below the water's surface. It stopped moving and returned his gaze, as if it had a face. But that was impossible, wasn't it? Spatchcock leaned further over the railing, stretching a hand down to touch the water below. If he could reach it, maybe–

"Spatch! What are you doing?"

The foul-smelling felon jerked his hand back, startled. Whatever had been below disappeared into the depths once more. Spatchcock looked up to see the slime-covered Flintlock approaching from the west tower. For the first time in his life Spatchcock felt obliged to pinch his nose shut, lest the smell from his friend overwhelm him. "What've you been doing?"

"Clearing a blockage in the drains beneath Wartski's quarters. I don't know what she's got in there but it gives off this green pus." Flintlock wiped a hand across his chest, pushing the upper layer of slime off his clothing.

"How can you stand the smell?"

Flintlock smiled and tipped back his head to reveal an orange shape wedged inside each nostril. "I kept pieces of carrot from last night's stew, shoved them up my nose. At least they've stopped me from vomiting too often." Flintlock gestured at the waters below. "What were you trying to touch before?"

"Thought I saw something moving down there."

"But nothing swims around this island, unless you believe the fishermen's tales about sea monsters."

Spatchcock shook his head. "Nah, this was something else. It had a face, almost looked human. Thought it was trying to talk to me."

"Spatchcock! Spatchcock, where are you?" Scullion's voice rang out from inside the kitchen. "Come out, my little helper!"

Flintlock's nose crinkled in disgust. "She still trying to get inside your trousers?" Spatchcock nodded disconsolately. "For once you've found someone who considers your unique aroma an aphrodisiac and you're repulsed by her touch! I find that rather ironic, old boy."

"I'm not even sure Scullion is female," Spatchcock admitted. He sized up the green-stained, slime-soaked appearance of his partner. "You want to swap jobs? I'd be more than happy working the sewers."

Flintlock shook his head. "Forget it. I almost smell as bad as you now. Scullion would probably think I was coming on to her. I'm staying put."

"Spatchcock? Get in here this instant!" Scullion shouted. "Doctor Fabergé is calling for his lunch. You'll have to take it to him."

"Lucky you," Flintlock teased. "Another afternoon of close encounters in the kitchens and an audience with the boss. Do give him my regards."

Spatchcock replied with a muttered curse before returning to the kitchen. Flintlock remained for a moment, contemplating the other man's suggestion. "I'm not sure that's physically possible," he decided before heading back to the drains, not noticing the hand breaking the waves below his feet.

In origami class Dante had exhausted his paper-folding repertoire after five minutes, creating an unimpressive hat, a dismal dart and an unrecognisable replica of a boat. Six students stared at their tutor in disbelief, the others being occupied in the next room with one of Professor Mould's tedious history lectures. Dante tried his most winning smile before admitting defeat.

"Okay, let's face it. Origami is not where my true talents lie," he said. "Perhaps we could spend the rest of this lesson on something else?"

"What do you suggest?" Carmen asked tersely. "What are you good at?"

"Have any of your ladies ever played poker?"

Zhang raised her hand to speak. "That is a card game, yes?"

"Yes, but it is much more than that. Poker teaches you life skills. You discover how best to observe others, to notice their strengths and weaknesses. You learn when someone else is bluffing or trying to conceal a winning hand. You develop your own ability to keep a secret, to outwit your opponent. All these talents will be useful in years to come, no matter whether you become the wife of a Tsar or the head of a corporation."

Carmen appeared intrigued by Dante's description. "Sounds interesting, sir. What are the rules for this game?"

Dante smiled broadly. "Well, I can explain the rules as we go along. Does anyone happen to have a deck of cards handy?" One of the pupils, a ravishing redhead from the House of Windsor in Britannia, put up her hand. "Tracy, isn't it? If you don't mind my asking, why carry the cards with you?"

She blushed a little. "I play solitaire during Professor Mould's classes to stop myself falling asleep."

Dante collected the pack from her and began fanning through the cards, ensuring all fifty-two were present. "Hopefully you won't have to resort to such tactics during my lessons. Now, who wants to play first?"

"Why don't we all play?" Helga suggested. "That would make it more interesting, ja?"

"Ja. I mean, yes." Dante began shuffling the cards expertly. "Of course, there is another way of making poker interesting. There's nothing like having something at stake, a slight hint of jeopardy, to increase your excitement and enhance the learning process," he added hurriedly. "Has anyone here ever heard of the forfeit system?"

The pupils all innocently shook their heads.

"If you lose a hand, you are obliged to perform a forfeit," Dante explained. "It can be anything from revealing a secret to removing an item of clothing. How would you all feel about that?"

Tracy nodded vigorously. "I think that would add to the learning experience. Don't you girls agree?"

Dante, are you sure about this? the Crest asked. *You seem to be placing a lot of trust in the word of your students.*

"What could possibly go wrong?"

EIGHT

"Food without salt is like a kiss without love"
– Russian proverb

Spatchcock returned to the kitchen to find Scullion waiting impatiently, a bowl of green soup clasped in one of her tentacles. "You're to take this to the institute's director in the north tower."

"But I thought only authorised personnel were allowed in that area?"

"True. Nevertheless, Doctor Fabergé still has to eat and I cannot risk leaving my soufflé. To make matters worse, that clot Flintlock has somehow succeeded in sabotaging the dumb waiter with his stumbling about in the drains. So you will have to deliver this soup personally."

Spatchcock took the bowl, wondering aloud what the pink lumps floating across the surface were.

"Pea and ham," Scullion snapped irritably. "Now get moving!"

"But how will I get through the security cordon?"

The alien removed a white plastic tag on a chain from round its neck. "Wear this, it will identify you as friend, not foe. Do not remove it, or else the laser grid will remove your head. Now get moving!"

"Which way do I–"

Scullion's only reply was a sternly pointed tentacle.

Natalia had not been this bored since Professor Mould's lecture series on the development of cold fusion and how it changed twenty-second century history. The ageing tutor had an uncanny ability to drain the life from any and all potentially fascinating subjects, rendering them as dull and inert as his features. Today's lesson was a case in point, sixty minutes of mind-numbing torture supposedly meant to illuminate the Neo Renaissance Movement of 2197 and its relevance to the rise of the Makarov Empire in modern times.

Mould's voice droned on and on, regurgitating whole chapters from set textbooks that Natalia had read whilst at university. Seven more days to go, she told herself over and over. Seven more days. A squeal of delight from the adjoining classroom was followed by wild applause and raucous cheering. That couldn't be right, could it? Surely Mr Durward was meant to be taking an origami class for the less academically gifted members of the elite group.

Natalia leaned back in her chair and sneaked a glance through a glass partition that linked the two rooms. All she could see were the backs of the pupils in the neighbouring class. They were gathered around the teacher's desk, clapping their hands and cheering somebody on. Natalia had opted out of paper folding after the first term, deeming it a topic beneath her contempt. What was raptly holding the attention of those next door? Had Mr Durward introduced some revolutionary techniques?

Suddenly the crowd of students parted to reveal the source of their fascination. Mr Durward was stripped to the waist, attempting a Cossack dance on top of his desk while wearing a brassiere over his head. Judging by the size of the cups, the bra had most recently been worn by the not inconsiderable chest of Helga. Whatever was happening in the next classroom, it had little to do with paper folding.

Natalia realised too late that she had leaned too far back in her chair. Her arms windmilled, trying to maintain a balance, but it was a futile attempt. Natalia's chair flipped over backwards and she was propelled into the desk behind her, crashing her head against its wooden edge with an almighty *thunk*. She slumped to the floor, white dots of light blinking before her eyes.

Mould looked up from his textbook for the first time during the lesson. "Is something wrong?" He studied the faces of his pupils and noticed one was absent. "Miss Sokorina? Where are you?"

Natalia scrambled to her feet, rubbing one hand against the back of her head. "Sorry, Professor Mould. I, er... lost control of my chair." She righted the seat and resumed her place in it. "Sorry."

Mould raised his eyebrows a fraction before returning to his textbook, seemingly oblivious to the noise from the next room. "Now, where was I? Ah, yes, the Neo Renaissance Movement of 2197. For many, the highpoint of this cultural revolution was the introduction of direct mind-to-computer terminals, enabling creators to translate imagination into action immediately..."

Spatchcock approached the north tower cautiously, a bowl of soup held in one hand, the white plastic tag in the other. While the kitchen held the homely scent of cooking, this part of the castle was filled by the musty smell of neglect – few came through these corridors. At the tower's basement entrance a wall of red light barred entry, its surface crackling menacingly. Spatchcock recalled how Wartski had opened and closed the castle entrance. He swiped the tag across a palm reader beside the energy barrier. After a short, metallic beep the red light faded away, allowing him to walk past. Once he had cleared the doorway, the energy barrier pulsed back into life. Getting out of the north tower was just as hazardous as getting in, it appeared.

The door to a lift stood open ahead. Spatchcock was about to walk in when he realised the security tag was missing from his hand. He eventually found it hidden in a side pocket. He had palmed it, Spatchcock realised – once a thief, always a thief. Retrieving the tag, he waved it in front of the lift doorway. Another energy barrier switched off, this one invisible to the naked eye. Satisfied the lift was now safe, Spatchcock entered.

Moments later he was being shot upwards by some unseen force, the walls of the lift shaft sliding down past him. "Diavolo!" he whispered, trying not to soil his trousers. The uplift began to slow, then stopped altogether. Spatchcock stepped out of the lift shaft, sure his stomach must be lodged somewhere below his knees by now.

A single door of frosted glass stood opposite. Spatchcock could see humanoid shapes moving beyond it, but not enough to make out their identity. After checking it was safe to touch, he rapped firmly on the glass with his knuckles. The door was abruptly pulled open to reveal the Strangelove twins inside, looming over the new arrival.

"Yes? What–"

"–do you want?"

Spatchcock held out the soup for them to see. "I brought Doctor Fabergé's lunch. It's pea and ham – I think."

The doctor was bent over a machine, examining something on a glass slide. "Yes, I ordered lunch more than an hour ago!" The laboratory was awash with shining glass and metallic silver, most of the workspaces choked with machines beyond Spatchcock's knowledge. The doctor gestured angrily at a nearby tabletop cluttered with papers, scribbled notes and data crystals. "Put it over there."

Storm glared at Spatchcock. "You heard the doctor."

He obeyed the instructions, walking uncertainly into the antiseptic air of the laboratory. Spatchcock approached the tabletop indicated by Fabergé and gently nudged some of the clutter aside to create space for the bowl. "Is there anything else I can get you?"

Fabergé did not bother to look up. "Yes – out."

Spatchcock nodded and scuttled from the room, careful to avoid the malevolent gaze of the Furies. Tempest slammed the door shut once he was outside, not noticing the glint of triumph in Spatchcock's eyes. He kept the security tag held up before his face, using it to summon the disconcerting invisible lift. His other hand nestled inside a pocket, clutching the data crystal he had palmed while inside the laboratory. It was tiny, little larger than a fingernail, and felt like a chip of warm glass to the touch.

Hopefully it contained information about what Fabergé was doing in his closely guarded laboratory. Now all Spatchcock need do was find a way of slipping the crystal to Dante so the Crest could analyse it.

I tried to warn you, didn't I? I tried to make you see sense. But no, you knew better. You were sure. You could handle a few innocent girls with limited life experience. What could possibly go wrong?

"Have you quite finished gloating?" Dante replied tensely.

Finished? I've barely begun. Besides, this isn't gloating. I'm attempting to teach you the error of your ways. Since you seem determined to ignore every piece of advice I offer, I've decided to take a fresh approach. Let you make your own mistakes and then try – repeat, try – to see whether you're learned anything from the experience.

"And how's that working for you so far?"

I trust this is not an experience you'll be reliving anytime soon.

Dante nodded his agreement. "That much we can agree on. Now, have you got any advice you'd like to offer at this juncture, Oh Great Oracle?"

Sarcasm does not befit a man who has only an abandoned brassiere between himself and complete nudity.

"I asked for advice, not for you to state the bloody obvious!" Dante shifted one of the cups so it covered his crotch more effectively. The other was clamped across part of his buttocks, while the straps dangled untidily between his legs. "Guess I should be grateful it was Helga who let me keep her bra. Some of the other students aren't so well endowed–"

Look who's talking!

"And I'd be in even more trouble right now." Dante peered round the doorway from the classroom where his poker lesson had gone so awry. The pupils had departed several minutes earlier, taking all his clothes as part of the final forfeit. Before leaving, Carmen revealed that the pupils often indulged in all-night poker parties, using Tracy's marked pack of cards to alleviate unsuspecting students from other classes of their allowances. At least that quelled Dante's embarrassment at losing twelve hands in succession, if not his shame at being left stark naked and with a hundred metre dash back to the safety of his private quarters. "Those girls are man-eaters," he muttered darkly.

And they had you for dessert.

"Crest, I think that's enough advice for the moment."

Do you think they'll still respect you in the morning?

"I said that's enough!" Dante realised shouting was not going to help and lowered his voice again. "Just tell me whether the coast is clear, alright?"

I sense no imminent danger approaching from any direction–

"Good. Now's my chance!" Dante decided. He started running towards the faculty rooms, looking back over his shoulder to make sure nobody had spotted him.

But there is someone just about to step into your path.

Dante clattered into Natalia as she emerged from the institute infirmary, clutching an ice bag to the back of her head. Teacher and student went both sent sprawling, their respective possessions flying into the air. Dante realised he had lost hold of the bra and made a grab for it as he tumbled over.

Natalia sat up and realised Helga's bra was draped across her own, less voluminous chest. More startling was the sight of the naked teacher holding a bag of ice against his crotch. "Mr Durward! What are you doing?"

Dante stood up, trying to look casual and failing dismally. "I might ask you the same question, young lady."

Natalia pointed at the infirmary door. "I hit my head during history and went to get something for the pain."

"I see."

She gestured towards Dante's crotch. "Could I have my ice bag back?"

"Actually, no."

"Why not?"

Dante shrugged helplessly. "Umm…"

Tell her you have an old war wound, the Crest suggested.

"I have an old war wound," Dante announced, a little too triumphantly.

And you need to pack it with ice once a day…

"And I need to pack it with ice once a day…"

To keep the swelling down, the Crest concluded mischievously.

"To keep the, er…" Dante smiled. "To keep my injury from getting worse."

Natalia was struggling to keep a smirk from her face. "Yes, I understand." She leaned forward and peered at the area Dante was trying to hide with the ice bag. "Well, then, your need is obviously greater than mine. I'd best find Helga and return this item of clothing to her."

"A good idea," Dante agreed hurriedly. "Now, if you'll just excuse me." He began backing away from her.

Natalia peered at one of his arms, her brow furrowing with thought. "Umm, Mr Durward?" she asked.

Dante stopped and raised his eyebrows. "Yes, Natalia?"

The student appeared to be planning another question, but changed her mind. "Nothing. I hope your, er, injury gets better soon." Natalia smiled helpfully. "It must be very painful."

"You have no idea. Good day to you."

Dante made it through the rest of the teaching day unharmed, except for the blows to his pride whenever students began whispering amongst themselves and giggling during his classes. He found himself looking forward to the evening meal when all the staff were gathered together, as it would offer another chance to assess Fabergé. So far the doctor had shown arrogance not uncommon in those who rate achievement above love or happiness. But how far did Fabergé's ambitions extend? The doctor's comments about the Tsar suggested Fabergé considered himself above the Empire's ruler, a dangerous belief for anyone.

Having lost his first choice of clothing to the unscrupulous poker players, Dante selected a plain black linen suit and shirt for the dinner table. But when he entered the staff library, the collective mood was decidedly more downbeat than the previous evening. Neither Fabergé nor the Strangelove twins were expected at dinner, and Wartski had refused to unlock the drinks cabinet. The female tutors muttered darkly amongst themselves while Mould sat disconsolately in an armchair reading a textbook. Dante approached the five women and tried to strike up a conversation.

"Hi! I'm the new self-defence and swordplay instructor. We didn't get a chance to talk during dinner last night."

The female tutors looked at him with a mixture of disgust and disdain. Dante put on his most winning smile and turned up the charm.

"My first day of teaching here was quite a revelation," he continued.

"So we've heard," one of the women said with a scowl. Dressed in a severe woollen twin-set and a string of pearls, the pinched expression on her face left Dante wondering if she had been sucking lemons between classes.

"I hope the students had good things to say about me, Miss…?"

"Ms Ostrov," she replied coldly. "No, they didn't."

"Oh!" Dante was surprised and rather hurt by this news. "I wonder why?"

"We do not encourage card games at this institution," another of the women interjected. Dante almost thought she might be a disciple from the House of Rasputin, so thick were the black hairs adorning her top lip. "Nor do we favour flirting with the pupils. It's most unseemly."

"This is a finishing school," Dante protested. "Isn't it, Miss…?"

"Ms Zemlya," she said.

"Don't you have a duty to prepare them for life in the real world?" Dante continued. "Flirting and games are part of that life."

"Not at this school," Ms Ostrov snapped. Her four colleagues nodded. "We believe in the power of learning and knowledge. A good education enriches the mind. Your sort of teaching can only harm the reputation of this esteemed establishment."

"Really? I thought I was bringing some fresh air to this place, blowing a few skirts up, injecting some excitement into the lessons."

Ms Ostrov's hands dropped to her own skirt and held it firmly in place, as if worried Dante was going to make good on his notions there and then. "All skirts should remain in their proper positions at all times!"

"I was speaking, you know, um…"

Metaphorically, the Crest prompted.

"Metaphorically," Dante said. "I was speaking metaphorically."

"Nevertheless," Ms Zemlya bristled, "we would prefer if you kept your distance from us. We don't wish to be contaminated by your errant ideas." The other women all murmured their agreement and turned their backs on Dante. He walked away shaking his head at their attitude.

"I wouldn't contaminate any of you with a ten foot barge pole," he muttered darkly. "Have all the distance you want." Dante approached Mould instead, hoping to have more success with the ageing academic. The professor was examining a textbook about noble families and their lineage through the centuries. "Anything interesting?" Dante asked.

"I've been trying to trace the name Durward in our historical texts," Mould replied. "I can't seem to find any mention of your family in the last two hundred years. Where did you say you came from?"

"I didn't," Dante replied hastily. "Mould is an unusual name. Where does that originate from?"

"It's an Anglo-Saxon name originally. My distant ancestors collected mould for use by apothecaries and alchemists."

"That's fascinating." Dante glanced round the room, searching for a way out of this conversational hell. "I wonder what we're having for dinner?"

A chime sounded and the faculty began moving into the dining hall. The seats normally occupied by Fabergé and Wartski remained empty, leaving Dante alone near the head of the table, with just Mould for company. The prospect of a long and tedious evening was crushing the last of his spirits when a familiar face appeared with the first course. An unusually clean and tidy Spatchcock entered from a side door, carefully balancing half a dozen plates of steaming, green soup on his arms. He served all the female staff first, then gave the final plate to the professor.

By now Dante was more than hungry but had to wait several minutes before Spatchcock returned with the final bowl of soup. The stooped servant put it down before Dante and made a point of engaging him in conversation. "I do hope you'll enjoy the soup, sir."

"I'm sure I will," Dante replied, picking up a spoon.

"It's pea and ham."

"Fascinating, I'm sure."

"I took a bowl to Doctor Fabergé for lunch today."

"Good for you." Dante wanted to make a start but Spatchcock's thumb remained on the side of the bowl, blocking his access.

"He seemed to enjoy it. The dish was empty when I collected it from his laboratory later in the afternoon."

"Yes. Good. Glad to hear it. Now, can I–" Dante tried to push his spoon past Spatchcock without success.

"I hope you'll enjoy it as much," Spatchcock continued, winking at Dante.

"I will if you'll give me the chance!"

"Make sure you go all the way to the bottom of the bowl." Spatchcock's winking continued, becoming ever more exaggerated.

"Yes, thank you. I get it. Enjoy the soup. Every last drop!"

"Exactly, sir. That's exactly right." Spatchcock nodded at Dante several times, adding a few extra winks for emphasis.

"Is there something wrong with you eye, Spatchcock? You seem to have developed a nervous tic."

"Just finish the soup," the servant hissed.

"I will, given half a chance!" Dante snapped, slapping Spatchcock's hand away from the bowl. "Now let me eat, why don't you?"

"Fine!"

"Fine!"

"Good!"

"Good!"

By now Mould and the other teachers were all staring at this hissing contest, regarding the new arrival and his servant with disbelief. Dante realised he was being watched and offered the others a warm smile. "Please excuse us. My manservant can be a little possessive sometimes."

Spatchcock rolled his eyes heavenwards. "Just eat the damn soup!"

"I will!" Dante snarled. "Haven't you got a kitchen to go to?"

"Fine! Choke on it for all I care!" The servant stomped out of the dining hall, slamming the side door on his way out.

Dante gave an exaggerated sigh. "You just can't get the staff these days." He turned back to his soup and began hurriedly spooning it into his mouth. "Still, this soup is delicious. What flavour did he say it is?"

"Pea and ham," Mould replied. "Don't see what all the fuss is about…"

Dante was slurping his soup eagerly; dribbles of the green liquid covering his chin and lingering in his beard. The female tutors watched his slovenly table manners with horror, but he kept shovelling. Such was his enthusiasm he didn't notice the glint of crystal in the final mouthful. After sucking the spoon dry, Dante slammed it down on the tablecloth and smiled broadly. "Yes, that was quite delicious. I must ask Spatchcock for–"

He stopped abruptly and grabbed at his throat. "Ackkk!"

Dante? What's wrong? the Crest demanded.

"Ackkk! Acckkk-acckkk!"

I don't understand. Are you unwell?

Dante's face was rapidly turning purple, while attempts to clear his throat were proving fruitless. "Mykk throackkkk! Stuckkk ikk myyykkk throackkkk!"

I can't detect any trace of poison in what you've ingested...

"Mykk throackkkk!" Dante gasped, blue replacing the purple in his face. He stood up, knocking his chair over backwards and startling the other staff. "Stuckkk ikk myyykkk throackkkk!"

You've got something stuck in your throat?

"Yekkkk!"

Mould looked up from his soup. "I say, are you quite alright Mr Durward?"

Dante shook his head and pointed at his throat. "I cankkk breaffkkk!"

"Sorry, I can't quite make out what you're saying," the professor replied.

The Heimlich Manoeuvre – tell them to perform the Heimlich Manoeuvre on you, the Crest suggested. Dante just gurgled in response. *Oh, I forgot, you can't talk properly. Sorry. Try miming it!*

Dante began performing an elaborate charade, all the while clutching at his throat and turning ever more blue around the lips. But his gestures for the other staff to help him were misinterpreted when Dante mimed one person thrusting themselves against another person from behind.

"This is too much!" Ms Ostrov protested. "I don't care what your sexual proclivities are, Mr Durward, I will not bear witness to such a display at the dinner table! Kindly cease and desist immediately!"

Dante gave up asking for help and instead began punching himself in the abdomen, trying to dislodge whatever was stuck in his throat. He did succeed in projectile vomiting viscous green bile across the table where it splattered Ms Ostrov's face and chest, but still could not shift the blockage.

Try drinking water. That should force the object down your throat!

Dante grabbed a carafe of water from the table and poured it down his throat, the liquid splashing against his features and soaking the surroundings. After one last swallow the obstruction was washed down his oesophagus. Dante collapsed on to the dining table, gratefully grasping breath into his lungs.

All five women had retreated back against the walls of the dining hall, their faces aghast at this violent spectacle. Mould sipped quietly at his soup. "Hmm, tastes alright to me," he commented.

"I had something lodged in my throat," Dante explained weakly. "Sorry."

Ms Ostrov looked at the hideous bile staining her white top, rendering the fabric transparent. "I've never been so humiliated in my life," she shrieked and ran from the room, the other women following her out.

Mould watched them leave. "Oh well," he shrugged. "All the more for us, eh, Durward?"

"What do you mean you swallowed it?" Spatchcock shook his head in disbelief. "How could you swallow it?"

"Believe me, it wasn't easy," Dante replied. After dinner he had gone down to the kitchens, ostensibly to pass his compliments to the chef. Scullion had already retired for the night, giving Dante a chance to consult with Spatchcock. They stood near the door to the external walkway but insisted Flintlock remain outside, where his stench was less likely to reach them. "What the hell did you put in my soup?"

"It was a data crystal I took from Fabergé's laboratory at lunchtime. I thought you could have the Crest read it. Maybe the information stored inside would give us some clues to this Strangelove Gambit."

"A good idea," Dante agreed.

"But I needed a less than obvious way of smuggling it to you."

"So he put the crystal in your soup," Flintlock chipped in. "I told him not to but Spatch wouldn't listen to me, as usual."

"You could have warned me," Dante said.

"I did warn you," Spatchcock wailed. "What did you think all that winking and nodding in the dining hall was about?"

"Muscle spasms?"

"Muscle spasms!" Spatchcock threw his apron across the kitchen in despair. "I give up, I really do!"

"Can the Crest analyse that crystal while it's still inside?" Flintlock asked.

Unfortunately, no, the Crest said. *The crystal is a sealed data storage unit. I'll need to access its contents via your bio-circuitry, Dante, and that can only happen once the crystal is outside your body.*

"Crest says no, not until I've expelled the crystal."

"In that case, may I suggest you keep a close watch on everything coming out of you?" Flintlock said. "I don't fancy having to sort through all the sewerage this place generates to find the crystal again."

"Good idea," Dante conceded. "How long will it take to come out?"

That depends, the Crest replied, *on what you eat for the next day or two. Plenty of roughage is the key that will help drive the crystal through your lower intestine and then out of your bowels.*

"It could take hours or it could take days," Spatchcock complained. "How long before the Tsar arrives?"

"The Imperial Palace is due to arrive on Sunday. That's six days," Flintlock calculated.

"What about some sort of laxative?" Dante asked. "Get things moving more quickly through my system."

"That crystal will take its own time," Spatchcock sighed.

"Maybe some liquorice?" Flintlock said. "Isn't that supposed to give you the runs?"

"I thought it made you more constipated?" Dante countered. "No, we'll just have to wait for nature to take its course. In the meantime, keep your eyes and ears open. Anything you can find out, anything at all could be valuable information. Spatchcock, get closer to Scullion, find out what she knows."

"Thanks a lot," the kitchen hand scowled. "Getting closer won't be any problem. It's keeping her away that's the hard part."

"Flintlock, I want you to investigate Madame Wartski. I've heard a few dark hints about what she does in her private quarters, maybe it's related to this Strangelove Gambit. Get in there and find out, okay?"

"Why don't you do that?" Flintlock asked. "Your quarters are much closer to her."

"I'm not exactly popular with the female faculty at the moment," Dante admitted. "I don't know what the girls have been telling them about me, but none of it has been positive."

"You couldn't keep your pants on for a single day, could you?" Spatchcock asked.

Dante shrugged. "These things always happen to me. I don't know why."

A classic case of denial if ever I heard one.

"What will you be doing in between trips to the toilet?" Flintlock enquired.

Dante smiled. "I think it's high time I paid a little more attention to Tempest and Storm. Since this weapon is called the Strangelove Gambit, it's a fair assumption the twins are involved in its development."

"They *were* working with Fabergé in his laboratory," Spatchcock recalled.

"I wonder if the Furies would be interested in joining me for a little ménage à trois action?" Dante asked.

"A little what?" Spatchcock looked to Flintlock for an explanation.

"In your gutter parlance," the exiled aristocrat replied. "He fancies having a three-in-a-bed sex romp."

"You lucky devil! And with twins, too!"

Dante smiled broadly. "It's a dirty job but someone's gotta do it."

Dante only remembered the rendezvous with Helga after returning to his private quarters. He hurried to the gymnasium, trying to think of some elegant yet subtle way of letting Helga down gently. If he was going to take on both the Strangelove twins, he would need all his energy. But the gymnasium door was firmly locked and Dante could see no sign of Helga through its glass window.

"Looking for someone?" a booming voice demanded. Wartski was stomping towards him, her nightgown flapping in the breeze. He caught a glimpse of what was hidden inside and hurriedly averted his eyes. The sight of that many warts on the human body was more than repulsive – it was obscene.

"No," he replied. "I left a piece of equipment behind when I was teaching in the gymnasium earlier and wanted to retrieve it before morning."

Wartski regarded him suspiciously and then peered in through the window while trying to door handle. Satisfied the gymnasium was both secure and empty, she folded her gown round her voluminous torso. "That area is locked for the night. Whatever is inside will still be there in the morning. I suggest you come back then to collect it. In the meantime, you should return to your room. Doctor Fabergé frowns upon new staff wandering the hallways at night. Better for your future here if you respect that."

"Of course," Dante agreed. "Well, I'll say goodnight then."

Wartski grabbed hold of his arm as he turned to leave. "Unless you wanted to come back to my private quarters for a night-cap? I have an interesting selection of sherry and sweet wines there, Mr Durward."

Dante yawned with great vigour. "Thank you for the kind invitation, but I think I'll follow your sage advice and retire to my room. Some of us need more beauty sleep than others."

Wartski withdrew her hand sharply. "What are you inferring?"

"Nothing, nothing at all," he replied quickly. "Well, goodnight!" With that Dante scurried away, counting his blessings at having escaped the matron's attention. He did not envy Flintlock the job of finding out more about her. Dante returned directly to his own room and fled inside, locking and bolting the door after himself. He listened intently for movement outside. A few moments later heavy footsteps approached the door and someone tried the handle. Unable to gain entry, they walked away again.

"That was a close call," Dante muttered to himself.

I don't think it's the only close call you'll have tonight, the Crest said.

"What do you mean?"

You have another visitor waiting for you on this side of the door.

A female voice was next to speak, her soft tones whispering across the room. "Poor Mr Durward. You must be tired. Come to bed."

NINE

"There's a time to chase, a time to run"
– Russian proverb

Dante spun round to see Helga lying in his bed, a single sheet pulled to just above her breasts, modestly covering her more outstanding attributes. "I thought we were supposed to be meeting in the gymnasium?" he asked.

"We were," she purred, "but it was already locked when I arrived for our private tuition. So I decided to see if you had another location in mind. You left the door unlocked, so I slipped inside and waited. I hope you don't mind…"

"No," Dante yelped. Realising his voice had climbed an octave, he cleared his throat before speaking again in a considerably deeper tone. "No, that's absolutely fine. Not a problem at all."

"Good," Helga replied coyly. "I wouldn't want to make you angry."

"True. I can be quite fearsome when I'm angry."

"Oh, yes, I can imagine. You might decide to punish me."

"Might I?" Dante was having difficulty in swallowing, suddenly aware that the collar of his shirt was constricting his breathing.

"Yes," Helga said enthusiastically. "I was rather a naughty girl after class, wasn't I? Flirting with you so shamelessly. Madame Wartski wouldn't approve."

"I take it she's against flirting."

Helga shook her head sadly. "She doesn't want us to have any fun at all."

"What a shame," Dante agreed. "Well, I must admit to being rather tired so perhaps we could hold our private session on another occasion…"

"You don't want to show me how a real fighter wields his weapon?"

"It's not so much that as–"

"I had so been looking forward to having you put me through my paces. The cut and thrust of a good duel, our bodies glistening with sweat as we strained to outdo each other, the battle of the sexes coming to an almighty climax in our combat," Helga enthused, her eyes alive with excitement. "Doesn't that sound inviting to you, Mr Durward?"

"Very inviting," Dante admitted, "but as I said, it's getting late and we both have classes in the morning."

"What would Madame Wartski say if she found us alone together in your private quarters?"

"I shudder to think."

Helga pursed her lips thoughtfully, pressing a forefinger against them. "It would be a shame if she found out what had been going on in here."

"But nothing is going on," Dante maintained. "Nothing's happened!"

"Nothing yet," Helga replied, letting her forefinger slip between her lips and into her mouth. Her tongue rolled around the sides of the finger, moistening it gently, before Helga withdrew the digit from her mouth with a sigh. "But I might feel obliged to tell her anyway."

"Tell her what?" Dante hurriedly wiped a beat of perspiration from his forehead, all too aware he was not in control of the situation.

"How you invited me back to your room," Helga said hungrily.

"But I didn't," Dante protested.

"How you ordered me to take off all my clothes and fold them across that chair," she replied, pointing at a neat pile nearby.

"But I never–"

"How you commanded me to get into your bed, wearing only a black silk ribbon around my throat," Helga continued.

"But I..."

"And then how you had your wicked way with me, over and over again." Helga suddenly sat up in the bed, the sheet falling away to reveal she was completely naked but for the silk ribbon around her neck.

"But–"

"Of course, I don't have to tell her all that."

Dante smiled weakly. "You don't?"

"Nein," Helga said. "I can be as quiet as you like, Mr Durward."

"That would be best, I feel."

"Or I can scream so loud everyone in this castle will come running." Helga rose from the bed and began walking slowly towards him. "It's up to you."

"Well, I don't think screaming will be necessary," Dante said hopefully.

"No?" Helga smiled and undid the strip of black silk from her neck. "We'll see about that. Now take off your clothes. I know the perfect place to tie this ribbon, somewhere that will keep you up all night if I wish."

You better do what she says, the Crest suggested. *Grin and bare it.*

Dante nodded and began tearing at the buttons of his shirt. "You have been a naughty girl, haven't you Helga?"

The House of Hapsburg's eldest daughter gave a tiny squeal of delight. "Yes I have, Mr Durward."

"Call me sir."

"Yes, sir!"

It was close to dawn before Dante finally got some sleep, having spent much of the night satisfying Helga's needs and wants. He stirred at six to see her hurriedly dressing. "Sorry, I didn't mean to wake you," she whispered. "I have to get back to bed. Madame Wartski checks all the dormitories just before seven, to make sure nothing has happened to us."

"You'll remember our little conversation, won't you?" Dante asked. "Not a word to her about what we did last night."

Helga looked horrified at the mere suggestion. "I'd never tell her anything of the sort! She'd have me expelled immediately."

"Oh," Dante said, realising he had been out-bluffed for the second time in twenty-four hours. "Oh well."

Helga unlocked the door and peered outside carefully. "But I'll certainly tell the rest of the girls! Everybody deserves one of your private lessons." She waved coyly and hurried outside, closing the door behind herself.

Congratulations, the Crest said as Helga's footsteps had faded into the distance.

"Thank you," Dante replied. "I thought it was a remarkable performance on my part too. I didn't realise you were such a connoisseur of lovemaking."

I was congratulating you on becoming Fabergé Island's new gigolo.

"You're exaggerating as usual, Crest. You don't honestly expect little Helga to tell her classmates about what went on last night do you?"

Of course she will, Dante. That woman left here with enough gossip to keep the students whispering for weeks on end. You can expect a steady stream of customers for your talents in the next few nights.

"Well, there are worse things than being a gigolo," Dante maintained. "I always fancied a career between the sheets. I could be the twenty-seventh century Casanova, the greatest lover of them all!"

Most gigolos get paid. All you got was an hour's sleep and a smug grin on your face. Do you honestly think you'll be able to keep that up all week?

"I'll have you know I survived the House of Sin's Hellraiser Gauntlet, a trial of male endurance that only two men in history have completed!"

I know, I was there, the Crest replied wearily. *Not a pretty sight. Anyway, it's time for you to get up.*

"I think I've been up enough for one night."

Maybe. But breakfast is already being served and your first class begins in an hour – self-defence with half a dozen sex-starved young women.

"Bojemoi," Dante muttered, climbing reluctantly from his bed. "How do teachers cope with this sort of schedule?"

They get long summer holidays and sleeping with their students is strictly forbidden.

"Well, that would make it a less strenuous profession, but rather less enjoyable too." Dante pulled on a pair of trousers and headed for the ablutions block. "Wake me if I fall asleep in the shower."

Dante spent much of his day fending off the attentions of his pupils, as word of his exploits spread through the elite class. Carmen from the House of Andorra kept dropping her pencil and asking Dante to pick it up for her, while Tracy from Britannia took every opportunity to pinch his rear as he walked past her desk. Helga was just as happy to see him, winking at the new teacher and giggling whenever she caught his eye.

Dante was examining the bruises on his buttocks after dinner when someone began knocking on the door of his private quarters. "I'm not here!"

"Yes you are," Spatchcock replied from outside. "I can hear your voice."

Dante let the kitchen hand in and then locked his door again.

"Why the extra security?" Spatchcock asked. "Has Fabergé figured out who you are?"

"No, I haven't seen him since Sunday night. I'm trying to keep out any unwanted visitors." Dante pulled down the waistband of his trousers to give Spatchcock a glimpse of the bruising. "See?"

"What have you been up to?"

Better to ask who he's been–, the Crest began.

"Yes, thank you, we get the idea," Dante snapped. "I'll do the smutty innuendoes."

Spatchcock looked askance at him.

"Sorry, just a little side discussion I'm having with the Crest."

"Flintlock wants to know if you've found out anything from the twins yet."

"Why?"

Spatchcock shrugged. "I'm guessing he's terrified of getting caught in Wartski's room. He doesn't want to get too close to her."

"I've seen her in a night-gown. He's got good reason to be scared," Dante agreed. "But he'll have to bite the bullet. Tempest and Storm have been locked away in the laboratory with Fabergé all day, so I haven't made contact."

"I'll pass the message on."

"What about you and Scullion?"

Spatchcock shook his head sadly. "I think she's falling for me, big time."

"Perfectly understandable," Dante said.

"Yeah?"

"Of course. You reek like a rotting corpse. How could she resist that?"

Spatchcock smiled. "I wonder what sex with an alien is like?"

"Just be careful where she puts those tentacles. The suckers on an octopus are strong enough to rip the skin from a human arm once they're properly adhered. Imagine what Scullion could do to you…"

"I hadn't thought of that," Spatchcock admitted. "Best be getting back to the kitchen. She wants me to start prep for tomorrow's meals. I'll pass on the message to Flintlock." Dante unlocked the door and let Spatchcock out. Seconds later an insistent knocking made him reopen the door.

"Spatch, I told you, I can't–"

His words were silenced by a slender female hand clamping itself across his mouth. Carmen appeared in the doorway, pushing Dante back into his room. Once they were inside the Andorran beauty pressed her back against the door, preventing Dante from trying to leave.

"Helga told us all about you, Mr Durward."

"Did she?" Dante smiled thinly. "Good for her."

"But we didn't believe her. No man could do all the things she claimed, as well as she claimed, for as long as she claimed."

"You're probably right. Well, now that we've settled that−"

Carmen suddenly ripped apart her blouse, revealing a red silk brassiere encasing two magnificent, deeply tanned breasts. A waft of perfume filled Dante's nostrils, powerful and intoxicating. "Perhaps such a man could satisfy Helga, for she has never known the fiery temperament of a true Latin lover. But we in Andorra pride ourselves on being the most passionate of people."

"An admirable quality," Dante agreed. "Perhaps we could discuss it further in the morning?"

"You are an animal, aren't you?" Carmen demanded. "You believe actions speak louder than words and now you want to prove it to me!" She clasped hold of her breasts and began to massage them through the brassiere. "Santa Maria, already I can feel my loins burning at the mere thought of your touch. Imagine what love we shall make tonight!"

"Perhaps it's best if we left it to our imagination. Reality can sometimes be a disappointment, I often find…"

Carmen shook her head. "You're right. Perhaps I should not be imagining such things." Her hand reached for the door, twisting the handle.

Dante smiled, relief flooding his features. "Good. Tomorrow we can−"

Carmen pulled open the door and whistled. The sound of approaching footsteps became audible outside.

"What are you doing?" Dante asked helplessly.

"I do not wish to imagine what love you and I shall make tonight," Carmen replied, licking her lips. "Instead I shall experience an even greater pleasure!"

Don't ask her what pleasure this is, the Crest urged.

But Dante couldn't help himself. "What pleasure is that?"

You had to ask her, didn't you?

Carmen pulled the door open a little wider and another of the pupils slipped inside. Her dark hair was cut in a bob, framing a heart-shaped face with warm hazel eyes. She was wearing a silk robe but it was obvious there was little on underneath it. "This is Mai Lin, a student from the Malaysian Provinces," Carmen explained. "She doesn't speak much English but we've discovered another way of communicating this past year. We talk to each other with our bodies, not with our voices."

Dante swallowed, twice. "I'm not sure you should be telling me this."

Carmen and Mai Lin began to advance on Dante, who was retreating towards the far corner of his room. Soon they had him against the wall, unable to escape. Carmen tore off the last of her clothing and began to remove his, while Mai Lin slipped out of her robe and began to rub her body against Dante. A heady smell of musk filled the air.

"We love you long time," Mai Lin whispered.

Bojemoi, the Crest whispered.

"You can say that again," Dante agreed.

It was just after breakfast on Wednesday that the data crystal departed Dante's body. After thoroughly washing the offending item, he took it back to his private quarters and locked the door. "Well, Crest, what do we do now?"

After last night I know there's not much you won't do, it replied.

"I meant with the data crystal," he snapped back.

Temper, temper. The Crest analysed the object silently for a few moments before speaking again. *Put your hands next to the crystal, then cede control of your cyborganics to me.*

Dante did as he was told, watching as tendrils of silver and purple biocircuitry began to extend from his fingernails, encircling the crystal. It was a strange sensation to feel your body acting under somebody else's control, a detached helplessness.

It's encrypted, the Crest announced.

"Meaning?"

I've been able to penetrate the outer shell and download everything stored inside the crystal. But the data itself has been run through a very sophisticated form of encryption, far beyond currently known technology.

"Something Fabergé has developed here on the island?"

Perhaps. That's not the important issue. I can break this coding, but it will take time – days at least, perhaps even weeks.

"We don't have weeks! The Tsar will be here on Sunday."

I know, I know. I'll have to devote all my energy and attention to this task until I find and crack the cipher upon which the encryption is based.

"In words I can understand?"

You're on your own.

"Crest? Crest!"

It replied after a long silence. *Yes?*

"Sorry – you just disappeared. I'm so used to having your voice inside my head, it was a little frightening," Dante admitted sheepishly.

Get over it. I'll contact you when I'm done. Understand?

"Yes. Do you still need the data crystal?"

No, I've extracted all relevant data. You'd best hide it for now.

"Okay." Dante waited for another moment, then realised the Crest had gone again. He concealed the crystal in his luggage before leaving for class.

Dante was pleasantly surprised to find Tempest at the faculty library when he went in for pre-dinner drinks that evening. Wednesday's classes had proven even more problematic than the day before, with Mai Lin and Carmen exchanging knowing looks and the other pupils trying to catch his eye. Dante pondered organising an orgy, simply to speed up the process of sleeping his way through the entire class, but decided that would be both risky and impractical. He might be all man but there was a physical limit to how many women even he could satisfy simultaneously. No doubt another of the students would be making a visit to his quarters tonight. If he could find somewhere else to spend the night, he might get some sleep.

"Mr Durward, I wanted to talk with you," Tempest said as Dante entered the library. "There's something we need to discuss."

"Indeed? Well, I'm all ears."

The red-haired woman raised an eyebrow at this statement. "I'm not sure I understand your meaning. I see only two ears and they do not appear any larger or more significant than most."

Dante smiled. "It's an expression. I was saying I'm all yours."

"All mine?"

"Er…" Dante cursed inwardly and realised how much he depended upon the Crest's help in such situations. For once, he'd have to sort this out for himself. "I meant I'm ready to talk with you about whatever you like."

"Good." Tempest nodded, looking down upon him. She noticed Dante rubbing the back of his neck awkwardly. "Is something wrong?"

"You're so tall, it's giving me a stiff neck."

"Then we should sit down." Tempest gestured at two armchairs in a corner of the library away from the others. Mould was snoozing in another chair, while Ms Ostrov and her cronies were watching suspiciously from the far side of the room. Once she and Dante were seated, Tempest smiled. "Is that more comfortable for you?"

"Yes, thanks. Now, what did you want to talk about?"

"You must excuse me. Sometimes if I fail to recognise colloquial expressions and vernacular phrasings."

"Now you've lost me," Dante said.

"Slang," Tempest explained. "Storm and I grew up here. The institute and those who pass through it, they comprise much of our life experience."

"You went to the Imperial Games, didn't you? I remember watching the highlights on the House of Bolshoi sports channel."

"True, but Doctor Fabergé insisted we keep ourselves to ourselves during the events. As a result, we do not have your knowledge of the world and its vernacular." Tempest chewed her bottom lip wistfully. "Sometimes I wonder what else we have missed out on."

Dante reached out a friendly hand and patted her on the shoulder. "Trust me, the world outside – it's no better than being here."

Tempest nodded. "That is what Doctor Fabergé always tell us."

"So, what did you want to talk about?"

"Your servant, Spatchcock. He's working in the kitchen, with Scullion."

"Yes. I understand she's quite taken with him."

"Two days ago Spatchcock delivered a bowl of soup to the doctor's laboratory. Soon afterwards we discovered an item was missing from one of the worktops. Storm and I have thoroughly searched the room, but can find no trace of the item. The only feasible explanation we can formulate is that your manservant took the item – either intentionally or otherwise."

Dante nodded, unsure of how to react. "I see…"

"The item is of little value, beyond a sentimental attachment for Doctor Fabergé and us – my sister and I. It is a crystal containing a recording of our mother's voice along with her likeness. We would very much like to retrieve it."

"Completely understandable," Dante agreed.

"Do you know anything about this crystal, its where-abouts?" Tempest stared at him intently, her eyes searching his face for a reaction.

"I can't say that I do," he replied carefully, "but I will approach Spatchcock and see if he can shed any light on the matter. It pains me to say it, but my manservant was once a thief. He came into my service during the war as a con-script, just like Flintlock, but both proved themselves worthy of my trust and loyalty. I would be mortified to think Spatchcock had lapsed back into his old, wayward habits." Dante smiled. "Thank you for mentioning this matter to me so discretely. I will ensure it is dealt with this evening."

"All three of us would be most grateful," Tempest said.

"One thing confuses me a little," Dante added. "You said the crystal contained recordings of your mother?"

"Yes."

"If I might ask, what happened to her?"

"She died giving birth to Storm and myself," Tempest said sadly. "It was a great loss for our father."

"And where is he now?"

"In the laboratory, at the top of the north tower."

Dante finally realised the truth. "Doctor Fabergé is your father?"

"Yes, of course." Tempest looked puzzled anyone could think otherwise. "He does not want it widely known, but I thought all the faculty knew."

"Well, I've only been here a few days," Dante said.

Tempest rose from her seat, towering over him. "I must return to the laboratory and tell the doctor what you have shared with me. When do you think you might have any further information?"

"Later tonight, I am certain of that," Dante replied. "Per-haps I could visit your quarters with an update?"

"That would be most kind of you. I share a room with my sister, on the top level of the west tower. Knock twice and I'll know it's you."

"I'll be there before midnight," Dante said.

Tempest nodded, acknowledged the others and then left the library. Dante smiled quietly to himself. Who says I need the Crest's help with everything? Tonight Quentin Durward will be making a house call.

After dinner Dante loudly announced he was going down to the kitchen to visit Spatchcock, making sure the other staff knew of his whereabouts. Although Wartski had not attended dinner, no doubt Ms Ostrov or one of her cronies was passing on news of Mr Durward's movements about the castle. It didn't hurt to act out the role he had created for himself as intermediary with the troublesome Spatchcock. Dante found the kitchen hand sulkily scrubbing pots and pans.

"Where's she of the many tentacles?"

"Went to bed early, complaining of a headache. More likely put too much sherry down her gullet instead of into that trifle."

Dante nodded. "It did seem a little lacking in kick. Now, did you steal a data crystal from Doctor Fabergé's laboratory on Monday?"

Spatchcock stared at him as if Dante had grown an extra nose. "Are you off your head? Why are you asking me that?"

"I'm worried that you might have reverted to your old ways."

"What old ways?"

"Don't try to play the innocent with me, Spatch. We both know you used to be a thief and a felon, along with numerous other offences."

"Yeah, so what?"

"Have you embraced that terrible life again?"

"I'm not getting this at all. What are you babbling about?"

Dante abandoned trying to be subtle, since such efforts were proving futile. Instead he explained about the conversation with Tempest, her explanation of the data crystal's contents and the belief the former thief might have accidentally purloined it.

"Oh," Spatchcock said slowly, at least showing signs of understanding. "I see. Well, er, now that you come to mention it, I might have accidentally picked something up – entirely by mistake you understand – when I was delivering the soup to the location you mentioned some two days ago."

"You're not giving evidence in court," Dante hissed.

"Sorry." He sniffed and then wiped a dribble of mucus from the end of his nose on the dishcloth. "So, er, what do we do now?"

"You give me the crystal and I return it to the Strangelove twins later tonight, no questions asked."

"So you get to play the hero–"

"And have a legitimate reason to visit them after dark in their room."

"Kill two birds with one stone," Spatchcock observed.

"Hopefully it won't come to that." Dante folded his arms. "So, where's this crystal then, hmm? Where have you hidden it?"

"Er, I'm not sure I remember."

"I hope you haven't hidden it in my private quarters," Dante hissed through clenched teeth, winking repeatedly at Spatchcock.

"What? Oh! Yes, well, it's funny you should say that."

"Somewhere near the bed? Or amongst my luggage?" Dante accompanied the latter suggestion with another flurry of winking.

"The luggage, it's definitely in amongst your luggage."

"Well, then I shall have to go and recover it." Dante delivered a firm clout to Spatchcock's head for good measure. "Don't you ever dare do something like this again, or I'll have your guts for garters! Got it?"

"Yes."

"Good." Dante began to leave, then stopped and came back. Spatchcock winced, fearful of another blow. "Where's Flintlock?"

"I think he's checking a blockage near Madame Wartski's quarters."

"Excellent. Well, I'd best go and find this data crystal. And remember what I told you, Spatch."

"What's that?" The kitchen hand was swatted with another blow.

"No more thieving!"

Flintlock had scrubbed himself clean before beginning his covert raid on Madame Wartski's quarters. He didn't want to leave any trace of his intrusion, and the lingering aroma of sewerage would not require a detective to identify the culprit. If he was honest, Flintlock would admit the elongated ablutions were merely a method of delaying his attempt at breaking and entering. But the message from Dante had been clear: they had to know what secrets the wart-ridden woman had hidden in her room and Flintlock was the man for the job. Besides, the exiled aristocrat had never been honest in his life, even with himself, and this was no time to start.

Taking what little courage he possessed and forcing himself forwards, the blond-haired burglar knocked on the matron's door. "Madame Wartski? It's Flintlock. I understand there's another blockage in the pipes near your quarters. I was wondering if I could come in and check for any signs of trouble?"

His hopes of being told to come back later proved fruitless, as no reply was made. After knocking and calling out several more times, Flintlock realised he couldn't linger outside the door any longer. He removed a sliver of flexible metal from a concealed pouch inside his trousers and used it to prise open the lock. The door swung open with an ominous creak but no lights were visible inside. "Madame Wartski? Are you in there?"

Flintlock could not hear the matron: neither her voice nor the heavy rasp of breathing that accompanied her everywhere. There was a different noise emanating from inside the room – a faint bubbling accompanied by a low rumble that defied easy identification. Perhaps she had left the

Imperial Net on? And what was that smell – like a swamp with a nervous disposition, noxious and nauseating. As Flintlock entered, the stench grew stronger and more cloying. He closed the door and stood still, letting his eyes adjust to the limited lighting.

The room had a green hue, illumination spilling in from another doorway. Wartski's quarters were sparsely furnished, just a bookshelf, wardrobe, dresser and vanity unit. No bed, so that must be in the adjoining room, Flintlock reasoned. He moved to the bookshelf and examined the spines on display: *Toads for Pleasure*, *Toads Across History*, *Tropical Toads*. The matron liked her friends amphibious, that much was certain. But the first room revealed few secrets. It was time to venture deeper into Wartski's privacy.

Flintlock edged closer to the other doorway, peering through the gap. Beyond he could see a double bed, its sheets rumpled and unkempt. A selection of plus size lingerie had been abandoned nearby, seemingly cast aside during moments of frenzy or passion. Pity the poor sod who gets caught in here while she's on heat, Flintlock thought, before remembering where he was standing. Best get on with the task in hand.

He ventured into the bedroom, its interior suffused with emerald. The source for this light was an entire wall of glass tanks, each containing a dozen toads of varying shapes, sizes and colours. Even more disturbing were the sexual implements arranged on hooks and handles in front of the tanks – whips, canes, harnesses, handcuffs, chains and a selection of rubber objects with intimidating proportions. Flintlock shuddered, backing away from the display of depravity. His legs collided with the bed and he twisted round in surprise. He noticed there were notches carved into the wooden framework, while chains and fur-lined handcuffs were attached to each corner.

That's it, I've seen enough, Flintlock decided. Wartski isn't doing any secret research for Fabergé in here – not unless it involves sexual deviancy and toads. Time to make a tactical withdrawal.

"Is someone out there?" a voice called.

Flintlock stopped, frozen with terror. He urged his legs to move but they seemed to have forgotten their normal functions. A door opened in a corner of the bedchamber and Wartski emerged, clad in just a thigh-length white camisole, towelling her hair dry. "I said is someone–" she stopped abruptly, surprised and perplexed by Flintlock's presence.

"Oh! What are you doing in here?" Wartski demanded.

Flintlock shrugged helplessly.

Wartski strode to the doorway between the bedchamber and outer room, waving her hand over the palm reader so the exit was sealed, trapping the intruder. "I said what are you doing here?"

Flintlock opened his mouth to speak and then remembered he was supposed to be a mute. Instead he improvised an elaborate mixture of mime and sign language, trying to communicate that he had wandered in by mistake while looking for a blockage in the drains but plainly there was no blockage here so it was for the best if he left now and–

Wartski stopped his spasmodic movements with a shout. Once Flintlock had abandoned his wordless attempts to communicate, the matron moved closer, an intrigued look on her wart-strewn features. "I can only think of three reasons you would enter my private quarters without permission. Firstly, you have come here on a mission from Scullion to investigate some blockage."

Flintlock nodded hurriedly at that suggestion.

"However," Wartski continued, "I know of no such problem, nor has Scullion mentioned it in our daily briefing. So that cannot be correct. Secondly, you came here to steal from me, hoping to find something of value to sell once the term is finished. Is that why you're here, mute?"

Flintlock shook his head vigorously, denying the charge.

"That just leaves the third reason. No doubt you've heard whispers about what I do here during the little spare time I have from the institute. You're curious. Can she really be the sexual deviant everybody says? Perhaps you have wondered whether you could share in my delight of the obscene, the obscure and the downright disgusting? Perhaps you would like a session in my chamber of delights and debauchery?"

Flintlock shook his head again, his face smeared with dismay.

Wartski reached down between the intruder's legs and grabbed hold of his genitals. "Your head says no but the rest of your body is saying yes. How delightful." She let go, smiling as Flintlock collapsed to the floor with a shriek of pain. "Good. It's a while since I've really enjoyed myself. Best of all, I've got the night off from patrolling the castle's corridors, so you don't have to leave before dawn. Isn't that wonderful?"

Flintlock whimpered helplessly, his eyes clenched shut to stop them seeing the vile woman standing before him. Wartski removed her camisole in a single movement, revealing her repulsive naked body in full. She licked her lips while contemplating the many options waiting in front of the toad tanks. "Let's get started then, shall we? Since you're already kneeling at my feet, you're in the perfect position for your first task of the evening."

TEN

> "Trouble appears without prior notice"
> – Russian proverb

Dante had drenched himself in cologne, pulled on his cleanest underpants and chosen the best-tailored jacket from among his meagre possessions. He examined his reflection in a mirror, running a hand through the luxurious mane of black hair. "Catnip for the ladies," he murmured, giving himself a wink. "The twins won't know what hit them." An itching sensation on his left arm forced him to pull jacket and shirt aside. The double-headed eagle symbol of the Romanovs was visible below the skin, like a faded tattoo.

"Crest?" Dante whispered. "Crest!"

What is it? I'm close to decrypting the data from that crystal, it replied tersely, *but I'll never finish if you insist on interrupting me.*

"You're becoming visible again," Dante explained. The tattoo was the only visible sign that he bore a Romanov Weapons Crest. The Crest was able to conceal itself when its human host was vulnerable, such as Dante being asleep or unconscious. This skill was more important than ever since the war, with anyone bearing a Crest was liable to execution by the Tsar's forces.

Sorry. The code breaking is taking all my concentration.

"I can't afford to have Tempest and Storm discover my true identity in a middle of a romantic moment, can I?"

You don't seem to understand how much effort is consumed by making myself invisible for such long periods of time. The Crests were not designed to go undercover for days on end.

"Just do your best, okay?" Dante watched as the double-headed eagle disappeared beneath his skin again, merging into the muscle. "Thanks."

Now, if you'll excuse me–

"Since I've already disturbed you," Dante interrupted.

Yes?

"How's the decryption coming along?"

I should have something for you before dawn.

"Good. Well, get on with it."

The Crest muttered a curse into Dante's mind and then fell silent again.

"Don't let your mother hear you talking like that," Dante replied before pulling his shirt and jacket back into place. After one last groom of his hair and stroke of his beard, he departed for the twins' room, whistling tunelessly.

In the kitchen Spatchcock had almost finished preparations for the next day's meals. All that remained was washing down the work surfaces and disposing of the scraps. Tired from a long day's labours, Spatchcock stared sourly at a massive tub laden with leftovers and other swill. Scullion insisted it be pushed through a grinder twice and then poured down a garbage disposal unit, both backbreaking jobs. But Scullion was still in bed.

"There's got to be a quicker way," Spatchcock muttered. "Just this once." He remembered the walkway that stretched over the waters surrounding the island and grinned. Nobody would ever know if he just emptied the scraps into the sea, would they? No sooner had the thought entered his head than Spatchcock was dragging the tub towards the walkway.

Outside a cold wind was slicing through the air, chill and bitter. Spatchcock got the tub halfway across the walkway before his energy and patience were exhausted. He fleetingly contemplated lifting the tub to tip its contents over the side railing, but his small frame could only raise it a few inches off the metal walkway. "Guess we have to do this the old fashioned way." Spatchcock dug both hands into the sloppy mess and scooped out the top layer, hurling over the rail and into the water. It splattered loudly on contact but soon sank into the inky black depths. Satisfied with his choice, Spatchcock continued lobbing kitchen scraps into the sea. "Much, much easier," he muttered. "Why doesn't Scullion do this all the time?"

His question was answered by a roaring sound from below. A shape burst from the water, vaguely humanoid but unlike anything Spatchcock had seen before. He cowered back in terror, aware of flailing limbs, rows of gnashing teeth and cold, dead eyes staring at him. The little thief fled for his life, screaming and shrieking, the slops bucket abandoned.

Dante bounded up the circular stairway, two steps at a time. At the top of the west tower he paused to catch his breath, then strode purposefully towards a heavy wooden door. It had to be the twins' room, as it was the only opening on this level. Adjusting his jacket one last time, Dante knocked twice. Footsteps could be heard padding towards the entrance and then the door swung open.

Storm was standing inside wearing a revealing black leotard. She mopped sweat from her forehead and chest with a towel while looking disinterestedly at Dante. "Yes, Mr Durward?"

The new arrival turned on the charm, giving her the benefit of his most winning smile. "Your sister asked me to pay a visit this evening."

"Did she?"

"Yes." Dante peered past Storm, not an easy task when the two-metre tall woman nearly filled the doorway. Beyond her he could see Tempest stretched out on a large square of padded matting. Like her sister she was dressed only in a leotard, its fabric stained with sweat from exertions. "And there she is!"

Storm folded her arms. "Why?"

Dante gave a little wave to Tempest but it went unnoticed. "Sorry?"

"Why are you here?"

"Well, it's a rather delicate matter."

"Could you be more specific?" Storm demanded.

At last Tempest noticed Dante at the door and called to him. "Mr Durward, you're here. Come in, come in."

Dante smiled at Storm again before pushing past her. The twins' quarters were considerably larger than his own, filling almost all of the west tower's top level. Much of the space was given over to a private gymnasium, with a steam room and sauna against one wall. Through an archway Dante could see a double bed in the next room, an inviting prospect.

Tempest continued to stretch and contort her body into new and ever more challenging positions while she talked to Dante. "Did you have any success with the matter we discussed?"

"Yes. Yes I did." Dante reached into his jacket pocket and produced the data crystal. "My servant says he inadvertently picked it up and I tend to believe him. It's been several years since he renounced thieving and he has stuck to that pledge. Nevertheless, I have given him a severe reprimand and you may be assured this sort of incident shall not happen again."

"I should hope not," Storm commented acidly from the doorway.

"Could I have the crystal?" Tempest asked from the floor, her legs doing the splits while she bent her torso forwards to touch the mat.

"Of course." Dante handed the crystal to her and watched as she examined its outer casing. He knew there was no visible evidence the Crest had breached the crystal. "I trust everything is in order?"

Tempest smiled. "Perfectly. Well, thank you for all your help."

"Yes, thanks," Storm agreed, opening the door ever wider so the visitor would have no problems departing. Dante frowned inwardly. This was not going according to plan. With most women he could charm his way into their affections a little, but the Strangelove twins appeared utterly immune to him. It was time to try another tactic.

"You obviously both spend a lot of time working out," he ventured.

"Yes," Tempest agreed. "Our athletic careers may have been quite short-lived, but we like to keep in shape. The body is a temple and no temple should be allowed to fall into disrepair."

"I know what you mean," Dante said, sucking in his stomach and puffing out his chest. "I find maintaining a rude health is essential for my teaching."

Storm arched an eyebrow at him. "You do?" she asked, her voice dripping with sarcasm.

"Most definitely. But I do worry about my levels of flexibility. Perhaps you could show me a few techniques for improving that?"

"We really don't have time for–" Storm began, but her sister cut in.

"It would be our pleasure," Tempest replied. "Storm, why don't you come and help me?" Dante thought he caught a look pass between the twins, but wasn't sure of its significance.

"Yes, I will," Storm said, shutting the door and approaching the mat. "This could be most educational for Mr Durward."

Flintlock opened his eyes and resisted the urge to scream. He had already been subjected to more degradation in one evening than he had experienced in a lifetime. Now he found himself stark naked and handcuffed to a bed while Madame Wartski sat astride his chest, her corpulent body pressing down on him. She was wearing nothing but a black domino mask while her hands caressed a large, brown skinned toad mottled with green spots. The matron stroked the creature tenderly with one hand while smiling down at her sex slave.

"I have a little secret. Would you like to know what it is, Flintlock?"

He shook his head from side to side but she ignored his wishes.

"Everybody knows of my passionate interest in toads, how I like to breed them. They all think that's the reason why I have so many warts on my body. But there's another reason."

Flintlock wished he could tear his hands away from the restraints and shove his fingers into his ears, to block out what was coming next. Wartski leaned forwards, her pendulous breasts brushing against his chest as she held the toad in front of Flintlock's face.

"The toads I breed secrete a powerful hallucinogenic from their sweat glands. Ancient tribes used to partake of it for therapeutic purposes. But via selective breeding I have developed a strain of toad whose secretions are a hundred times more powerful than anything which occurs in nature. All you need do is lick the back of such a toad and you will experience sensations beyond belief. Alas, indulge too often and you become very warty – like me."

Wartski gave her toad a kiss, then ran her tongue along its back, sucking the sweat into her mouth. "The best part about this particular toad is that its glands also secrete a strong sexual stimulant amidst the sweat. Not only do you see visions beyond imagining, you will also reach a state of sexual ecstasy unlike anything before in your life."

Tears began seeping from Flintlock's eyes, running down either side of his face. Wartski smiled benignly at him. "That's right, I also wept with joy when I discovered this delight. Now I am going to share it with you. Ah, Flintlock, if only you could speak and tell me what you are feeling right now."

Wartski turned the toad around so its back was close to her slave's lips. "Lick my beauty's back," she commanded. But Flintlock kept his mouth firmly closed, not wanting any part of the matron's ecstasy. Wartski smiled and reached behind herself to grab hold of his testicles, squeezing them between thumb and fingers. "I said lick!"

Flintlock darted out his tongue and made the tiniest of licks.

"More!" the harridan ordered.

Flintlock licked once more, rolling his tongue back and forth across the toad's back. Wartski released his privates from her grasp. "That's better. Now, we wait. In just a few moments you will begin to see me as the most beautiful creature you have ever encountered. You will do anything I desire, freely and without hesitation, debasing yourself in ways you never thought possible. The best part of it all? Afterwards, you will remember every moment, every wonderful second of pleasure and pain. Let the fun begin!"

Flintlock closed his eyes. Maybe it won't affect me, he hoped. Maybe I'll be immune. Maybe I'll... Then the spots started dancing in front of his eyes.

Dante had stripped off his jacket, shirt and boots, leaving just his trousers to take the strain. Storm and Tempest were already stretched out on the padded mat, bending and twisting their bodies into the unlikeliest of shapes. "Do you know yoga, Mr Durward?" Tempest inquired politely.

"It can be nice with honey," he replied, smiling at his own joke.

"She meant the Hindu system of philosophy aiming at the mystical union of the self with the Supreme Being in a state of complete awareness and tranquillity through certain physical and mental exercises," Storm chided.

"Oh, yoga. Well, I've experienced a few mystical unions in my time, but wouldn't call my body a supreme being. Yet."

"Let's begin with a basic position, shall we?" Tempest replied.

"Let's. I can certainly handle the basic positions," Dante said.

Five minutes later he was starting to have serious doubts. His body had been twisted, stretched and strained in ways he didn't think possible. Muscles and tendons screamed for relief, while his face tried to maintain a relaxed look. Sweat was pouring down the back of his legs and chest, creating unsightly damp patches on his trousers.

By comparison Tempest and Storm were laughing as Dante's attempts to keep up grew more feeble. Finally he collapsed altogether, arms and legs flailing through the air before his body thudded to the floor. After lying still for half a minute he pulled himself up into a sitting position.

"Well, that wasn't bad for my first attempt, was it?"

"Pathetic," Storm replied.

"Abject, to be perfectly honest," Tempest added.

"Still, practice makes perfect," Dante maintained, wiping the sweat from his eyes. "Shall we hit the showers now or later? I could do with a little steam..."

"We prefer to continue our exertions here on the mat," Tempest said, one hand reaching out to stroke her sister's face lovingly.

"Is that a fact?" Dante could feel his energy returning rapidly. "Well, I'm sure I can rise to the occasion."

"After a good workout, we like to keep pushing each other to the limit," Storm continued, her own hands hungrily exploring her sister's body.

"So I can see. Perhaps I can help out?" Dante asked hopefully.

"I don't think..." Tempest said between kisses with Storm, "that will be necessary... Mr Durward... Ohhh."

Storm began peeling off her leotard to reveal the perfect body underneath. "Please close the door on your way out." The twins flung themselves at each other, rolling over and over across the matting. Dante jumped to his feet to get out of their way, retreating to the doorway.

"Well, I can see you've both got your hands full, as it were."

The two women began moaning loudly as they writhed in ecstasy.

"So I'll be off," Dante said, all too aware he was surplus to requirements. He opened the door and stepped outside, looking back wistfully at the spectacle inside. "Try to get *some* rest tonight." He closed the door and began back down the stairs to his own room.

Dante, I've done it, the Crest announced. *I've broken the code.*

"Good, then at least tonight won't be a complete waste of time. What data was stored on the crystal?"

I'm still sorting through it all. The crystal appears to house a virtual reality simulation, made as a dry run for a presentation to the Tsar.

"The Tsar was here?"

No, he must have sent a representative to relay the report.

"What does this presentation say?"

I can do better than tell you, the Crest offered. *I can insert your mind into it, so you can witness what Fabergé wanted the Tsar to see.*

"Do it." Dante opened his door and slipped inside. "Then we can–"

"Then we can do what, Mr Durward?" a female voice asked.

"Oh, no," Dante groaned. "Not another one!"

"Not another what?" his visitor replied. "Don't tell me I'm not the first of your pupils to come inside your private quarters outside school hours?"

Dante found Natalia draped across his bed. Unlike his previous visitors, she was wearing an old fashioned pair of striped pyjamas. As he watched she began undoing the first button of her top, exposing naked skin underneath. "Look, just stop, okay?"

Natalia smiled at him coyly. "Why should I?"

"I don't know what Helga has told you…"

"Helga?"

"Or Carmen. Or Mai Lin." Dante thought back, trying to remember if he had bedded any of the other students, but his mind had gone blank. "Or anybody else for that matter. I am not some gigolo willing to provide you with a night of pleasure free of charge!"

"You mean I have to pay?"

"No, of course you don't have to pay!"

"That's good," she replied, rising gracefully from the bed. "I didn't bring any money with me, as you can see from my attire."

"What I'm trying to say is–"

"Yes?" Natalia asked, moving a step closer.

"Is that I am not merely some kind of stud–"

"That's not what I've heard," she continued, her fingers undoing another button on her top to reveal the swell of her breasts.

"What happened before cannot happen again," Dante insisted. "It was a one-off occurrence, that's all!"

"A one-off? I'm told you're capable of more than that – when roused." Natalia stepped nearer to her teacher, close enough to reach out and touch his jacket. "Much more than that."

Dante tried backing away but the closed door prevented that. "Look, Natalia, I'm not sure this is a good idea. How old are you?"

She smiled. "Just seventeen."

"Bojemoi!" he gasped. "It wouldn't be right, wouldn't be proper if I..."

"Who said anything about being proper?" Natalia sighed, pushing Dante's jacket off and stroking her hands across his chest. "I've got a surprise for you, Mr Durward."

"Really? What's that?"

"I've never been with a man – not a real man. You'll be my first." Natalia licked her lips and slipped her hands inside his shirt.

"I'm sorry, but you're just too young," he protested weakly. "The others, they were women, but you're just..."

"Just a girl?"

Dante nodded meekly.

"We'll see about that!" Natalia ripped his shirt apart at the middle, tugging the material away from his shoulders and down the arms. She leaned close to him, pressing her young body against his squirming form.

"Please, don't do this," Dante whispered.

Natalia looked him in the eyes and began to giggle.

"I don't understand," he said in bewilderment.

Natalia was laughing out loud now, staggering away from Dante as her whole body descended into hysterical guffaws.

"Hey! What's so funny?" he demanded.

Natalia collapsed on the bed, still laughing heartily, one finger pointing at Dante. "Your face! If you could have seen your face!" Another fit of hilarity overtook her, making further speech impossible. Dante waited until she had regained her breath before asking another question.

"You mean you didn't come here to seduce me?"

Natalia's face crumpled with disgust. "Euwwww! You're old enough to be my father. Gross!"

"I am not old enough to be your father," Dante protested. "Well, only if I had been a very early developer. Which I was." Natalia was shaking her head so he abandoned that train of thought. "So why are you in my room?"

"I need your help. I know the institute is a finishing school for young ladies of the Empire, but there's something else going on here."

Dante sat beside her on the bed. "Such as?"

"I'm not sure," Natalia admitted. "Fabergé hardly ever comes out of his laboratory, and when he does visit our classes it's more like he's looking at prized exhibits in a science fair instead of students."

"You can't accuse someone because of the way they look at you, otherwise most of the Empire would be in a gulag."

"It's more than that. I think he's conducting secret experiments on us."

Dante, she may be right, the Crest said.

"What sort of experiments?"

"Everyone but me in the elite class has been given a detailed medical examination by Doctor Fabergé."

"That's not so unusual…"

"Under anaesthetic?" Natalia began nervously pacing the room. "I talked to each of the girls when they came back from these medicals. Their memories about what happened were fuzzy, at best – as if they'd been drugged. And the examinations themselves. From what the other girls described, I believe Doctor Fabergé has been removing unfertilised eggs from each of them."

"Why? Why would he do that?"

"I've done some research into his background. Fabergé was a co-founder of GenetiCo, the scientific research company. Have you heard of it?"

Dante nodded. He had visited GenetiCo's orbital headquarters just before the war, with his half-brother Konstantin. The owner, Raoul Sequanna, had committed suicide rather than side with the Romanovs against the Tsar.

"I think Fabergé has been continuing his genetic research on the island ever since, establishing the finishing school as a front for his activities. Whatever he's been working on, it must need unfertilised human eggs as raw material. The doctor has been taking them from his students, using us like white mice in a laboratory!" Natalia burst into tears.

What she has just told you tallies with my findings, the Crest confirmed. *But the Strangelove Gambit is far more terrifying than she could ever imagine.*

Dante went to the seventeen year-old and put a comforting arm round her shoulders. "If what you told me is true, it must be stopped, Natalia. But why choose me as your confidante?"

"That's simple," she replied between sniffles. "I've read all about you, your exploits, the way you battle for lost causes and hopeless cases. You might act first and think last, but you're exactly the right man to stop Doctor Fabergé."

"I don't understand," Dante maintained. "I'm Quentin Durward, a humble teacher. I may be one of the best swordsmen in the Empire but–"

Natalia rested a hand against his lips, silencing him. "Hush. You don't have to pretend for me. I know you're Nikolai Dante."

ELEVEN

"Seeing is easier than foreseeing"
– Russian proverb

"I don't know what you're talking about," Dante maintained. "I'm a substitute teacher here on probation."

"I saw it on your arm," Natalia replied.

"Saw what?"

"The symbol of the Romanovs, the double-headed eagle. It was visible on your left arm that night we met in the corridor, when you were holding my ice bag against your groin."

Oops, the Crest mumbled. *I told you it was problematic trying to maintain stealth status round the clock.*

"That's just an old tattoo," Dante said lamely.

"A tattoo that appears and disappears?" Natalia asked. "Why do you think I ripped your shirt off earlier?"

"I thought you were flinging yourself at me…"

"I was searching to see if the symbol was still there." Natalia twisted Dante's left arm round to show the place where his Crest normally was. "It's gone, invisible to the naked eye."

"Maybe I was wearing a temporary tattoo?"

"It was a Romanov Weapons Crest, the kind that can be subsumed beneath the skin when necessary to protect its host from detection."

The colloquial expression for this situation is: 'the jig's up'.

Dante sat back down on his bed. "Have you told anyone else about me?"

Natalia shook her head. "I wouldn't. I had to be sure first."

"Then don't," he pleaded. "You're right, Doctor Fabergé has been continuing his experiments – that's why I'm here. He is unveiling a new weapon for the Tsar on Sunday. I'm trying to stop that."

"I knew it! I knew you coming here couldn't be coincidence," Natalia said excitedly. Dante beckoned for her to sit beside him on the bed.

"Natalia, it's important nobody else discovers who I am or why I'm here. You must know about the bounty on my head."

"Yes. Don't worry, I wouldn't know what to do with all those roubles."

Dante nodded. "I guess your family is rich enough already to send you to a place like this?"

"No, I got in on a scholarship. The House of Sokorina is almost bankrupt, has been since before the war."

"Oh. Well, anyway, the important thing is–" Dante's words were cut off by the sound of someone screaming in the corridor outside. "Stay here," he hissed at Natalia, hurrying to the door. Biocircuitry was already starting to extrude from his right hand, forming itself into a sabre.

A naked man was running along the corridor towards Dante's quarters, babbling and gibbering wildly. As the figure got closer Dante realised it was Flintlock, the aristocratic face filled with terror and horror in equal measure.

"Flintlock? Flintlock, what's happening?" Dante hissed, as his travelling companion raced past. But the man from Britannia kept running, as if intent on getting back to his homeland before dawn.

"Nikolai? What's happening out there?" Natalia asked.

Dante waved her to be silent. Another figure was running towards him. This one was slower and heavier, judging by the sound of the footfalls. Suddenly Madame Wartski burst round a corner, clad only in a harness of leather straps, much of her body wobbling freely in the night air. She was clutching a black rubber truncheon, but it looked surprisingly flexible. Dante pushed his door shut before she ran past, not wanting to catch her eye.

"Well?" Natalia demanded. "What was it?"

"You mean *who* was it," Dante replied. "In cases like this, I operate a strict policy of 'Don't ask, don't tell', okay?"

"You're not trying to keep secrets from me?"

"No. Look, Natalia, there's two things I have to ask you to do."

"Just name them, Nikolai."

"First of all, don't call me Nikolai or Dante, even when we're alone together. I don't believe this room is under surveillance but we can't take any risks. If Doctor Fabergé discovered who I really am he would not hesitate to have me killed or handed over to the Tsar. You would suffer a similar fate for not having turned me in."

"Alright, I understand."

"The other thing is even more important. Let me investigate what is going on in this castle. You don't have my experience at covert missions and you don't have a Weapons Crest."

"You're saying I'm just a girl and can't be trusted."

"No. I don't want to see you hurt because of me. You've got your life ahead of you. Don't throw it away."

"I suppose you're right."

Dante took her chin in one hand and tilted her face up so she was looking into his eyes. "Promise me you won't do anything to endanger yourself."

"I promise," she agreed reluctantly.

"Good. Now you'd better get back to your dormitory. I don't want to explain why I've got a seventeen year-old pupil in my room this late at night."

"That didn't bother you with Helga. Or Carmen. Or Mai Lin."

"I'm not taking the same chance with you, okay?"

"Okay. Well, goodnight." Natalia bent forward and gave him a quick kiss on the left cheek before hurrying out of the room.

Once she had gone Dante locked his door for the night, not wanting any more surprise visitors.

"Do you think she'll listen to me, Crest?"

I hope so, it replied, *for her sake. Are you ready to see Fabergé's report?*

"I guess so," Dante agreed. "What do I have to do?"

Close your eyes and let me interface with your subconscious mind. It'll be like walking into a dream – a very sinister dream.

Dante lay down on the bed and followed the Crest's instructions, emptying his mind of all conscious thought. Blackness soon engulfed him...

"Welcome to Fabergé Island!" Dante was startled to see Doctor Fabergé striding towards him, arm outstretched, ready to shake hands. "You've arrived on a most propitious day. Follow me, follow me!" Fabergé marched away towards the doors of the castle. Dante looked around and found he was outside again, on the island's landing pad.

"Crest! What's happening?" he hissed under his breath.

You're inside the report, it replied. *Don't worry, this isn't the real Doctor Fabergé, just a simulation that will guide you around the castle. I'll skip past the guided tour and take you to the key section of the report.*

Dante's surroundings shimmered out of existence and then reappeared in a new form. The doctor was standing in front of his laboratory, holding the door open for the visitor to enter. Dante walked past Fabergé and into the room, studying its high ceiling, gleaming work surfaces and phalanx of research tools. "Very impressive," Dante said, unwittingly falling into the role of tourist.

"You're too kind," Fabergé simpered in response. "How much do you know about my experiments, codenamed the Strangelove Gambit?"

"Surprisingly little," Dante admitted. "When did you first get the idea for it?"

"The Year of the Tsar 2660. I heard one of the fabulous Imperial Easter Eggs was coming up for auction. I had long been fascinated by those masterpieces of the jeweller's art. When word leaked out the fabled Steel Military Egg was going to be auctioned, I determined to buy it at any cost. That egg inspired me to create an entirely new branch of scientific research, which I call Fabergénetics."

"Tell me more," Dante prompted, taking a seat in the virtual laboratory.

"Each of the Imperial Easter Eggs contained a miniature surprise, some made of clockwork, others exquisite jewels or tiny portraits. I decided to adopt this idea on a genetic level, engineering human embryos so they too would contain a surprise. But my surprises would not be made of clockwork or jewels. No, mine would be far more valuable in years to come."

"Sounds fascinating," Dante said, even though his mind recoiled in horror at the thought of someone like Fabergé playing God.

"I am creating the finest in genetically-enhanced children, each one artificially augmented with weaponry that makes the Romanov Weapons Crest look like a plaything. I won't presume to bore you with the fine details of this research, it can be rather a dry subject for those who have not devoted their lives to the field of genetics."

"A wise decision."

"But suffice it to say the last twelve years of my life have been devoted to this task. There have been many failures – many, many setbacks – but also one glorious success in the earliest days of my research. Now, at long last, I have made the final breakthrough. Unfertilised eggs have been taken from the elite class of pupils here at my finishing school, one from all the most important noble houses. These eggs are being genetically modified to create my little surprises. Once fertilised with sperm from a suitable donor, the eggs will be implanted back into the students before they graduate. The young women shall return home to their families, unaware they are pregnant with the next generation of bioweaponry.

"When their relatives become aware of these unwanted babies, some may attempt to abort the foetus. That cannot be allowed. Your forces must ensure the noble houses remain loyal by letting these pregnancies continue. The babies will be vulnerable until the end of the second trimester. After that the mother can be discarded, her usefulness as a vessel for my Fabergénetics at an end." By the end of this speech the doctor had raised his arms skyward, as if raising himself to the level of a god. Eventually he dropped his hands back to his sides. "Well, are there any questions?"

"How much more of this horror show do I need to watch?" Dante asked.

"I'm sorry," Fabergé replied. "I don't understand the question."

That's enough, the Crest interjected. *Shutting down the presentation.*

Dante's eyes snapped open. He was back on his bed in the castle. "Diavolo! Is what Fabergé has planned feasible, Crest?"

Apparently so. He wouldn't have invited the Tsar here otherwise. That's too great a risk, even for someone with such a bloated view of his own importance.

"I need to find a way into that laboratory," Dante decided. "I don't want to risk a frontal attack, but unless I can past Fabergé's security system soon..."

Fools rush in where angels fear to tread, Dante.

"Yeah, well, I'm no angel."

That much is certain.

A hammering on the door cut short their debate. "Not another late night visitation," Dante complained. "Even I can only stretch so far." He went to the door and listened intently. The knocking resumed. "Who is it?"

"Spatch," a voice hissed urgently. "Let me in, quick!" Dante unlocked the door and the kitchen hand hurried inside, his face full of fear. "We have got to get out of this madhouse!"

"Why? What have you seen?"

"For a start, Flintlock ran past me on the stairs, screaming blue murder and clutching his privates, closely followed by a nearly naked Madame Wartski. You don't get many of those to the pound, let me tell you."

"They went past here before," Dante agreed. "What else?"

Spatchcock detailed his attempt to throw kitchen scraps into the sea, struggling to describe the creature that reared up at him from the water. "It was half human, half fish – teeth like razors, hundreds of them. And its eyes, dead they were, black as coal and colder than the night. Horrible, it was, horrible." His hands were shaking as he recalled the incident.

Dante retrieved a hip flask from his luggage and let Spatchcock take a drink from it. "Enough, that's enough!" he growled when the former felon tried to steal another sip. "Crest, in his presentation Fabergé talked about having had many failures during his years of research. Do you think Spatch encountered one of them, still alive in the waters round the island?"

The good doctor may be using his failures like guard dogs, letting them scare away curious fishermen and tourists, the Crest speculated.

Dante nodded. "Spatch, I need you to find Flintlock. Try and keep him quiet, he's supposed to be a mute. One of the students has already figured out who I am, we don't need anyone else discovering why we're here."

"Alright," Spatchcock said. "But I ain't going near water again. Ever."

"It's not like you had that close a relationship with washing before, is it? Now, off you go!" Dante urged. He let the kitchen hand out and locked his door once more. "Crest, there's something that's still troubling me."

Only one thing?

"We know where Fabergé keeps some of his failed experiments. But in the presentation he mentioned an early success. Where does he keep that?"

. . .

Natalia had lain awake in her bed most of the night, tossing and turning, going over in her mind the conversation with Dante – Mr Durward. She knew she was right about letting him investigate what Doctor Fabergé was doing, that was the sensible course of action. But she had spent her whole life being sensible, doing what others told her, always following the rules. For the first time she was close to something important. She couldn't just lie here and pretend nothing was happening. She had to do something, but what? The answer came to her at dawn.

When the other pupils went for breakfast, Natalia headed directly to the north tower and waited outside the basement entrance. A few minutes later the twins arrived to start work. "What are you doing here?" Storm demanded.

Taking a deep breath, Natalia approached the intimidating women. "Doctor Fabergé sent for me," she said boldly. "I'm overdue for my check-up."

"He never mentioned it to us," Tempest replied.

"Are you sure about this?" Storm demanded.

"Yes," Natalia maintained, trying to keep the fear from her voice. "All the elite class has been given a full medical examination, except me."

The twins exchanged a look before nodding. Storm passed her hand over the palm reader, deactivating the security systems. "Come with us," she said coldly, pushing Natalia toward the lift.

Dante arrived at his first class of the day, a fencing session in the gymnasium. But when the students split into pairs for practice, Helga was left without a partner. "Where's Natalia?"

"She didn't come to breakfast," Helga replied sadly. "Maybe she is sickening for something?"

"Guess she's becoming a woman at last," Carmen said sarcastically, getting a snigger from the other students. "Not before time if you ask me."

Dante turned on her. "Nobody did ask you, so keep your opinions to yourself," he snarled. A chiming sound cut through the air, surprising teacher and class. Dante looked around, perplexed. "The lesson can't be over yet, we've only just started…"

Wartski's voice issued from the Tannoy speakers, grating and metallic. "Mr Durward, come to my office immediately. Mr Durward, come to my office immediately. All other teachers and students are to return to their rooms." Another chime signalled the end of the message.

"Who's been a naughty boy then?" Helga whispered on her way out. "The last person called to her office was Mr Russell, and we never saw him again."

Dante escorted all the pupils outside and locked the gymnasium. "You heard the announcement, go back to your dormitories. Hopefully we'll be able to resume this class later in the day." He watched them wander back towards the east tower.

If you're lucky, Wartski is only going to reprimand you for sexual antics with the students, the Crest said.

"She's in no position to preach after what I saw last night."

Could Natalia have betrayed you?

"No," Dante replied firmly. "She believes in me. Natalia would never betray our secret – at least, not willingly."

Doctor Fabergé was already at work in his laboratory when Natalia arrived, escorted by the twins. "What is this girl doing here?"

"She claims you asked her here for a full medical examination, just like the other members of the elite class," Tempest explained.

Fabergé shook his head. "I made no such request."

Natalia smiled nervously, all too aware of the powerful hands gripping both her arms. "Well, I might have, er, exaggerated a little. I was just curious, I guess, about what happened in here. Maybe feeling a little left out, since all the other girls… you know." Realising she was out of her depth, Natalia tried to leave but the twins refused to release her. "Perhaps I should go?"

The doctor regarded her thoughtfully. "No, my dear, you shall have your examination. Tempest, prepare the instruments. Storm, you will sedate young Miss Sokorina, while I perform the procedure." Fabergé approached Natalia, staring intently into her eyes. "You should be careful what you wish for. Now, remove your clothes and get up on to that examining table."

Dante stood before Wartski in her office, a cold room cluttered by administrative paraphernalia. The matron sat behind a broad oak desk, dressed in her usual blue and white uniform. She glared at him for a full minute, arms folded across her more than ample chest. "First things first," she said, "I want to know why you lied about one of your servants, Flintlock."

"Lied? I never lied," Dante replied, determined to maintain his pretence of innocence as long as possible. Better to let Wartski make her accusations than offer any unnecessary admissions of guilt.

"Soon after arriving on the island you told me he was a mute."

"That's correct."

"Yet last night he was shouting and screaming at the top of his lungs – in the accent of a Britannia native. How can you explain that?"

"I can't." Dante shrugged. "May I ask, what were the circumstances of Flintlock regaining his voice?"

"You may not."

"I just wondered if he was undergoing a painful or pleasurable experience at the time. You see, my servant lost his voice as a result of post-traumatic stress disorder suffered during the war. He was trapped for four days alone in no man's land, during the Battle of Vladigrad. When finally rescued by his comrades in arms, Flintlock was no longer able to speak."

"Is that so?"

"Yes. I hate to think what horrors he must have faced, to rob the power of speech from him. That's· why I asked about the incident that led to his speaking again, I thought it might be relevant."

"The circumstances are irrelevant. Suffice to say, he has regained his voice, although he is not yet making much sense. I believe your other servant is trying to coax him into forming sentences," Wartski said.

"Well, whatever incident triggered his recovery, it can only be considered a miracle cure. Just a shame we don't know what did the trick, as it could be recommended as a treatment for other sufferers of post-traumatic stress." Dante suppressed a smile, enjoying teasing the matron.

Wartski rose from her chair and began to walk around the office, circling Dante. "After witnessing your servant's sudden recovery, I began to have my doubts about you, Mr Durward. So I instituted further enquiries into your background, with a more thorough check of data on the Imperial Net."

She may be on to you, the Crest warned. *Prepare for evasive action.*

"On the mainland you claimed to be a close personal friend of Grigori Arbatov," Wartski continued, "the man originally appointed to your post. I contacted the Arbatov family, but none could recall such an acquaintance–"

"Well, Grigori and I were–"

"Do not interrupt me!" Wartski bellowed. She was standing to one side of Dante, her face quivering with rage. "You told me Captain Arbatov had suffered a fencing accident that prevented him joining the institute's faculty. I could find no record of any such accident. The captain was last seen in the village near our landing pad on the mainland, asking for directions on the day he was due to catch Doctor Fabergé's shuttle to the island."

Dante waited for a pause in her accusations before speaking again. "I can explain all of this, you see–"

"I did not give you permission to speak," Wartski spat at him, resuming her circling. "Early this morning I sent Tempest and Storm across to the mainland in search of the elusive Captain Arbatov. It did not take them long to discover his body, buried in a shallow grave, along with some of his discarded belongings."

"The Black Sea coastline is notorious for its bandits," Dante offered.

"Meanwhile I was scouring the Imperial Net, delving deeper than I had on my first search. A cursory enquiry would find plenty of evidence to support the claims of Quentin Durward. But something far more interesting came up when I was granted permission to access the files of the Tsar's Raven Corps."

Here it comes, the Crest warned.

Before Wartski could continue, an insistent knocking rattled her office door. "Come!" she commanded. Tempest entered and approached the matron, whispering something into her left ear. Wartski nodded, a cruel smile playing about her lips. "Very well. Thank you for that." Tempest departed again, glaring at Dante on her way out.

Wartski returned to her desk and opened a drawer, withdrawing a sheet of paper from inside. "Quentin Durward does not exist, but the name has been used as an alias by members of the Vorovskoi Mir over the years – among them one of the most wanted men in the Empire." She turned the paper round to show Dante the image on the other side. It was a picture of him, all too familiar from wanted posters erected in the Tsar's name. "Quentin Durward is an alias of this man, Nikolai Dante, and this man... is you!"

Dante smiled, determined to try one last bluff. "You've got me all wrong. I know I look a lot like that rogue, but–"

"Spare me any more of your lies," Wartski replied, reaching into her desk drawer. Before she could pull out the weapon inside Dante kicked at the desk, driving it and Wartski backwards across the office, pinning her to the far wall. She screamed an obscenity at him, struggling to free herself.

"I hope you don't kiss anyone with that mouth," Dante replied, then leapt towards the office door. He tore it open to find Storm and Tempest waiting for him outside, wielding syringes filled with a luminescent liquid. Dante threw both hands up to protect himself, biocircuitry already extending outwards from his fingers to form blades. But the twins stabbed the needles into his palms, ramming the plungers down to inject the syringes' contents.

Dante staggered backwards, a chilling numbness shooting up his arms.

"Crest, what's happening? What was in those needles?

That was, the Crest started to reply, but its voice was fading inside Dante's mind. *That was...*

"Crest? Crest, I can't hear you!" Dante shouted. The twins stepped into the office, standing over their target as he collapsed to his knees. Dante's arms hung uselessly at his side, the numbness now spreading across his chest and down his spine. He looked up at Wartski as she approached, a malicious grin on her face. "Help me," he said weakly.

"Help yourself," she replied, slapping him across the face with the back of her hand. The blow twisted Dante sideways and he fell, unable to stop himself. His head thudded into the floor and then blackness closed in...

TWELVE

"He that masters his wrath can master anything"
– Russian proverb

Natalia regained consciousness slowly, as if swimming up from the bottom of a dark river towards the surface. Even when she opened her eyes, the surroundings were at odds with her expectations. The last thing she could remember was shivering on the cold metal examination table in Doctor Fabergé's laboratory, her nostrils filled with the smell of rubber from the gas mask being clamped over her face by Storm. Then all was darkness.

Now she was sat on the floor of a small stone chamber without windows, just a single wooden door set into one wall. She was shaking, her fingers almost blue at the tips, while her teeth kept chattering together. A heavy metal manacle was clamped around one leg, a chain leading from it to a barred grille in the floor. The smell of seawater and rotting fish hung in the air like a pall. Natalia pulled the thin cotton of her patient's gown closer, trying to keep in some warmth. What was this place? Why had she been put here, it didn't make sense. After the other students were examined by Doctor Fabergé they had spent a night in the infirmary recovering before being allowed to rejoin the elite class. None of them had ever mentioned this place.

"Hello?" she called out. "Can anybody hear me?" No reply came, just the echo of her own voice mingling with the sound of waves beneath the grille in the floor. "Can anyone hear me? Hello?" Natalia felt a rising note of panic in her voice and told herself to stay calm. A terrible mistake had been made, that was all. Somebody would soon realise and let her go.

As if in answer to her thoughts, the sound of approaching footsteps became audible. A heavy key twisted inside a lock and then the door swung inwards. Storm stood in the entrance, her face as cold as the stone beneath Natalia's legs. "I have bad news and good news," the towering woman said emotionlessly. "Which do you want to hear first?"

"What am I doing in here?" Natalia demanded. "Where am I?"

"The good news or the bad?" Storm repeated impatiently.

"The bad news."

"During your medical examination, Doctor Fabergé removed one of your eggs, but it proved to be infertile – you can never have children."

Natalia was numb to this, still unable to grasp what has happening. "And the good news?"

"You won't have to live with your infertility much longer. Since you are no longer of any use to the doctor, he has decided you can no longer remain as a student at this institute. Your academic career is being terminated."

"Are you expelling me?"

"Not exactly. This chamber is one of the lowest points of the castle. Every time the tide rises, it floods this room with seawater. Within the next few hours you will suffer a tragic drowning – at least, that is what your grieving family will be told. It's the most convenient option for your disposal."

Natalia shook her head in disbelief. "But why? Why are you doing this?"

"Patients often say things as they are being sedated. You kept saying two names over and over, mixing them up."

"Oh no," Natalia gasped.

"The name of our new fencing tutor, Quentin Durward – and the name of a wanted criminal, Nikolai Dante. You confirmed what my sister, Madame Wartski and I had discovered during the night. These men are one and the same. How long have you known that?"

Natalia didn't answer, the reality of her situation becoming too much for her. Tears were welling in her eyes, her hands clasping each other helplessly.

"It doesn't matter," Storm concluded. "You cannot be allowed to leave Fabergé Island alive, but your death must also appear to be accidental."

"Please," Natalia begged. "I wouldn't tell anyone, I promise!"

Storm ignored her, pulling the door closed and locked it again.

"Please, you've got to let me out of here!" Natalia screamed. But she could hear Storm walking away, footsteps fading into the distance. "Help me," Natalia sobbed as water ebbed at the grille in the floor. "Someone, help me…"

"Where are they?" Wartski demanded. She was standing in the middle of the kitchen, snarling at Scullion. The alien cook ignored her, continuing to stir a huge saucepan filled with a fragrant stew. "I said where are they?"

"Where are who, matron?"

"Your kitchen hand and his partner in crime – Spatchcock and Flintlock," Wartski replied. "They were here earlier. The blond one was babbling in a corner and your little friend was feeding him vodka."

"I'm not surprised if what he was raving about was true," Scullion said. "He seemed to have hallucinated the most unlikely scenario. It involved you, actually. You, a toad and something about leather and rubber. I didn't get all the details, sounded like nonsense to me."

Wartski made a cursory attempt to search the kitchen but soon abandoned her quest. "If either of those two miscreants come back here, you are to send them to my office. Is that clear?"

"Painfully so," the alien replied dryly. She stopped stirring and turned to face the matron. "Was there anything else, or can I get back to doing my job?"

Wartski didn't bother to reply, storming from the kitchen. Once she had gone Spatchcock emerged from a cupboard in the pantry, unfolding himself from the cramped space. "Has the dragon gone?"

"For now," Scullion said. "What have you and Flintlock been up to?"

"Better you don't know." Spatchcock bit his fingernails hesitantly. "You won't hand us over to her, will you?"

Scullion laughed, a guttural sound full of strange mirth. "Wartski and I have never seen eye to eye. The day I make her life easier is the day I die."

Spatchcock gently stroked one of the cook's tentacles. "Don't let it come to that. I don't want you to suffer because of me or Flintlock." He looked around the kitchen. "Where is he, anyway?"

The alien smiled. "Inside the main drain. I knew that even Wartski wouldn't go looking for him down there."

Dante came to in a room of blazing light, humming machines, cold steel and glass. He was lying on a metal examination table, heavy clamps pinning his wrists beside his head. Antiseptic was the overriding smell in the stonewalled chamber, the air harsh and acrid. More metal clamps encased Dante's torso, which was stripped naked to the waist, but he could raise his head to look round the room. This must be Fabergé's laboratory, he thought, recognising it from the presentation. Not exactly the homeliest of places to visit.

"Crest, I need you to analyse the surroundings, see what you can find out about the security system in here," Dante whispered. But no reply entered his thoughts. "Crest? Crest, can you hear me?" Still nothing. Then Dante remembered the needles stabbing into him, the Crest's voice fading away, the numbness creeping up his arms. "Crest?"

"It can't hear you," a supercilious voice responded. Doctor Fabergé was standing behind him. "Nor can you hear the Crest. All communications between the two of you have been severed. You're on your own, Nikolai."

"We'll see about that," Dante snarled, concentrating his mind to activate the biocircuitry within his hands. Once the bio-blades were extended he could easily cut his way free and take on the gloating Fabergé.

"Your ability to create weapons from your hands is also defunct. Tempest and Storm injected you with a suppressant of my own concoction that nullifies all the gifts bestowed upon you by the Crest. For the next two hours you are just as human as I. Even your enhanced healing abilities are in remission." Fabergé walked towards the examination table, a gleaming scalpel held in one hand. "Most surgeons use laser cutters these days, believing them to be more precise than metal blades like this. Laser cutters cauterise a wound while they slice. Personally, I prefer the old-fashioned method." The doctor laid the edge of his scalpel against Dante's chest, letting it nestle amidst the coarse black hairs. "Allow me to demonstrate."

Fabergé ripped the scalpel sideways, slicing open skin. Blood began flowing freely from the wound. Dante cried out in pain, cursing repeatedly as he twitched involuntarily against his restraints. "See?" Fabergé asked. "You can bleed like anyone else now. If I cut deep enough, you'll bleed to death."

"I get the point," Dante replied. "What do you want?"

"From the likes of you? Nothing. Your precious Crest, the fabled weapon of the Romanovs, is old news. After the war the Tsar let me participate in the vivisection of one of your half-siblings. I used the results of that to develop my suppressant, storing it carefully should I ever encounter another Crest's living host. But now I have developed a process that far surpasses your alien biotechnology, that shall beget the next generation of bio-weaponry."

"Spare me the lecture," Dante said. "I saw your show and tell routine on the data crystal Spatchcock stole."

"An unfortunate lapse of security," Fabergé admitted, "and one for which your two associates shall be punished. Severely punished."

"One thing you didn't mention in that sick little presentation," Dante said. "Whose sperm are you using to fertilise the students' eggs? Not your own, I hope – that hasn't been a great success so far, has it? Spatchcock saw where you keep your failures, swimming round the island as underwater sentries."

"I unsuccessfully tried using stem cells from marine mammals," the doctor admitted. "But all scientific research is a process of trial and error. I have used my own seed quite successfully, adapting eggs taken from Wartski. She's quite devoted to me, in her own way, and gratefully donated them."

"Better than having sex with her. I'm not sure Flintlock will ever recover."

Fabergé twisted the scalpel in Dante's wound, eliciting another scream from the captive. "No need to be nasty, Nikolai. We all have our flaws."

"Speak for yourself," Dante spat back.

"We also have our successes. You've already met two of mine, Tempest and Storm. I called them the Strangelove twins, for their conception was the product of unusual circumstances – my seed and science, together with Wartski's eggs. The Furies are my genetically-engineered daughters."

"But they're almost thirty. How long have you been working on this?"

"The twins were force-gestated to the age of eighteen, given accelerated growth hormones, along with learning implants and simulated memories of their childhood. The sperm for this stage of my experiments has been provided by the Tsar."

Dante's eyes narrowed as he realised the implications of this. "Your elite class will go home on Sunday carrying his bastard offspring in their wombs."

"Pre-programmed to be loyal only to him once they are

born, the perfect soldiers to enforce his regime," Fabergé said. "Sadly, not all the class will be making the journey back to their families. Young Natalia proved infertile when I examined her earlier today. And since she unwittingly revealed knowledge of your true identity, I had no choice but to arrange an accident."

"What have you done to her?" Dante demanded.

"Nothing. The rising tide will cause her drowning, not I."

"You bastard! She's done nothing to you. She's no threat to the madness you've been brewing in here!"

"I beg to differ."

"What about the other students? Won't they notice she's gone missing at the same time as me? Won't that ring any alarm bells?"

"I've had the rest of the class sedated. I need all the time between now and the Tsar's arrival to implant the fertilised eggs back into their wombs."

Dante shook his head, steely resolve in his eyes. "It's taken me this long to figure you out, Fabergé. You're clinically insane. You've been playing God for so long you've starting to believe your own legend."

"I'm not playing God," Fabergé replied. "I *am* a god, or close to becoming one. I can recreate mankind in whatever image I see fit. Soon the children I have engineered in this laboratory shall rule the Empire. Is that not the definition of a god?"

"I take it back – you're not mad."

"Thank you."

"You're barking mad!" Dante spat. "Wartski should put you on a leash and take you for a walk. She'd probably enjoy that, too."

Fabergé smiled. "Goad me all you want, it won't change anything. When the Tsar arrives on Sunday he shall reward me handsomely for having caught the notorious Nikolai Dante, a task that everyone else has singularly failed. Whether you are still alive when the Imperial Palace arrives is entirely up to you. The reward for your corpse is almost as generous as that for delivering you alive, so I don't mind which bounty I receive." The doctor placed the scalpel on Dante's chest, then walked to the laboratory entrance. "Don't go anywhere, I'll be right back. I've something to show you. A blast from the past, I believe the phrase is." He left the room, the frosted glass door sliding closed behind him.

"Crest? Crest, can you hear me? Crest, respond!" Dante hissed, but no reply came. The suppressant must still be in effect. To escape from this place, he would need to rely on his own skills and talents, instead of letting the Crest save him as usual.

The laboratory door opened again and Fabergé returned, carrying a familiar object – the Steel Military Egg. Dante had not seen it since his painful visit to the doctor's hotel suite, twelve years earlier. "Remember this, Nikolai? I paid a fortune for this at auction and within a few hours it was stolen from me by a grifter and his apprentice. I became a laughing stock, a cocktail party joke across the Empire, and the living embodiment of that old adage that a fool and his money are soon parted. So I vowed to find the two men who duped me and punish them for my ignominy. I never realised the apprentice was the infamous Nikolai Dante, bane of the Empire. You looked very different as a callow youth. At dinner on the first night you arrived, I knew I had seen you before, but couldn't remember where. It's taken me far too long to put the pieces together, far too long."

"I know what you did to Di Grizov," Dante said, disgust in his voice. "I was with him when he died, cursing your name. He's the reason I came here, to avenge his death and to stop you completing this new weapon for the Tsar."

Fabergé began laughing, merely a chuckle at first, then a full-throated roar of hilarity, throwing his head back. "How wonderful! And what a roaring success you've made of that mission! Really, Nikolai, you are priceless."

"Stop calling me Nikolai," Dante warned. "We aren't friends and we aren't lovers. You don't know me, so don't pretend that you do."

"And who's going to stop me, Nikolai? You?"

"Remember this, Fabergé: I'll be there when you die screaming. That egg puts a curse on anyone who touches it and you'll be next to suffer."

The doctor put down the egg and began applauding. "Bravo! Your machismo is almost as admirable as it is pointless. I do hope the Tsar will let me dissect your corpse once he's finished killing you."

Dante cursed Fabergé, who picked up his prized objet d'art and strolled towards the door, still smiling. "Goodbye, Nikolai. One of the twins will be back in a few hours to inject you with a fresh dose of suppressant. We don't want the troublesome Crest helping you make an escape bid, do we?" Fabergé left the laboratory, still chuckling to himself, the door sliding closed behind him.

Dante strained against the restraints binding his arms, but they were too strong for him to break unaided. There must be a way out of here, he thought, there must be. Bojemoi, I trained with the best escapologist in the Vorovskoi Mir, I should be able to—

A broad smile spread across Dante's face as he looked at the scalpel still resting on his bloody chest.

Natalia had given up calling for help. Nobody was coming to rescue her, she knew that. If Doctor Fabergé knew about Dante, he was probably dead already and none of the other pupils would question explanations about her own absence. They were products of their upbringing, trained from birth to follow orders, to do what they were told, to conform. If only I'd done the same, she thought ruefully, I wouldn't be waiting to drown in here.

The tide had long since bubbled through the metal grille in the floor and was now inching its way up the walls. She was standing in the corner, the cold seawater already lapping around her knees. The chain restraining her movement did not even have enough slack for Natalia to reach the wooden door. She was trapped on the far side of the stone chamber, shivering from the cold. I should just lie down and accept my fate, let the waters wash over me, she thought, but I can't. I have to stay alive as long as possible, even if it is hopeless. I have to give myself every chance...

Dante pushed his chest upwards, arching his spine. This pulled apart the slice on his skin, sending stabs of pain through him, but also dislodged the scalpel from its position. The sliver of metal slid down his chest towards his throat, point first. Time this wrong and he would get a scalpel in his neck. As the blade moved closer Dante shoved his chin down into his chest and opened his mouth. The scalpel picked up speed as it slid, hurrying towards his face–

"Got it!" he hissed after catching the handle between his teeth. Dante twisted his head sideways and passed the scalpel into the grasping fingers of his right hand. They nimbly rotated it so the tip of the blade was facing the locking mechanism that clamped his wrists to the table. Now for the tricky part: picking the lock without knowing anything about its style or manufacture.

Twelve minutes later Fabergé returned to his laboratory, still carrying the Steel Military Egg. He breezed inside, not bothering to seal the door behind himself. "Sorry to bother you again so soon," the doctor said cheerfully, "but I seem to have misplaced my scalpel. And since this was the last place I used it..." His voice trailed off as he noticed the empty examination table, a pool of blood and open clamps telling an eloquent tale.

"Is this what you're looking for?" Dante asked.

A right hook sent Fabergé sprawling. Moments later Dante was on top of the doctor, punching him repeatedly in the face, pummelling him with blow after blow until Fabergé stopped fighting back.

Satisfied the doctor was unconscious, Dante produced the razor-sharp blade so recently used on himself. He kneeled on Fabergé's right forearm and began hacking at the wrist with the scalpel, slicing through skin and flesh, tendon and bone. It was a messy job, with blood spurting from the lacerated limb. Towards the end of the operation Fabergé came to and began screaming for help. Dante rammed his spare knee down on the doctor's throat, threatening to crush the windpipe. "Keep quiet or it won't just be your hand I cut off!" Eventually he succeeded in severing the hand completely, holding it up in the air to admire his efforts.

"Now I can get through any lock or door in this castle," Dante said with grim satisfaction.

"What about me?" Fabergé whimpered, his eyes fixed on the bloody stump where his hand used to be.

"I haven't finished with you yet," Dante replied, a wicked glint in his eye. "Where's Natalia, you bastard?"

The stone chamber was now almost completely flooded, only an inch of air remaining below the ceiling. Natalia had let the chill waters float her to the top, treading water despite the chain restricting her movements. It couldn't be long before the tide stole away the last pocket of air and then she would be left holding her breath, hoping and praying. She wished she'd paid more attention during mass on Palm Sunday, maybe there were some words of solace read out that might have been a comfort. But she hadn't planned on drowning less than a week later. I'm only seventeen, I was supposed to have my whole life ahead of me, she thought.

Natalia felt another surge of water rising past her feet, towards the ceiling. She took a final, desperate gulp of air before it was all gone, then let herself drift downwards again. How could she hold her breath for? Thirty seconds? A minute, at most. Not much time, not nearly enough.

Suddenly a dull thudding sounded through the water. Someone was banging on the door outside. Or maybe I'm just imagining it, Natalia thought? She'd read that drowning people who were revived often recalled vivid hallucinations. Maybe the sound was one of those, just an oxygen-starved brain taunting her with a final hope…

Dante slammed his fists helplessly against the door, but the thick wooden beams resisted him. "Natalia? Natalia, can you hear me? Hold on!" Water was pouring out through the ancient lock. Fabergé's severed hand had opened every door between the laboratory and this place, but it could not undo the final barrier. The scalpel, he remembered, I've still got the scalpel. He retrieved the blade from a pocket and stabbed it into the old lock, carefully pushing the tumblers aside one by one. After a final click the lock was undone and Dante began pushing the door, fighting against the weight of water pressing back from within. But once the door had opened more than a crack, the sea found a new space and began rushing outwards.

Dante shoved and shoved against the door, stumbling forwards into the chamber. It was still half-filled with water but that was draining out rapidly now. A forlorn female figure floated face down in the cold liquid, the material of a patient's gown billowing out around her. "Natalia!" Dante cried in anguish.

He rushed to her side and tipped the girl's body over, lifting her out of the water. She appeared lifeless, her skin cold and lips blue, eyes staring sightlessly past him. Dante slapped her face once, twice, but got no response. "No, no, you can't die," he insisted. "Not like this!" Dante dropped into a crouch amidst the receding water, resting Natalia across his knee. He bent forwards to listen for signs of breathing, but there were none. Dante pinched her nose shut and pressed his mouth over hers, blowing hot air into her lungs. "Come on, breathe! Don't give up on me now. Breathe!"

But there was no response. Natalia was dead.

THIRTEEN

"When the time comes, all will go to their grave"
– Russian proverb

Dante cradled Natalia's body in his arms, rocking her slowly, not caring about the tears on his face or the seawater stinging his chest wound. "I could have saved you if Fabergé hadn't deactivated the Crest," he whispered. "You didn't have to die today, not like this." Then words failed him, leaving him alone with his grief. Another person was dead because of Doctor Fabergé and his insane ambition, another murder to be avenged.

"Nikolai? Are you down here?"

Dante recognised the voice. He wiped his face dry and laid Natalia's body on the cold, wet floor. "I'm in here," he called.

Spatchcock appeared in the doorway, holding a severed hand. "I figured you must be. This looked like something you'd…" His voice trailed away as he saw Natalia's corpse. "What happened?"

"Fabergé had her drowned. I wasn't fast enough to save Natalia, but I can make her murderer pay. I can stop Fabergé's experiment."

"What do you need us to do?"

"Get the other students off the island. I doubt Wartski will let you take the shuttle–"

"We'll convince her," Spatchcock said, a sly grin on his face.

"Try to get the teachers on board too. None of them are involved, except the twins and Wartski."

"Got it. What will you be doing?"

"Stopping this madness, once and for all," Dante vowed. The sound of a siren cut through the air, its wailing echoing along the castle corridors. "I guess Storm and Tempest have found their mentor."

Spatchcock looked at the severed hand he was clutching. "So this is...?"

"A useful way of getting through security doors. Take it with you and go!"

Near the kitchen Scullion was helping Flintlock back out of the drain, where he had been hiding from Wartski. "Are you sure it's safe?"

"Yes, yes," the alien replied, using one of her tentacles to drag him onto the floor. "She was summoned to the north tower, some emergency up there." The wailing of security sirens cut off her voice.

"I decided the twins could deal with that problem," Wartski announced. The massive matron was blocking the only door out of the drainage room, a meat cleaver held in one of her fists. "You'll suffer for hiding this one from me," she promised the cook. "I have plans for Lord Flintlock."

"How do you know my name?" he quailed.

"I know all about you and your master," Wartski sneered. "The Tsar will pay handsomely for the head of Nikolai Dante. But you and Spatchcock – you have no value, except as sport."

"I won't let you touch Spatch," Scullion warned. "He's mine!"

"Don't tell me you're getting attached to the little gutter-snipe? Does the appalling odour he gives off excite you that much, freak?"

Scullion pushed Flintlock to one side and threw herself at Wartski, tentacles coiling around the matron's bulky body. Wartski fought back, hacking at Scullion with the meat cleaver. Green blood flew through the air, spattering Flintlock's face. "I say!" he spluttered unhappily.

"Flintlock, over here!" Spatchcock was in the doorway, waving with Fabergé's severed hand for Flintlock to join him. Meanwhile Scullion and Wartski's brawl continued, the two fighting females staggering about the room, battering each other with all their might.

The alien was retreating towards the open drain, Wartski advancing on her rapidly. At the last moment Scullion sidestepped the charging woman, leaving a tentacle behind to trip her up. Wartski tumbled forwards into the hole; face first, screaming in rage. "No! Nooooooo!"

The cry was abruptly cut off when her vast torso became wedged in the circular hole, half in and half out, legs kicking helplessly in the air. Flintlock delivering a kick to her copious buttocks. Wartski howled with rage but remained stuck fast. The former aristocrat savoured the ugly spectacle. "You know what that's called where I come from? Toad in the hole."

But Spatchcock wasn't there to appreciate the joke, having helped Scullion out into the kitchen. He was trying bandaging her wounds, deep slices cut into many of her tentacles, green slime pulsing from the injuries. Flintlock joined them, still enjoying the sounds of Wartski's furious screams. "If the tide keeps rising, so will the levels inside the main sewerage pipe. With any luck that vile woman will drown in effluent."

"Forget about Wartski," Spatchcock urged. "Dante asked me to evacuate the teachers and pupils. He's tackling Doctor Fabergé and the twins by himself, and doesn't want anyone else caught in the crossfire. I'll help Scullion out to the shuttle. Can you fetch the others?"

Flintlock did not look convinced. "What happens if I run into Storm or Tempest? They'll tear me to pieces!"

Spatchcock slapped Flintlock across the face. "Show some backbone for once in your life!"

Dante was surprised to find all the north tower's security systems had been switched off. No doubt the Crest would have warned him to be careful, suggesting it was all part of an obvious trap. Well, so be it. Dante stepped into the lift shaft and let it raise him to the top level. Even there he could see no obvious danger or threats. The frosted glass door to the laboratory stood open, the sound of something dripping audible from inside.

"Please, do come in," a voice beckoned. "I have a surprise for you."

Dante moved cautiously to the door and peered inside. Doctor Fabergé was sitting on the examination table, a strip of leather tightly fastened above the stump on his right arm. Blood was still seeping slowly from the wound, falling into a crimson pool on the metal table beside him. "You needn't worry, I'm quite unarmed." The doctor smiled bleakly at his own pun.

"What's the surprise?" Dante asked, venturing carefully into the laboratory after checking there was nobody hiding in wait for him.

Fabergé gestured at the Steel Military Egg atop a nearby workbench. "When my namesake designed his Easter Eggs, he concealed a surprise within each one. I have done the same with my genetically engineered eggs."

"I've already seen your presentation," Dante replied.

"But did you stop to think why I called this project the Strangelove Gambit? My daughters, Storm and Tempest, were the first successful attempt at this procedure. I have waited more than a decade for the right moment to trigger their transformation." Fabergé spared a glance for his wounded arm. "I think this is the perfect moment, don't you? Girls, why don't you come out and show Dante exactly what you can do."

The twins emerged from behind a workbench, holding each other's hands. They were naked, their statuesque bodies glistening with sweat.

"I've already seen how these two spend their spare time," Dante said.

"This is not about sex, you fool!" Fabergé spat. "This is about life and death – your life and death, to be precise." He turned to the twins and nodded. "Activate the Strangelove Gambit!"

Dante took a step backwards, towards the door. He had no weapons, no Crest and no plan. The hunger for vengeance had driven him to this moment, but now it had arrived he was ill prepared. The Strangelove twins began striding towards him, their eyes glowing angrily. "Fuoco," Dante whispered.

For all her life Tempest felt like she was holding something back, never being true to herself. Childhood had been a blur of memories, growing up with her sister and Doctor Fabergé, blossoming into a woman. Even when she and Storm were allowed to make their public debut at the Imperial Games, their father had forbidden them from revealing more than a fraction of what they could do. Afterwards it was back to the island, back to a life of containment and waiting and stifling claustrophobia. Deep within her there was something squirming and twisting, fighting to break free – no, to escape.

When the doctor gave the command to activate, Tempest's reaction was purely instinctive. She reached down inside herself and let go, let the creature within take hold. It was an orgasmic release, flooding outwards through her body, searing the fingertips and extremities, exploding from the inside out. She shuddered with relief as the last boundaries were broken. The waiting was over. She was becoming her true self at last.

The twins began to glow, their skin radiating pure light. Within seconds Dante could not look directly at them, such was the brilliance of the light. He continued backing away, hands in front of his face to stop himself being blinded. Even then, he could still see the outline of what was happening to the twins.

Tempest and Storm were changing, mutating, their bodies convulsing and warping. As the process accelerated the twins begin screaming, pain and ecstasy given voice, the sound searing into Dante's brain until blood was dripping from both his ears. Stumbling backwards, he found the doorway and retreated through it, unable to tear his gaze from the blazing light in the laboratory.

The twins' screaming grew louder still, its pitch rising note by note until finally passing beyond human hearing. Light flooded the corridor outside the laboratory as Dante flung himself into the lift shaft. It pulled him down towards the basement. As he descended, Dante saw an explosion of light and sound at the top level. Then there was nothing but the air whistling past Dante as he descended.

"WE'RE COMING TO GET YOU," a metallic voice whispered.

"WE'RE COMING TO TEAR YOU APART," another voice echoed.

"RUN, DANTE! RUN, NIKOLAI."

"RUN AS FAST AS YOU CAN!"

"IT WON'T BE FAST ENOUGH."

"YOU CAN NEVER ESCAPE THE FURIES!"

Dante gave one last glance upwards before stepping out of the shaft. Something was moving above him, sleek and silver. Tempest and Storm were coming for him, but what had they become?

Helga was woken by sound of screaming. She sat up in her dormitory bed, the other students sharing her confusion. "What's happening?" Helga asked Carmen, who was looking out of a window to the north tower.

"I don't know," the Andorran woman admitted. "I was dreaming and then there was some sort of explosion in Doctor Fabergé's laboratory."

"You have to get out of here!" shouted a male voice. Helga pulled the bedclothes up to cover herself as a blond-haired man ran into the dormitory. "You have to evacuate the island," he yelled, gesticulating wildly at the students.

"Why?" Carmen demanded. "What's happening? I saw an explosion–"

"It isn't safe!" the intruder shouted. "Dante said we have to get everyone out while there's still time!"

"Dante?" Helga asked. "Nikolai Dante?" Everyone had heard of him, even if few knew what he looked like. The images taken of him during the war showed a bitter-faced man with a shaven head and angry features.

"I mean Mr Durward," the man said, correcting himself. "Mr Durward is evacuating everyone from the island."

"Mr Durward is Nikolai Dante?" Carmen said, a sly smile of satisfaction spreading across her face.

The blond man rolled his eyes. "We haven't got time for this," he snapped. "I have to get you out–"

Another explosion shook the castle, this time echoing upwards from below. The students screamed in terror, all trace of sleep purged from their systems. Flintlock was almost crushed underfoot as the eleven women stampeded for the doorway.

"Everybody, make for the shuttle!" he shouted after them.

Dante was retreating to the kitchen in the hope of finding a weapon, any weapon. He looked back and glimpsed a blur of silver approaching. The shape threw a fist-sized ball of fire towards him. Dante hurled himself sideways and it flashed past, exploding against the end of the corridor. Electrical energy sparked outwards from the blast, tendrils of high voltage stabbing into everything within twenty feet. Dante was caught in the periphery of this, the shock jolting through his body.

Once the detonation had begun to recede, he continued running, knowing the kitchen was just round the corner. Where the fireball had struck was now a void, a circular hole larger than Dante in the castle floor and walls. Fabergé had been right, the bio-weaponry wielded by the twins made the Romanov Crest look like a child's plaything. I don't even have the Crest to help me, Dante thought ruefully. How long before the suppressant drug wears off, minutes or hours? If it was only minutes, he might have a chance. Otherwise...

A rumbling, scorching noise was rapidly advancing towards Dante as he ran. A glance over his shoulder confirmed the worst. Another of the fireballs was accelerating towards him. He raced into the kitchen, flung the door shut and dived for cover.

Another explosion detonated inside the castle, shaking stone dust from the ceilings. Flintlock was almost grateful to hear the sounds of nearby battle again, as it made convincing the fearful female teachers to flee much easier. He grabbed one of them by the arm as she passed, a hatchet-faced woman with far too many hairs above her top lip. "Is there anybody else left?" Flintlock shouted.

"Professor Mould," Ms Zemlya replied before tearing herself free. "He's in the last room on the left!"

Flintlock hurried to Mould's quarters and barged through the door. But the ancient tutor was already dead, his face twisted in an image of pain and anguish. "Poor chap," Flintlock muttered. "Must have died in his sleep."

A tiny movement in one corner caught his eye. A toad emerged from the shadows, its colouring and shape all too familiar for Flintlock. He looked at Mould again, the horror in the dead man's eyes, the telltale signs of a struggle. No, the professor hadn't died in his sleep. He hadn't been that fortunate.

"Poor sod," Flintlock said and fled from the room.

When the second fireball had finished exploding, Dante risked a glance at what remained of the kitchen doorway. A massive circular hole had been created in its place, the door and surrounding stonework vaporised. Two figures were standing in the space created by the blast, holding hands. They were the same size and shape as the Strangelove Twins, but there the resemblance ended.

Both were encased in what looked like living metal, shimmering with crazed reflections of their surroundings. Blank, featureless surfaces remained where once had been faces. Each was missing a hand. Instead, the left figure had an arm that ended in a ball of fire, while the right one had a crystalline gauntlet. Ahead of them the kitchen table lay on its side, tipped over to provide cover.

The fire-fisted creature looked at its mate. "SHALL I?" it asked, the metallic voice still recognisable as that of Tempest.

"LET ME," Storm replied, her voice also warped by their transfiguration. She pointed her gauntlet and a ball of ice shot forwards, engulfing the wooden table and freezing it. Storm stepped closer and kicked at the object, shattering the table into thousands of tiny, frozen fragments.

Dante watched from his hiding place in the drainage room. He retreated further into the shadows, almost tumbling backwards into the main sewer. "Bojemoi, who left this open?" he muttered, before silently cursing himself. Maybe the Furies hadn't heard him, maybe his hiding place was still safe.

"WE KNOW YOU'RE IN THERE," Storm snarled. "NOW COME OUT AND FACE YOUR DEATH LIKE A MAN, DANTE."

The fugitive smiled ruefully. So much for playing hide and seek.

Spatchcock was helping Scullion towards the shuttle where the screaming students emerged from the castle, running for their lives. "Flintlock's done his job," the little man observed, straining to keep the badly wounded cook from falling. "Scullion, who normally flies the shuttle?"

"There's a pilot," she replied weakly, "but this is his day off."

"Wonderful." By now the students were running past them, towards the shuttle. The fleeing teachers were also spilling from the castle entrance, searching for a means of escape. "The shuttle! Everybody make for the shuttle," Spatchcock shouted.

"But how...?" Scullion asked.

"Worst come to worst, Flintlock can get us off this rock. He flew a Sea-Hawk during the war – not very well, but it's better than nothing."

"Only one problem with that idea," the alien said. "Where's Flintlock?"

Spatchcock searched the faces of those outside the castle. "I hope he hasn't gone back to the kitchen looking for us..."

"Spatch? Scullion? Are you still down here?" Flintlock strode towards the kitchen. He stopped short of the entrance, startled to find there was no doorway – just a void where it had been. Flintlock walked through the hole into the kitchen, careful not to touch anything with his hands. Sparks of electricity still danced in the air. "What the blazes happened here?"

"WE DID," an ominous voice replied. Two menacing silver creatures emerged from the drainage room to confront the new arrival. "WHERE IS HE?"

"W-where's who?" Flintlock stammered, backing away from them.

"OUR QUARRY."

"OUR PREY."

"NIKOLAI."

"DANTE."

"Looking for me, by any chance?" Dante appeared from behind Flintlock, his face and clothing smeared with sewerage. He dragged the terrified Flintlock away from the advancing Furies by the collar. The two men fled from the kitchen, out onto the external walkway.

"W-Where did you come from?" Flintlock gasped.

"Crawled along the drain beneath the kitchen – not elegant, but effective. The Furies need to recharge their weapons between each discharge, that gave me enough time to rescue you. But they'll be–"

Dante! Evasive action!

"Get down!" Dante shouted, throwing himself and Flintlock down on the metal walkway. A frozen blast chilled their backs as it passed overhead, slamming into the far wall of the castle. "Crest – I can hear you again!"

A massive increase in adrenaline levels accelerated your recovery from the suppressant, it replied. *Just in time too, judging by your precarious–*

"Enough pontificating," Dante hissed. "Just find us a way out of here!"

What will you be doing?

Bio-circuitry surged from the end of Dante's hands, forming itself into two razor-sharp blades. "Turning the tables."

Storm emerged onto the walkway, expecting to see the frozen remains of Dante and Flintlock floating in the water below. But the blond man was alone, standing nervously in the centre of the walkway. "Hello," he said. "Sorry to disappoint you, but I'm still alive."

"NOT FOR LONG," Storm snarled, raising her weapon to fire again.

Dante jumped from his hiding place above the doorway, both bio-blades slicing through her weapon arm. Storm howled in agony, the severed limb spurting metallic liquid into the air.

"Like father, like daughter," Dante quipped.

"YOU! YOU SHALL PAY FOR–"

"Yeah, yeah," he replied, bio-blades flashing through the air. One of them cut through Storm's neck, removing her head. The other severed a leg, causing the body to topple sideways so it fell into the water. "Tell it to your relatives!"

Tempest felt her twin sister's death as if it were her own, the shock too much for her to absorb without warning. She sunk to her knees in the kitchen, a chilling numbness spreading through her, dulling the fire in her soul. Storm couldn't be dead, she couldn't be…

Flintlock watched in horror as Storm's torso was torn apart by the creatures guarding the sea around Fabergé Island. Dante used a boot to nudge the dead twin's head and severed leg over the side of the walkway. The face bobbed briefly in the water before it too disappeared, swallowed by hungry mouths. "One down, one to go," Dante said grimly.

Dante, the shock of her sister's death has debilitated Tempest, but I doubt the effect will last for long, the Crest said. *You should attack her now.*

"No," he replied. "The twins were Fabergé's victims, as much as Jim and Natalia. It's the doctor who deserves a taste of his own medicine."

"What about me?" Flintlock asked.

"Get to the shuttle," Dante commanded, already running towards the kitchen doorway. "Fly everyone off the island."

Doctor Fabergé fumed in his laboratory. What was taking them so long? The twins should have despatched Dante by now. He was an inferior being, not worthy of consideration. Even his bond with the Crest was weak, because Dante only had half the Romanov family genes. The fugitive should have been an easy target for Tempest and Storm's first hunt.

Fabergé examined the stump where his hand had been with clinical detachment. The twins would have to assist him implanting the altered eggs back into the pupils, otherwise the process would not be finished before the Tsar's arrival. *After that I'll create another hand for myself*, the doctor decided, using growth-accelerants to clone a replacement. *Shouldn't take more than a few days.*

He reached across to the Steel Military Egg and stroked his remaining hand lovingly across its surface. So much he had sacrificed for this beautiful object. Now he would never be parted from the egg again. Ideally, Fabergé would have preferred to kill Dante himself. But the thief was useful sport for the twins. The doctor frowned. What was keeping them?

Another face appeared beside his own reflection in the egg, a man's face. Fabergé slowly turned to find Dante holding a bio-blade at his throat. "Not dead yet?" the doctor asked. "How regrettable."

"I beg to differ," Dante replied. "Your elite class has escaped, the castle is in ruins and one of your precious twins is dead. The experiment is over, doctor. The Strangelove Gambit is a failure."

"Never," Fabergé snapped. "You could never beat one of my creations!"

"A god would never create something fallible, is that it?"

"You are an inferior, no match for my beautiful twins."

"One of your beautiful twins is providing a snack for several of your other creations in the sea. They were eating her face, last time I looked."

Dante, be careful! Tempest is approaching from behind Fabergé.

"I don't believe you," the doctor maintained.

"Don't you?" Dante asked. "The twins, they were just guinea pigs, weren't they? A laboratory experiment that succeeded, against your expectations."

"What of it?" Fabergé replied. "They were the first, a happy accident that showed me the way. The next generation are a vast improvement upon them."

"Every child wants to be loved by their parents, don't they?"

Fabergé shook his head. "Those freaks aren't my daughters, they were experiments. Nothing more, nothing less."

"HOW CAN YOU SAY THAT?" Tempest demanded. She had walked silently into the room, observing Dante and her father. "STORM IS DEAD! YOU SHOULD BE MOURNING HER!"

Fabergé whirled round, shocked at her appearance. "If you were truly my daughter, you would have killed Dante by now! He is your inferior – destroy him! Prove yourself to me! Prove yourself worthy of the name Fabergé!"

Tempest looked at Dante, hatred burning in her eyes.

Flintlock ran out of the castle towards the shuttle, where the evacuees where gathered. "Quick, everybody on board! Dante says we've got to get away!"

"Only one problem," Spatchcock whispered when Flintlock reached him. "Somebody else got here before us." He jerked a thumb towards the shuttle door, where a familiar figure was sat clutching a pulse pistol.

"Who wants to die first?" Madame Wartski asked.

"I will," Scullion replied, attacking the matron from behind.

Dante backed away from Tempest, bio-blades held up to defend himself from the coming attack. "You heard what he said about you and Storm! He called you freaks, experiments!"

"MAYBE WE ARE," Tempest snarled, the fireball weapon at her wrist growing hotter by the moment.

"Destroy the weakling!" Fabergé shouted. "Embrace your destiny! Show him the power of the Strangelove Gambit!"

Tempest loomed over Dante, her hand drawn back, ready to strike – but she hesitated. "What are you waiting for?" her creator bellowed. "Finish him! Or are you as pathetic as your twin sister?"

The silver creature spun round to face Fabergé. "WHAT DID YOU SAY?"

"I ordered you to kill Dante!"

"WHY SHOULD I TAKE ORDERS FROM YOU?" Tempest asked. "IF ANYONE IS A WEAKLING, IT'S YOU, FATHER. IF ANYONE HERE IS INFERIOR, IT'S YOU – NOT HIM."

"What are you talking about?" Fabergé spluttered. "Do as I say!"

"I DON'T HAVE TO FOLLOW YOUR ORDERS ANYMORE," Tempest replied. "I'VE EVOLVED INTO WHAT YOU ALWAYS WANTED ME TO BE."

"You *must* obey me," he maintained. "I am your father, your creator!"

"BUT STORM AND I WEREN'T YOUR DAUGHTERS. WE WERE JUST FREAKS, EXPERIMENTS GONE RIGHT."

"You misunderstood what I was saying!"

"I UNDERSTOOD YOU PERFECTLY." Tempest drew back her arm, ready to strike. "I'LL GIVE YOU A CHOICE, FATHER. I CAN DESTROY YOU OR I CAN DESTROY YOUR PRECIOUS EGG."

"What?"

Tempest pointed her weapon at the Steel Military Egg. "YOU LOVED THAT MORE THAN YOU EVER LOVED STORM AND I."

"But–"

"LEAVE NOW AND I'LL LET YOU LIVE – BUT THE EGG STAYS HERE. TRY TO TAKE IT WITH YOU AND I WON'T BE RESPONSIBLE FOR THE CONSEQUENCES."

"I'd do what she says," Dante suggested.

The doctor glared across the laboratory at him, then turned to leave. At the last moment he lunged past Tempest and grabbed the egg. "You won't kill me," he maintained. "I'm your father. I can make you a god like me, giving and taking life as you see fit–"

"YOU ALREADY HAVE," she replied sadly, and fired.

Spatchcock watched as Scullion and Wartski fought each other, grappling for control of the pulse pistol as they rolled across the landing pad. The alien cook had clamped tentacles across the matron's face, stifling her breathing. Wartski's movements grew jerkier and more desperate as the life was crushed from her lungs. There was a last feeble spasm, accompanied by the muffled sound of a weapon firing – then neither of them moved again.

Spatchcock ran to Scullion's side, rolling her away from the matron's corpse. "Scullion? Scullion, talk to me, say something!"

The alien cook opened her single eye and looked at him sadly. "You'll make an Arcnevan a fine husband some day," she said. Her tentacles sagged to the ground as the last breath escaped her lungs.

Dante approached Tempest, who stood over the remains of her creator. "You did the right thing," he said. "I know it wasn't easy, but you did the right thing."

Be careful, the Crest warned. *There's no knowing what she will do now.*

"GET OUT OF HERE WHILE YOU STILL CAN," Tempest said. "YOU DIDN'T KILL ME WHEN YOU COULD HAVE DONE, SO I'M GIVING YOU A CHANCE."

"What are you doing to do?"

"DESTROY THIS PLACE – THE LABORATORY, THE EGGS, ALL OF HIS NOTES. THESE EXPERIMENTS CAN NEVER BE REPEATED."

"And what about you?"

"I SAID GO!"

She's preparing to fire her weapon again. I'd do as she suggests.

Dante paused at the doorway. "Goodbye, Tempest. And… thank you."

Spatchcock was still with Scullion when Flintlock leaned out of the pilot's window. "Spatch, get into the shuttle! Everyone else is on board, we have to go. There's nothing more you can do for her."

"I know," he replied.

Dante emerged from the castle entrance, running as if his life depended upon it. "What are you still doing here?" he shouted. "I told you to get everyone away from this place!"

Spatchcock stood up. "We were just… saying goodbye."

Dante checked his stride as he saw the bodies of Scullion and Wartski. "Are they both…?" Spatchcock nodded. "Then we'll have to leave them here, like Natalia. There isn't time for two trips. Now, come on!" Dante bundled

Spatchcock into the crowded shuttle. "Flintlock, take off! Now!"

The shuttle rose creakily into the air, a warning alarm sounding in the cockpit. "We're overloaded," Flintlock shouted. "I can't get any more elevation!"

"Just fly towards the mainland," Dante yelled back. "Skim the top of the waves if you have to, but get us gone!"

The shuttle banked slowly to the left and chugged slowly over the water. A white light ballooned outwards from the north tower, rapidly spreading to engulf the castle and then the entire island. A sonic boom of noise flashed past the shuttle, jerking it forwards through the air.

Dante looked back at what was left. "Crest?"

No signs of life, it replied. *Tempest destroyed everything.*

"Then it's over."

EPILOGUE

"Where there's a beginning, there's an end"
– Russian proverb

The Imperial Palace reached the Black Sea before dawn on Easter Sunday. There had been no contact from Fabergé Island for several days but this was not unusual as the doctor preferred the institute to keep itself to itself. The Tsar was ill prepared for what he saw when emerging onto his viewing platform at dawn. Instead of a welcoming party standing outside the castle, the island was little more than a smoking crater. Its outer edges remained, but the ground where the castle had stood was gone, utterly destroyed.

A team of Raven Corps flyers were sent down to investigate the ruins while the Tsar raged through his palace. He stormed into his daughter's bedchamber, throwing aside Jena's ladies-in-waiting to confront her. "Who did you tell, daughter? Who?"

"What are you talking about, father?"

"We are above Fabergé Island – what little remains of it. The castle was destroyed by enemy action."

Jena pulled her sheets closer. "And what has that to do with me?"

The Tsar stalked around the side of the bed, moving closer to his daughter. "Only a handful of people knew about today's event. Even fewer knew what Fabergé was doing on that island – you amongst them."

She looked directly into her father's eyes. "I would never betray you," she said, no trace of fear in her voice. "You know I am utterly loyal to the House of Makarov, just as you know I would never dare reveal our secrets."

The Tsar glared at her for fully thirty seconds, searching for any trace of duplicity, before turning away furiously. "Then who...?"

Jena let herself breathe again. "Perhaps there was no enemy attack. You said it yourself, Fabergé had a rampaging ego and questionable loyalty. Either he over-reached, destroying himself and the castle in the process..."

"Or?"

"Or he created the explosion to conceal his treachery."

The Tsar reflected on both of these suggestions until a knock on the door of Jena's bedchamber. "Come!" A member of the Raven Corps entered, gave a note to the Tsar and then hastily departed. Vladimir read the note, his face growing redder by the moment, before crumpling the piece of paper in his fist. "It seems most of the pupils and teachers got out just before the island exploded, thanks to the efforts of one man."

"Who was this man?" Jena asked. But her father strode from the room without answering, leaving the crumpled note on the floor. Jena bent forwards to pick it up, smoothing out the paper on her bed. The final two words caught her eye: Nikolai Dante. "He has his uses, after all," she whispered.

At the bar of Famous Flora's, Dante was sharing a bottle of Imperial Blue with Spatchcock and Flintlock. "We did what we set out to do," the exiled aristocrat offered, his words slurring together. "We stopped the Fabergé experiments, all the genetically engineered eggs were destroyed and the girls are returning to their families, safe and sound."

"Not all of them," Dante replied darkly. "Natalia can never go home."

"Nor can Scullion," Spatchcock said.

Nor can Di Grizov, the Crest added.

Flintlock tipped the last of the vodka into their glasses. "I want to propose a toast, for all those who died – their sacrifice was not in vain."

"You know, we never saw if Tempest died," Spatchcock observed.

"True," Flintlock agreed, downing the contents of his glass. "But she couldn't have survived that blast... could she?"

Dante pushed his drink away. "I've got to go," he muttered.

"Where?" Spatchcock asked.

"To find a church," he replied. "I want to light a candle for Natalia. She deserves to be remembered in a better way than this." Dante staggered away from his companions.

"Will we see you later?"

"I don't know," Dante admitted. "I just don't know."

ABOUT THE AUTHOR

David Bishop was born and raised in New Zealand, becoming a daily newspaper journalist at eighteen years old. He emigrated to Britain in 1990 and became sub-editor of the *Judge Dredd Megazine*. He was editor from 1992-1995, a period when the title was voted Britain's best comic every year. He edited *2000 AD* weekly from 1996 to 2000 before becoming a freelance writer. His previous novels include three starring Judge Dredd (for Virgin Books) and four featuring Doctor Who (for Virgin and the BBC). He also writes non-fiction books and articles, audio dramas, comics and has been a creative consultant on three forthcoming video games. If you see Bishop in public, do not approach him – alert the nearest editor and then stand well back. Bishop's previous contribution to Black Flame was *Judge Dredd: Bad Moon Rising*.

ABC WARRIORS
THE MEDUSA WAR

1-84416-109-9
£5.99/$6.99

WWW.BLACKFLAME.COM
TOUGH FICTION FOR A TOUGH PLANET